THE FRASERS:
CLAY

Rebecca Elliot: She's a young, adventurous widow heading West to see her brother. But an unexpected love might set her on an entirely different path.

Clay Fraser: He and his brother Garth are chasing their runaway sister. But suddenly a breathtaking woman with a passionate spirit is steering Clay on a new course—toward love.

"One of the most exciting Western romance series of all time."
—*Romantic Times* on THE MACKENZIES

THE
FRASERS
CLAY

ANA LEIGH

POCKET STAR BOOKS
New York London Toronto Sydney

This book is a work of fiction. Names, characters, places and incidents are products of the author's imagination or are used fictitiously. Any resemblance to actual events or locales or persons, living or dead, is entirely coincidental.

An *Original* Publication of POCKET BOOKS

 A Pocket Star Book published by
POCKET BOOKS, a division of Simon & Schuster, Inc.
1230 Avenue of the Americas, New York, NY 10020

ISBN: 0-7434-6994-1

First Pocket Books printing May 2004

10 9 8 7 6 5 4 3 2 1

POCKET STAR BOOKS and colophon are registered trademarks of Simon & Schuster, Inc.

Illustration by Gregg Gulbronson

Manufactured in the United States of America

For information regarding special discounts for bulk purchases, please contact Simon & Schuster Special Sales at 1-800-456-6798 or business@simonandschuster.com.

To Micki Nuding,
for giving me the hope and belief in new beginnings.

THE

FRASERS
CLAY

1

Independence, Missouri
1865

"I'm sorry, Mrs. Elliott, but I don't allow any woman to join the wagon train who is not accompanied by an adult male member of her family."

"But Mr. Scott, I don't need a man's help. I can drive my own wagon. I often drove the bakery wagon back home in Vermont," Rebecca said.

"A woman alone creates other considerations, ma'am. Delicate ones."

"Such as?"

"It's a long journey, ma'am, at least four months, or as many as six if we run into trouble. In that length of time, a man . . ." He looked away and cleared his throat. "Let us say, a single woman can become a distraction to a man, whether he's single or married. The married women prefer that their husbands are not subjected to that kind of temptation."

Rebecca was getting angrier by the minute. "Mr. Scott, I'm a widow. My husband was killed during the war and I'm still grieving his loss. I am not interested in . . . in attracting other men, particularly another woman's husband. All I want to do is get to California and join my brother."

"Then why not go by sea? A sea journey is much safer for a woman alone."

"And takes almost a year, sir."

For the past fifteen minutes Rebecca had been arguing with this stubborn man. She could only hope he knew more about the Oregon Trail than he did about women. She may not be as physically strong as a man, but she certainly had as much grit and stamina as any she'd met—even more than some.

"Mr. Scott, I've already purchased a wagon and team."

"Then I suggest you either sell them or find yourself a husband real fast if you want to join this train. We leave at first light the day after tomorrow." He tipped a finger to his hat. "Ma'am."

Rebecca folded her arms across her chest and watched the wagon master disappear into the crowd filling the streets. It was clear to see there was no changing the man's mind.

Returning to her hotel, she went into the dining room and sat down and ordered a cup of coffee to calm down.

She felt like screaming. She'd made some foolish mistakes in her life, but maybe this was the worst. Maybe she never should have left Vermont.

No, it wasn't a mistake. She'd been miserable there. And after Charley's death, there was nothing to keep her there. She'd wanted to get as far away from Vermont as she could, and the letter from her brother in

Sacramento made the city sound like a golden land of opportunity.

So now she was faced with two certainties. One, she had spent most of her money; and two, she did not intend to give up and go back East. She'd come all this way to start a new life, and she wasn't about to give up without a fight.

Since this was the last train out until next spring, no doubt she could find employment until then. But even if she did, she'd still be faced with the same problem if she didn't have a husband. And Lord knows she didn't want one.

But desperate situations called for desperate measures. From what she could see, there was only one obvious solution—she had to find a husband quickly.

Because by hook or crook, she intended to leave with the wagon train.

With steadfast determination she left the dining room and stopped at the desk to get the key to her room.

"Good morning, Miz Elliott," the desk clerk said.

"Good morning, Jimmy."

"You sure are up and around early, ma'am," he said.

"Yes, I had an errand to run."

"Heard tell you came here to join up with that wagon train. Thought they didn't allow any unescorted ladies on the train."

"So I was just told. I still intend to go."

"I sure wouldn't mind heading out to California," he said. "Heard tell you can get rich there real quick."

"Yes, that's what my brother said in his letter."

Rebecca took a long look at the young man. This could be manna from heaven. "That's why I'm going there."

Tall and lanky, the young man couldn't be much more than seventeen or eighteen. A boy that young would be easier to control than an older man might be. And she could talk him into making it a business arrangement. It would be robbing the cradle, but Scott never said anything about how old her husband had to be.

"How old are you, Jimmy?"

"Short a few days of eighteen," he said.

"Do you have a family or a girlfriend, Jimmy?" If he had a girlfriend, she wasn't about to break up the course of young love.

"No folks, or a girlfriend that I'm sweet on, ma'am."

"And you're sure you really want to go to California."

"Oh, yeah. Been saving up for it. Oughta have enough by next year."

"Jimmy, how would you like to accompany me to California?"

"What do you mean, ma'am?"

"I have a business proposition for you."

At that moment several people approached the desk. Rebecca whispered, "Come up to my room when you're off duty, and we'll discuss it."

He broke out into a wide grin. "Yes, ma'am!"

The next two hours Rebecca paced the floor of her room, wondering if the boy would lose his nerve and not show up.

When a knock sounded on the door, she took a deep

breath and opened it. Jimmy stood there with a sly grin on his face.

"Come in, Jimmy." Rebecca stepped aside so he could enter. "I'm glad you're interested in my proposition."

"Just what is it, Miz Elliott?"

"Well, as you know, a single woman is not permitted to travel alone. Inasmuch as you said you want to go to California, I thought you could accompany me."

"You mean as a body guard or somethin' like that?"

"Well, something like that. As my husband?"

"You mean we'd pretend to be married?"

"No, I don't think Mr. Scott would be naïve enough to take our word for it. We would have to get married legally. When we get to California, we can have the marriage annulled and go our separate ways. I'll furnish the wagon and food for the journey, and when we reach Sacramento, you can have the wagon and mules. I'd pay you more, but I'm afraid the food and supplies will take most of my remaining money."

"And this won't cost me anything?" he said.

"Not a cent. Whatever you've saved so far is yours to keep. All I want is a husband."

"Yeah, and I know what for."

Before she realized his intent, he shoved her back onto the bed and kissed her. She struggled to free herself and managed to hold him off.

"Jimmy, you don't understand. I meant this as a *business* proposition."

"Sure, I understand what you want. But I ain't gonna buy no pig in a poke. I wanta try you out first." He started to lower his pants.

"Get off me, you misguided oaf!" She managed to shove him away and scrambled off the bed. Looking around for a weapon, she grabbed her face mirror from the top of her dresser. "You come one step nearer and I'll smack you in the face with this." Opening the door, she said, "Now get out of here, you depraved little pervert, or I'll call the sheriff."

Trying to hold on to his pants, Jimmy stumbled past her. Rebecca put her shoe to his rear end and sent him sprawling right into the path of two men in the hallway. They almost fell over him, but managed to keep their footing. Jimmy got to his feet and managed to trip and fall again in his haste to get away.

Both men tipped their hats. "Is there a problem, ma'am?"

"Nothing I can't handle," she declared, and slammed the door.

Manna from heaven indeed! she fumed. That devil's disciple was strictly from hell! Where did young men get such ideas? It was no wonder they called this the Wild West.

She decided to go back to where the wagons were assembled. Maybe she would see a prospect there. She would try one more time to be forthright, and if she was unsuccessful, she'd have to resort to deceit.

The area was jammed with people packing up wagons in preparation for the departure. The incessant clang of blacksmiths' hammers rose above the cacophony of women's chatter, the shouts of men, and the laughter of children playing tag as they darted among the throng. Her nostrils stung from the pungent odor of horses, mules, oxen, and cattle.

A buckskin-clad man, his grizzled beard stained with tobacco juice, slammed into her. He grabbed her arms to prevent her from being knocked off her feet.

"Sorry, lady," he said.

She was assailed by the foul odor of his breath and body. Before moving on, he spat a stream of tobacco juice that was immediately trodden into the dirt by the boots of the passing swarm.

Rebecca stepped over to the protective wall of a blacksmith's shed and her gaze swept the crowd. It was easy to discern the married men from the single ones. Most of those without a woman at their side looked as if they'd forgotten what the inside of a bathtub looked like—if they'd ever known to begin with. She could smell them from a distance.

Rebecca forced herself to walk among them. Surely within the horde, there had to be one unmarried man who made an attempt at personal hygiene. She saw Mr. Scott talking to two tall men and recognized them as the men in the hotel hallway.

She took a longer look. There was a bachelor quality about them—and more important, they were relatively clean looking. Neither wore stained buckskins, and both men were clean shaven, but for a two- or three-day growth of whiskers.

She stepped into a secluded spot where she could study them more closely. It was impossible to hear what the three men were discussing, but from their gestures she sensed it related to joining the wagon train. She was sure of it when they each signed a form, and the wagon master led them over to a corral and pointed out two horses to them. The three conversed for several minutes more, then shook hands. Mr. Scott left them, and the two men walked away.

Rebecca followed her quarry back to the hotel and waited from a distance as they registered and then climbed the stairs. As soon as they were out of sight, she went up to the desk clerk on duty, who fortunately was not Jimmy. While he turned to get her key, she glanced at the register: Clay and Garth Fraser. *No Mrs. Frasers. Thank you, God, thank you.* For the first time since arriving in Independence, Rebecca felt her luck had changed.

She quickly walked upstairs, peeked around the corner, and counted herself doubly blessed when the men entered the room just before hers. She hurried to her own room and put her ear to the door connecting their rooms.

From their conversation, it appeared they intended to go downstairs to eat dinner as soon as they cleaned up. *Cleaned up!* Music to her ears. Yes, indeed, she had definitely made a wise choice.

Rebecca rushed to the dresser and put her hair in order, then put a light dusting of powder on her face and pinched her cheeks to give them color.

With loving care she extracted a fancy bonnet from her trunk, the only real luxury item she owned. Rebecca perched the bonnet at a cocky angle on her blond hair and stepped back to view the result. She shifted the hat several times until she was satisfied with the angle, then returned to the connecting door. Timing was of the essence. When Rebecca heard them about to leave the room, she hurried to her door and stepped out in the hallway at the same time as they did.

"Ma'am," one said politely. The two men stepped aside.

Rebecca offered a sweet smile and nodded as she passed them, very pleased with herself. They certainly were gentlemen, and better yet, she couldn't smell them!

"I must apologize, gentlemen, for our earlier meeting—as brief as it was," she said with a quick smile. "I didn't thank you for your offer of help."

"Well, ma'am, from where I was standing, it appeared you didn't need it," one said.

"I can't believe that young man. I intend to report his actions to the hotel's manager." She quickly changed the subject. "My goodness, I think this is the busiest town I've ever been in," she said with a pleasant smile as they followed her down the stairs.

"It surely is, ma'am," said the man who'd spoken before.

She hoped they intended to eat in the hotel's dining room, and smiled when they followed her to the entrance. A quick glance revealed there was only one empty table. It was too good to be true. She glanced heavenward and winked.

Looking harried and overworked, a waiter came over to the entrance. "Table?"

"Yes, please," Rebecca replied.

"You all together?" he asked.

"No, we're not," Rebecca said. "I'm alone."

"If you fellas want a table, you'll have to wait," he said.

"Oh, my! I'm so sorry to be taking the last one." She hoped her frown looked contrite enough. "You gentlemen are welcome to sit at mine."

"That won't be necessary, ma'am, but thank you for the offer," the second man said.

His companion immediately spoke up. "Why not accept the lady's offer, Clay? We've still got a lot to get done before leaving."

"What's it gonna be, folks?" the waiter asked. "I've got customers to take care of."

"Well, if the lady doesn't mind," the one named Clay said.

"Of course not," Rebecca said, jumping on the offer. "Understand, gentlemen, I insist on paying for my own meal."

Once seated, the more talkative of the two said, "Since we're going to be dinner partners, ma'am, my name is Garth Fraser, and this is my brother, Clay."

"How do you do. I'm Rebecca Elliott. Where are you gentlemen from?"

"Virginia, ma'am," Garth said. "And you?"

Virginia! Drat the luck! Those *were* southern accents. "I'm from the north, from Vermont," she replied.

"What brought you to Independence, Mrs. Elliott?" Garth Fraser asked, glancing at the plain gold wedding band on her finger.

So they were observant, too. Obviously it was going

to be harder to fool them than she had anticipated. It was clear that Garth was the more outgoing of the two, and Clay was making her nervous. He sat in silence and just looked at her—with a stare that bored into her.

"I'm on my way to California. My brother lives in Sacramento, and I plan to join the wagon train. And you? This is pretty far from Virginia." She turned her head and directed the question to Clay, hoping to break his steady stare.

Garth spoke up instead. "We're heading to California on the wagon train, too. That makes us neighbors, so to speak, for at least the next four months." He offered a wide smile, his teeth even and white against the deep tan of his face.

Oh, they were attractive, all right—even if they were Johnny Rebs. Both were tall with dark hair, ruggedly handsome faces, and compelling brown eyes. An air of confidence about them made them even more appealing.

Garth had a friendly, gregarious personality, while his brother was more reserved. And besides those probing eyes, there was a set to his jaw that suggested a stubborn streak.

Of course, she was in no position to criticize since no one had ever accused her of being complaisant.

By the time they finished their meal, Rebecca had found out that both had been cavalry officers in the Confederate army, and that neither of them were married. What she failed to find out was the reason why the two men had joined the wagon train.

Rebecca hated Rebels. And with good cause. Her husband had been killed by one—maybe one of these very men.

So now, with time running out with every tick of the clock, not only did she have to make a choice between the two men, she had to decide which would be worse on the long journey: tolerating a stinking Rebel, or a Yankee who literally stank.

She glanced up and discovered Clay was staring at her again. There was a mysterious gleam in his eyes, one that was dangerously seductive. Common sense warned her to avoid him at all costs. But his reserve made him a better candidate for annullment than Garth, whose engaging warmth suggested that he'd want more than a business arrangement. So she decided on Clay. Stubborn jaw or not, he was less talkative and would probably not encourage a real relationship between them.

Having made the choice, she had one final decision to face: Did she really have the fortitude to go through with the outrageous scheme? Or the selfishness to affect someone else's life—even that of a damn Rebel secessionist—to serve her own purpose?

On the one hand, she wouldn't be in this predicament if they hadn't started the miserable war. On the other hand, she had to live with her conscience. And the Lord knew how desperation often brought out the weakest qualities in one's character, rather than the finest.

But she had sold everything she owned and had nothing to return to back East. The only way to get to

California was on this wagon train. And the only way to be able to do that was to find a husband and . . .

She glanced up again and met those seductive, dark eyes.

Didn't the woman ever shut up? She'd talked incesssantly throughout the whole meal. And even though she was doing a damn good job of trying to disguise it, he could tell that something was bothering her.

Clay glanced at his brother again. Garth appeared smitten with her, but he always did around an attractive woman. And she was pretty enough, with that blond hair and those incredible green eyes. His own taste had always run to dark-haired women. Like Ellie, with her blue eyes and hair as shiny and dark as black silk. But Garth liked women any way they came, and right now he was gobbling up her words like a mouse in a grain trough.

They stood up when she finished and excused herself. True to her word, she had left the seventy-five cents on the table to pay for her dinner. It was a good thing, too; they were down to their last few dollars. The hotel room was a luxury they really couldn't afford, but Garth had convinced him it might be the last bed they'd get to sleep in for six months.

"The way you were nestling up to the widow, I figured you had the same plans for the night as that desk clerk," Clay said when they sat down again.

"I do have plans," Garth said, "but they don't include the widow. I'm all set with a little redhead down at the Alhambra."

"The Alhambra! Dammit, Garth, are you going to waste what little money we have on a whore?"

"We've got a long drought ahead of us, Clay. You heard what that wagon master said. If we're signing on as riders, we're not allowed to say much more than hello and goodbye to any woman on the train. So I'm not about to get mixed up with the Widow Elliott. Six months, Clay! That's a long time to go without a woman. Tonight's the last opportunity we might have, and you ought to be considering it yourself. It'll be money well spent."

"I've already let you talk me into a hotel room we don't need. Besides, the last thing I need right now is a woman," Clay said, disgruntled.

"You'll be singing a different tune a couple months from now."

"I doubt that. Thanks to Ellie, I wouldn't trust any one of them. Like they say, 'One bad apple spoils the barrel.' "

Garth chuckled. "Women aren't apples, Brother Clay. They're like peaches—rosy and round, and delicious to the taste." He slapped Clay on the shoulder. "Don't wait up for me."

Clay had no intention of waiting up for him. He was tired and might as well get his money's worth out of that bed they'd rented. He paid the bill and went back to the room.

2

He was about to enter it when Rebecca Elliott ran out of her room, wearing a dressing gown that offered a good idea of the curves that were filling it. Her blond hair was brushed and hanging in a golden mantle to the small of her back, and the sight of her reminded him of how very long it'd been since he'd been with a woman. Maybe Garth had the right idea, after all.

She rushed up to him. "Oh, Mr. Fraser, thank goodness! There's a huge bug in my room. Will you kill it for me? It's just too horrible!" Her shudder drew his immediate gaze to the bounce of her breasts beneath the satin robe.

"It's most likely just a cockroach, Mrs. Elliott. I suggest you get used to bugs, ma'am, because you're likely to encounter a lot worse than a cockroach in the next six months."

He walked over to the doorway of her room in time to see the insect scurry under the door separating their two rooms. "I guess it's my problem now."

"Well, I appreciate your willingness to help just the same. May I offer you a drink to show my gratitude?"

What is she up to? For damn sure, that bug was just an excuse. His instinct—which had gotten him through some pretty tight squeezes during the war—told him that this woman wouldn't be afraid of a charging elephant, much less a cockroach. The way she was dressed showed plenty enough to heat his loins, and he'd bet his last buck she knew it, too.

What the hell—if her purpose was to seduce him, why not take it? After all, six months *could* be a hell of a long time.

He stepped into her room and closed the door. "It would be my pleasure, Mrs. Elliott."

"My name's Rebecca. Do drop the formality, Clay."

He sat down in the only chair, and as she poured the drinks his hungry gaze swept the length of her. Her neck was shapely and inviting above the low-cut dressing gown. His mouth suddenly felt dry, thinking about sliding his lips down that slender column and along the silky curve of those shoulders. Her breasts were high and firm, her waist narrow, and her hips were slim. He was suddenly itching to get his hands on those breasts and on the rounded buttocks outlined beneath the clinging satin garment.

She turned and approached him with a glass in each hand, the undulating sway of her hips giving him glimpses of her long, slim legs peeking out from the side slits of the gown. He was getting harder by the second.

"We're going to be friends, aren't we, Clay?" she asked in a throaty invitation as she handed him the glass.

Her eyes were twin pools of seduction as she raised the glass to those luscious lips he was now dying to taste. "Here's to new friendships."

"To new friendships." He took a sip. "You didn't drink. That's no way to finish a toast."

She smiled and took a sip. Her lips were moist when she lowered the glass, and he leaned forward and placed a light kiss on them. They were as soft as velvet and tasted of whiskey.

His gaze focused on her swaying hips again as she moved away and sat on the edge of the bed. His mouth went dry when she crossed one leg over the other, revealing a bare limb that drew his attention like a magnet. Her leg was long, and smooth, and lily white. He couldn't take his eyes off it.

"Since we're going to be traveling together for a long time, I think we should get to know each other better, Clay."

He smiled. "Oh, we're going to get to know each other real well, Rebecca."

She was ready and willing, so why waste time with idle chatter? He stood up and quaffed the liquor in a single gulp. It burned like hell going down, but it felt good when it hit. "No time like the present. Right, honey?"

Her mouth curved in an inviting smile. "Oh, I like 'honey' much more than Rebecca." Her tongue darted out and moistened her lips. "Much more, Clay."

God, she hadn't put a hand on him yet, but she had him hard and hot.

"But look at that, your glass is empty," she said.

"And you've barely touched yours. I don't like to drink alone, Rebecca."

She downed her drink, then began to choke and

cough. "This isn't very good whiskey, but it's the best they had," she said when she was finally able to speak.

She rose and took his glass from him, then moved to the dresser. "I bet you think I'm being very forward." She refilled the glass and handed it to him.

"Not at all. I like an honest woman." He thought of Ellie and took a deep draught of the whiskey. This time it went down smoother and felt even better. "There's nothing worse than a lying female who deceives you into believing she's in love with you. It's all business and no pleasure, with some gals." He finished off the drink.

"Did some woman do you wrong, Clay?" she asked.

"She sure did, honey."

She refilled his glass again. "Tell me about it," she said.

"While I was away at war, she up and married another man." He took another drink. "A damn Yankee, on top of it."

"She must have been a fool to pass up a good-looking fella like you."

"I was the fool, to ever think I loved her," Clay said as she refilled his glass yet again. He felt a little dizzy and sat down on the bed.

"Some women don't know when they have it good. I'd never run off and marry another man if you asked me to marry you."

"Ha! I'll never make the mistake of asking any woman to marry me, ever again."

His loins felt on fire as his gaze followed the sway of those hips again. He downed his liquor, hoping to squelch the fire, but it stoked it instead. Setting the empty glass aside, he cocked a finger, "Come here, honey."

When Rebecca approached, Clay pulled her down on his lap and covered her mouth with a hot kiss.

Maybe it was the whiskey she'd drunk, but to Rebecca's surprise, the kiss wasn't altogether unpleasant. As a matter of fact, it was . . . mind-numbing, toe-curling delightful! This man could kiss all right, and it had been a long time since she'd been kissed.

The next kiss was even more potent. His tongue slid past her lips, and the hot, darting sweeps sent shivers of excitement through her. Charley had never kissed her like this. It felt far too good to stop.

With a smothered groan, she slipped her arms around Clay's neck when he pressed her back to the bed and cupped one of her breasts. The heat of his palm was an added weapon against her dwindling resistance.

When he brushed aside her dressing gown, shivers of arousal raced up her spine. Ignoring the thin barrier of the nightgown, he drew both the fabric and her nipple into the moist heat of his mouth. Oh, that felt *so* good. It had been so long since she'd felt a man's touch.

Rebecca's eyes popped open. What was she doing? This wasn't part of her plan! She pushed him away and sat up.

"Slow up, Handsome, we've got the whole evening ahead of us," she said, fending off the hand cupping her breast.

To her relief, the whiskey finally caught up with

him; he was having trouble sliding the dressing gown off her shoulders.

"Let's get that off you, honey."

She smiled teasingly. "Let me do that before you rip it." Slipping out of his grasp, she stood up. "I think you could use another drink."

"I don't want another drink. I want you."

"And I want you, but I'm ready for another drink." She refilled his glass, and then picked up her own barely touched one. "Let's drink to us, lover; then I'm going to make you feel so good." She tipped up her glass. "To us."

"To us," he slurred.

They clinked glasses and Rebecca brought hers to her mouth but didn't drink, watching as Clay gulped his down. He had to have a cast-iron stomach. What was keeping him from passing out? Those weren't single shots she'd been pouring him.

She put her glass on the dresser and went back to the bed. Slowly she removed her robe. He was finally so drunk he couldn't do much more than stare at her.

"Lay back so I can get your boots off," she said. It was a struggle, but she finally succeeded in removing his boots and stockings. As she was about to toss a stocking aside, a shiny object caught her attention. A closer look at it revealed a small, diamond-studded wedding band tacked by thread to the top of his stocking.

Had he intended the ring for this Ellie woman he'd planned to wed? Rebecca began to feel sick in the pit of her stomach. The whole situation was becoming worse by the minute. She wasn't proud of what she was doing to begin with, and now she felt she was no better than the woman who had betrayed him.

"Now the shirt and pants," she said lightly, feeling heavy with guilt. She had to fend him off as he groped at her breasts when she leaned over and worked the shirt over his head.

Clay rolled over, his body pinning her to the bed. Drunk or not, those hands of his had a will of their own as his mouth captured hers in a hot, moist kiss. The thin fabric of her gown was no deterrent against the warmth of the palm caressing her breast, or the other hand sliding up her thigh to nestle between her legs. She squirmed beneath him and tried to budge him off her while trying to fight off his hands, but one or the other always found its mark.

Her chest was heaving from breathlessness when he finally broke the kiss.

"Let's get rid of this, baby." His fingers tucked around a strap of her nightgown and began to slip it off her shoulders.

Drawing a deep breath, Rebecca succeeded in shoving him off her and onto his back just as his fingers got caught in the strap. It tore lose, ripping the gown down the front from neckline to hem.

Clutching the gown together, she bolted off the bed.

"Come on, baby, I'm waiting."

Though his speech was heavily slurred, he didn't show signs of passing out. She began to worry that maybe he wasn't drunk enough to implement her plan. And who knows if his brother might show up at any minute. Rebecca pulled a dress over her torn gown.

"Where are you going, baby?" he slurred.

"Just down the hall to the bathroom. I'll be right back."

Rebecca hurried downstairs, and after a hushed conversation with the desk clerk, she returned to the room.

God had delivered her! Clay was fast asleep.

For the next quarter hour she paced her room nervously, sparring with her conscience. It wasn't too late to abort her plan, which was shameful and self-serving. But in truth, as long as he was heading out on the wagon train anyway, she couldn't see how she was doing him any harm. They could have the marriage annulled once they reached California, and neither would be worse off then they were now.

She opened the door in response to a light knock.

"Rebecca Elliott?" the caller asked.

"Yes."

"I'm Judge Wilkins. Sam said you have a problem and that it's important that you wed tonight, is that correct?"

"Yes, please come in, sir."

He stepped inside and looked around at the figure in the bed. "Is this your intended?"

"Yes. You see, Clay and I planned to get married and leave with the wagon train. Unfortunately"—she blushed appealingly and lowered her eyes—"in our excitement we . . . ah . . . we got overly . . . ah, well, you know. My poor mama and daddy would turn over in their graves if they thought I'd . . ." She bit her lip. "You understand, it's best we marry right away. Please, Judge Wilkins, will you marry us now?"

"I have to say it's most unusual, young lady, and it appears the intended groom is sleeping."

"He said to wake him when you arrive."

"Very well, madam. But under the circumstances, it will cost you ten dollars."

"Ten dollars!" Her money was dwindling quickly.

"There is the matter of my services, certificates to issue, and the marriage to be properly registered, young lady. Now, if you wish to go through with this marriage, I suggest you wake up the intended groom."

Rebecca went over to the bed and shook Clay by the shoulder. "Clay, darling, wake up."

"Come to bed, honey," he mumbled.

"Clay, Judge Wilkins is here to marry us."

"Marry us? Okay, Ellie."

Ellie? Oh, no, he was going to ruin her plan! She helped him up and he staggered to his feet.

The judge frowned. "He appears inebriated, madam. Are you sure it's his wish to marry you?"

"Of course," Rebecca declared. "Clay's a gentleman, Your Honor. He would never have compromised my reputation if he didn't intend to marry me. Clay, darling, you want to marry me, don't you?"

He pulled her back against him and put his arms around her. His breath ruffled the hair at her ear. "Of course I do, sweetheart. You know that." He began to nibble at her ear, and she sucked in her breath. "Thought of nothing else for the past five years. Now, let's get back to bed, Ellie."

He started to tickle her sides chanting, "Ellie, Ellie, with the ticklish belly." She giggled and tried to ward off his hands but only succeeded in putting her neck in a vulnerable position for him to trail a string of kisses down the column of it.

"Darling, behave yourself," she said breathlessly. "You're embarrassing me in front of the judge." Her legs were trembling. "You must excuse him, Judge. He's had too much to drink, celebrating our intended nuptials."

"Hello, Judge." Clay extended his right arm for a handshake, as he pulled her tighter against him with his left one, so tight she could feel his arousal.

"Glad to meet you, Judge." He blew lightly in her ear, making her shiver.

"Shall we proceed, Judge Wilkins?"

The judge eyed her dubiously. "He calls you Ellie. I thought your name was Rebecca."

She didn't even blink. "Yes, it is. Ellie is a nickname . . . from my last name, Elliott." The lies were coming faster and easier. *Dear Lord, please forgive me.*

Clay's hands crept upward to her breast, and Rebecca's eyes widened in shock. "Can you hurry this along, Judge? He's, uh, very eager."

The judge shut the book he held. "I think we'd better get you two married right away. Do you . . ." He looked questionably at Clay.

"Clay Fraser," Rebecca said.

"Do you, Clay Fraser—"

"Clayton Fraser," Clay corrected. His warm breath was at her ear again, sending more shivers down her spine. "Captain Clayton Hunter Fraser, Confederate States of America."

"Do you, Clayton Fraser, take this woman to be your lawful wedded wife?"

"Yes, I do," Clay responded. "Can we go back to bed now, honey?"

"And do you, Rebecca Elliott, take this man to be your lawful wedded husband?"

"I do," Rebecca replied.

"By the power invested in me by the sovereign State of Missouri, I pronounce you man and wife."

Rebecca released Clay and he fell back down onto the bed.

"If you want this marriage to be legalized, your husband has to sign the marriage certificates."

Rebecca managed to get Clay in a sitting position, and helping to guide his hand, she succeeded in getting Clay's signature on the marriage certificates.

Judge Wilkins handed her two copies. "One's for you and the other's for the happy groom." With a twinkle in his eyes, he nodded at the sleeping Clay. "I trust you will see that he gets his copy in the morning."

"I certainly will, Judge Wilkins. It will be my pleasure."

"And I want you to know, Ellie, Ellie with the ticklish belly, that you haven't fooled me one bit. I can tell this isn't the first time the two of you have been intimate."

Rebecca wanted to collapse in relief. "Oh, there's just no fooling you, is there, Judge Wilkins? Thank you for your trouble." She handed him a gold eagle and practically shoved him out the door.

Then she leaned back against the door and took a deep breath. It was done.

She dug out her other nightgown, a plain white muslin she was used to wearing. That fancy one she'd foolishly bought to wear on her honeymoon was ripped, anyway. She walked over to the bed and gazed down at her new husband, unable to resist the temptation of looking at his body. His shoulders were broad, his chest muscular and dusted with dark hair.

Releasing his belt, she pulled the trousers off his legs. Thank God he had on drawers; the bulge of his male organ was still hard, despite his being asleep and the alcohol he'd consumed.

Now came the hardest part, the moment she dreaded the most. But she had to do it. She had too much New England mettle to back down now.

Rebecca touched the gold band on her hand. Though Charley had been dead for four years, she had never considered removing the ring he'd slipped on her finger the day they were married. Her eyes misted as she fought back tears, and slipped the ring off her finger.

She picked up the diamond-studded band and slid it onto her finger.

Then she climbed into the bed.

3

Clay opened his eyes slowly, but the glare of sunlight caused him to snap them shut again. For a long moment he lay motionless. His head felt as if a horse had kicked him, and he couldn't raise it from the pillow. He didn't want to. He just wanted to lie there and die.

The previous night's events began to bombard his mind like a cannon fusillade. Dinner. Garth leaving. Rebecca Elliott calling him into her room. Good Lord! How much had he drunk? He could never remember a headache like this before.

He finally gave it another try, and this time he managed to keep his eyes open. "First things first," he murmured.

Raising his head, Clay realized there was another sleeping figure in the bed.

"Garth, wake up. We've got a lot to do."

He reached over to shake his brother awake, and his hand encountered a shoulder considerably smaller and softer than his brother's. He shot to his feet, then groaned and grasped his head. His brain felt as if it were slamming from one side of his head to the other. The room finally stopped spinning enough for him to focus on the sleeping figure.

Garth didn't have long golden hair that fanned out on a pillow; Garth didn't have a lovely face with delicate features, and wide, sensual lips that tempted a man to cover them with his own. No, Garth didn't have any of that—but Rebecca Elliott did. He must have had a great time last night, but he couldn't remember a single moment, dammit

He began to gather up his clothes. As he pulled on his socks, Clay realized the ring he'd bought for Ellie was gone. He had carried it throughout the whole war, and after he'd learned she'd married, he'd figured it would be a source of money if they ran out when they came west. For now they'd gotten jobs with the wagon train, but there was no telling what would happen after they caught up with Lissy.

Where in hell was the ring? Clay shook out his boot, then got down on his knees and crawled painfully around on the floor in search of it. But no luck.

Could the Elliott woman have taken it? If she thought she'd get a diamond ring for her services, she had another think coming. He riffled through her purse, then her suitcase, but there was no sign of the ring. Where in hell could she have hidden it?

He strode over to the bed and shook Rebecca's arm.

"Where is it? Give it to me *now.*"

"Wh-What are you looking for?" Rebecca asked, startled awake by the abrupt move.

"The ring. Where did you hide the ring?"

She blinked and held up her left hand. "You mean this ring?"

Shocked, he stared at the band sparkling on her finger.

"You gave it to me." She sat up and slid out of the bed.

"I don't remember giving you the ring—or even getting in bed with you. But whatever we did, it wasn't worth the cost of that ring. So take it off," Clay demanded.

She looked good in that sheer nightgown, with her hair all tousled like a vixen. Damn good—but still, not worth-a-diamond-ring good.

Rebecca picked up a piece of paper on the dresser and handed it to him. "Maybe you should read this." She gathered up her clothes as he began to read the document. "I'm going to take a bath. We'll discuss this when I'm through."

As she left the room, Clay sat down on the edge of the bed, holding his aching head in his hands. The marriage license slipped through his fingers and fell to the floor.

Married! How could he have been so drunk that he'd married her? He racked his brain, but the last thing he vaguely remembered was her starting to undress him. How did it get from that to a marriage license?

Lord, what a development! Married to a woman he didn't even know, much less love. How did he ever get into this mess? What was he even doing in Missouri?

It had all begun last month—which felt like a century ago. The war had ended and he'd returned to Fraser Keep . . . .

Clay propped an arm on the saddle horn and leaned forward; his weary gaze swept the valley below.

Spring had rejuvenated the Virginia countryside with a fresh look of rebirth. Perhaps it was a sign that his beloved homeland would be reborn, too.

Sun gleamed off the gabled windows of the house, set upon a sprawling lawn lined with ageless oaks. Beyond the house, the James River flowed past in soothing tranquility.

Whatever the season, massive oaks, elms, dogwood, cypress, and holly offered an ever-changing kaleidoscope of color. And although a closer look might reveal that the majestic columns of the house needed a whitewash and the roof a repair, from a distance, the stately dwelling had not lost its grandeur.

Fraser Keep had been the ancestral home of his family for two centuries. Through the years two wings had been added to the original structure, rooms enlarged, and stained-glass windows had replaced wooden shutters, but its exterior walls of red bricks set in Flemish bond had not been altered since 1676.

Seven generations of Frasers had grown up within those walls, which had withstood Indian attacks, two wars with England, and now this tragic war between the States.

Located between the James and York rivers, the original three thousand acres had grown to six thousand. And within those boundaries lay some of the best bottomland in Virginia—hundreds of acres of rich cotton and tobacco fields.

Clay's sad gaze fell on the distant fields. Only a few showed signs of recent sowing. The rest were barren. He could make out the figure of his brother Will, his two nephews, his brothers Jedidiah and Colt, and the half dozen Negroes who had remained at Fraser Keep plowing and seeding one of the fields. Thank God Jed and Colt had returned. There was no sign of Garth, yet.

His eyes deepened with sadness. His parents and Will's youngest child had died of cholera during the war. His brother Andrew had died at Gettysburg, and Will's sixteen-year-old son at Sharpsburg. God grant that Garth had not perished, too, in the closing days of the war.

It had levied a costly toll on not only his family, but on the entire South. Could the South rise again, like a Phoenix from the ashes? He doubted it.

Clay straightened up in the saddle and started to descend the hill.

The joy of his arrival was increased tenfold when a weary Garth arrived home a few hours later. They all gathered around the family's graveyard as Will lead them in a prayer of thanks for those who had been spared.

Clay glanced around at the assembled group. Like him, his younger brothers Garth, Jedidiah, and Colt were exhausted, but time would heal that condition. His sister Melissa, who had been fourteen when the war began, had now developed into a woman.

Although only thirty-four, Will appeared to have aged the most. Keeping the plantation going for the past four years while the rest of them had gone off to war had been a grueling task, and at times a hopeless one. The heartache of the loss of both their youngest and eldest child showed on the faces of Will and his wife, Emmaline.

When they returned to the house, Will called his brothers into the library. The large room had once boasted an enormous oak desk, stuffed chairs, couches, and paneled walls lined with bookshelves; now the room was barren of all furniture, the panel stripped from the walls, and only a few scattered books remained on the shelves.

"It's not going to be easy," Will said, "but we've held on this long. When the Confederacy passed the Impressment Act two years ago, they cleaned us out of all our livestock and stored grain, along with practically anything of value worth selling. And what the Confederacy didn't take, some of those Yankees did when they were quartered here last month.

"By the way, Clay, Captain Grange, the Yankee officer in charge, said to say hello. He said you were classmates."

"Colin Grange?" Clay asked.

Will nodded. "He was kind enough to give us a horse when the Yankees pulled out. That's how we were able to plow the fields."

Clay's carefree days at West Point now seemed a century ago. There'd been so many friendships made—and so many of those classmates had ended up on opposing sides during the war.

"We've got three fields of cotton planted," Will continued, "and there's time to get a couple more done, now that you're all back. God willing, next year *we ought to be able to plant twice as many. I promised Dad before he died that Fraser Keep would rise again."* His eyes misted. *"It sure is great to see you all back in one piece. In a couple of weeks you'll feel as healthy as ever."*

"Will," Clay said, *"I know I'm speaking for all of us when I say we're grateful to you for keeping our home going. We've all seen the destruction in the South, so we know what you've gone through to do it."* He slapped Will on the shoulder. *"You've got some help now."*

"Amen, brother," Garth said. *"I don't know about the rest of you, but right now I'm beat. I'm going to bed."*

As they started to file out, Will stopped him. *"Hold up a minute, Clay. I have to talk to you."*

"Okay, but make it fast. I want to ride over and see Ellie."

Ellie, his beloved betrothed. He'd thought of nothing else for the past hour. He and Ellie had been sweethearts for five years, and as soon as the war ended they planned on getting married. The thought of her beautiful face had helped to lighten his darkest moments during the war, and he wanted to wed her as soon as possible. He was already thirty years old and it was high time he got started on a family.

Will closed the door. *"I'm afraid I've got some bad news."* He went to the safe and pulled out an envelope. *"This is for you."* Will handed it to him and then walked over and stared into the fireplace.

Clay's name was written in Ellie's neat script on

the envelope. With a sense of foreboding, he opened it and read the enclosed letter. And felt as if he'd just taken a bullet in the gut.

"How could she?" he murmured, not realizing he'd said it aloud.

Will turned around, his eyes filled with compassion. "They were married two months ago."

Clay felt numb—too numb to even be angry.

"I'm sorry, Clay. Buford had a wealthy aunt who lived in Vermont. She died and made him her heir because he hadn't joined the Confederate army. They moved up North right after the ceremony."

When Clay continued to remain silent, Will said, "I wish there was something I could say to comfort you, Clay. You know how Mom always said that everything happens for a reason. It's been hard holding on to that thought for the past four years, because I don't know what purpose all this death and devastation could serve. The issue of states' rights and slavery could have been fought out in Congress—not on bloody battlefields."

"Yeah, I know," Clay said. He shook his head. "I know my loss can't compare to yours and Emmaline's, but Lord, Will, the thought of Ellie got me through the worst of this wretched war. And now—"

"And now the war is over, Clay, and you start building a new life."

"Yeah. A new life," Clay said desolately.

Later in his room, once the shock and numbness of Ellie's betrayal wore off, anger set in. He couldn't understand how she could have married another man, especially one who wasn't even willing to defend Virginia from an invading army from the North. Elias Buford had claimed he had asthma and therefore could not serve in the army—although no one, including the local doctor, had ever been aware before of his malady. Instead, the shopkeeper had remained home and gotten rich by overcharging his neighbors as much as three hundred dollars for a barrel of flour or two hundred dollars for a plain pair of shoes.

"The damn bastard should have been shot for the lowdown, sneaking spy he probably was," Clay ranted the next day to his family.

"His wealth would have attracted Ellie easily," Emmaline said. "She always did love pretty clothes and luxuries, Clay."

"Yes, and she always let the rest of us know how much better hers were than the rest of ours," Melissa declared.

Before the war, Clay had been able to lavish Ellie with expensive gifts, so smitten with her that he had overlooked her shallowness and the warnings of Will and Garth. But what young man in love ever heeded the advice of others? Wisely, neither brother reminded him of this now.

And one thing he knew for certain: He'd never trust a female again.

By the end of the week four more of the Negro families had come back, willing to work for food and lodging. Will agreed, with the promise to pay them in the fall if the crops came in.

At least no one here would go hungry, Clay thought as he prepared to retire for the night. They had succeeded in planting two more fields of cotton and a field of vegetables.

"Come on in," he said, in response to a light tap on the door.

Melissa entered the room. "Clay, I have to talk to you." Her usually lively eyes were grave.

Despite the twelve-year difference in their ages, he and his sister had always been exceptionally close. From the time she'd been a dirty-faced little imp trying to keep up with her brothers, Melissa had always run to him with her bruises or hurts. He'd hold her and comfort her, then send her on her way with a hug and a kiss to the top of her mop of curly dark hair.

Now he saw what a beautiful woman she had become in his absence, and was sad that he had missed the metamorphosis.

"What's wrong, Lissy?"

"Clay, I'm in love."

He couldn't help smiling. "Well, don't look so happy about it. Who's the lucky fellow?"

"His name is Stephen Berg."

"I don't remember the name. Have I met him before?"

"Stephen's not from here, Clay. His home is in Wisconsin. He was one of the Yankee soldiers quartered here."

"Good God, Lissy! What are you thinking of? First

Ellie, and now you—did every young girl in the South become beguiled by the damn Yankee invaders?"

"I love him, Clay. And Stephen loves me. He's asked me to marry him."

Clay groaned. "Oh, Lissy." What could he say to her? It was her life, but . . . "Honey, you know as well as I that after losing so many loved ones during the war, we could never welcome a Yankee into the family."

Melissa began sobbing, and he took her into his arms and held her trembling body.

"We need time to heal, Lissy."

She looked up at him, tears streaking her cheeks. "Doesn't it matter to any of you how I feel? Aren't I a member of this family, too?"

"Of course it matters to us." He tipped up her chin. "They say time heals all wounds, honey. You just have to give us some time."

"I don't have time, Clay. You see, I'm . . . I'm going to have a baby." She turned and fled from the room.

The next morning she was gone. In the letter she left behind, Melissa assured them she was not going up North to live. She and Stephen had decided that rather than make a choice between the North or the South, they would head west to California on a wagon train.

Clay told the grim-faced family about Melissa's condition and declared his intention of going after her to bring her back home. All agreed, and with the exception of Will, his other brothers drew lots to determine who would go with him.

The following day he and Garth left Fraser Keep.
Clay sold his horse and the gold watch his grandfather
had given him. The money brought them river pas-
sage to Independence, Missouri, the debarkation point
for wagon trains heading west on the Oregon Trail.

Clay picked up the marriage license and stood up.
The first thing he'd do was to see if this was authentic.
He *never* drank so much that he didn't know what he
was doing. Something was mighty fishy here, and
maybe he hadn't been the only fish in that pond.
Maybe she'd had some help baiting that hook.

One thing was for certain. He wasn't going to let
that scheming little Yankee out of his sight until he
learned the truth.

In the meantime, he'd better break the news to
Garth.

Then a light tap sounded on the connecting door,
and he didn't have to guess who that would be.

"Come on in, Garth."

4

"Married!" Garth spouted, after reading the marriage certificate Clay had handed him.

"That's what it says," Clay replied.

Garth began laughing. "I don't believe it."

"I'm glad you find it amusing."

"You actually got liquored up and let Rebecca convince you to marry her?"

"I know I was drinking pretty hard, but I swear I don't remember any marriage or the mention of one. I woke up this morning in bed with her. She was wearing a nightgown and the ring I'd bought. And that damn marriage certificate was on the dresser."

"You bought a ring?" Garth asked.

"I bought it for Ellie, intending to get engaged, and when the war broke out, I held off in case I was killed. Then I figured we could sell the damn thing out West when we ran out of money."

Garth chuckled. "I leave my big brother alone one night, and this is what happens."

"If you don't wipe that grin off your face, so help me, Garth, I'm going to smack you."

Garth shook his head. "You always were naïve when it came to women, Brother Clay. Ellie was a good example."

"I've been around women long enough to know when they're offering something, and what that is. Rebecca Elliott—"

"Rebecca Fraser," Garth corrected.

"Over my dead body!"

"More like naked body, Brother Clay." His grin couldn't have been any wider.

Clay glared at him. "You're a damn lot of comfort. The woman came to me dressed in a robe and nightgown that left nothing to my imagination, and said there was a bug in her room. She knew exactly what she was doing, and didn't fool me for a minute. Then when she invited me for a drink, I figured why not? Especially after your talk about the long drought ahead of us."

"You're blaming me because you let yourself get rooked into a marriage?"

"I'm not blaming you. This just doesn't make sense. If she was out to roll me after she got me drunk, why didn't she just take off with my money and the ring?"

"Maybe you read her wrong, Clay." Garth said. "Maybe she was on the up-and-up. The two of you drank a little too much, had a tumble in bed, and since she's a decent woman, you decided to do right by her." He patted Clay on the shoulder. "I'm proud of you, Brother Clay. You held up the family honor."

Frustrated, Clay had all he could do to keep from socking his brother right in the middle of his amused grin. "Dammit, Garth, how long have we been brothers?"

"All of my twenty-six years."

"And did you ever know me to run off and do anything as half-cocked as this?"

"No. But on the other hand, people do some pretty crazy things when they're on the rebound. Any woman might have looked good to you. And let's face it, Brother, Rebecca is a damn good-looking woman."

"I can assure you, Garth, marrying *any* woman was the farthest thing from my mind, much less one I didn't know. I've learned how little you can trust a woman. And as soon as my *wife* finishes bathing, we'll check out the legality of that marriage certificate."

"And if it is legal?"

"Then this will be the shortest honeymoon on record, because I have no intention of taking her with us, on that wagon train."

"If she's your wife, Clay, you can't just take off and abandon her. Dad and Mom would turn over in their graves."

"I'll sell the damn ring and give her the money. It was expensive and it will pay for a ticket back to Vermont with plenty left over. Then as soon as I return from California, I'll hire a lawyer to dissolve the marriage."

"Sounds kind of heartless to me, Clay. Rebecca's no whore, but you're treating her like one. And my hunch is that the certificate is legal," Garth slapped Clay on the shoulder. "What the hell, Brother Clay, it's time you got married anyway. I like the gal. And even if you don't remember last night, things could have been worse. It might have been Ellie you woke up with this morning, instead of Rebecca." Garth picked up the torn nightgown and quirked a brow. "And you don't re-member anything beyond the first couple of drinks?"

Clay knew exactly what was going through his brother's mind. It was impossible to sustain anger around him for any length of time; Garth found a lighter side to almost every situation.

Clay shook his head and tried not to grin. "Nope, nothing—That's the damnedest part of the whole thing—I sure hope I had a good time."

After the bathroom attendant had filled the tub and left, Rebecca climbed in, leaned back, and closed her eyes. The soothing effects of the hot water began to relax her. If only she could appease her soul as easily.

It had been such an ugly scene with Clay Fraser. No one—man or woman—had ever spoken to her like that before. Not that she hadn't anticipated his anger, and didn't deserve his wrath. But when faced with it, she had felt like the deceitful whore he believed her to be, trading sex for an expensive ring.

She opened her eyes, raised her left hand, and stared at the glittering band. She wasn't a common thief and never intended to keep the ring. As soon as the wagon train was underway, she planned on returning it to him. She'd only used it as a prop to support her story.

For a long moment she continued to stare at the ring. It was clearly valuable. Much more valuable than her quick inspection last night had led her to believe. The five stones encircling the band appeared to be real diamonds—not imitation. The corners of her lips curled in a deprecating smile. Certainly not intended for the hand of a woman prepared to undertake the rigors of the Oregon Trail. No indeed. The ring was meant for the hand of one of those dainty southern belles serving tea in the drawing room of a big Virginia mansion, surrounded by slaves who did everything except eat and sleep for her.

Rebecca wondered what the woman was like, whom he'd bought the ring for. And why she'd married someone else. Which was why he was so bitter against women, of course.

Hmmm, you might have bitten off more than you can chew, Rebecca Elliott . . . ah . . . Fraser. She reached for the soap and began to sponge herself.

After bathing, she hurried back to the room and dressed quickly. There was a lot remaining to do, now that she knew for certain she'd be leaving with the wagon train.

She had just put on her hat when Clay knocked on the connecting door.

"Are you about ready?" he called. "We'd like to get some breakfast, and we're not going anywhere without you, lady. So hurry up."

"You sure have a way of ingratiating yourself with your new wife," Garth said.

Clay was convinced Rebecca took her time getting dressed, knowing full well they were waiting for her. Back home, a woman could have donned a crinoline and six petticoats in the time it took her to appear in a plain gingham dress—no crinoline, no half dozen petticoats, and not even a small bustle. Garth might be willing to cut her some slack, but she wasn't going to make a fool of him again. No matter how beautiful she was.

Garth and Rebecca kept up a running conversation throughout the meal as if they were old friends. Blood was supposed to be thicker than water, and Clay was beginning to wonder whose side his brother was on.

Sure, maybe he was being unchivalrous toward her, but who wouldn't be, in his shoes? He knew damn well he had not asked this woman to marry him.

Judge Henry Wilkins's office was located in the Independence courthouse, a redbrick building that stood in the center of the town square. The judge recognized them at once, and to Clay's further disappointment informed them that he'd just had the marriage officially registered.

"You're looking considerably sounder than you looked last night, Captain Fraser." The judge winked at him and poked him in the arm.

Clay took Rebecca firmly by the elbow and steered her out of the office. "What the hell was that all about?"

"It might have something to do with 'Ellie, Ellie, with the ticklish belly,' " Rebecca said, and walked on.

The woman was mind-boggling. By the time he caught up with her, the streets were too filled with people and livestock to pursue the matter any further.

They returned to the hotel, and Garth joined them in Rebecca's room. As she sat down, Garth leaned back against the wall with his arms folded across his chest, and Clay began to pace the floor.

"Unfortunately, Mrs. Ell . . . ah, madam—"

"Just call me Rebecca—or, if you prefer, *honey*, like you did last night."

Flushed, Clay cast a guilty glance at his brother. Garth's expression was inscrutable. Clay cleared his throat and began again. "Rebecca, unfortunately the events of last night—"

"Are you referring to what we did before we were married or the marriage itself?" she asked.

"Dammit, woman, will you stop interrupting and let me finish what I have to say?"

"Excuse me. Please go on, sir."

She looked like a cat with canary feathers hanging out of her mouth. That uppity Yankee attitude of hers was beginning to really annoy him.

"You do understand it's my intention to leave with the wagon train tomorrow morning."

She didn't reply, but continued to stare at him with her hands folded neatly in her lap.

He arched a brow and looked at her questioningly. "You do understand, don't you?"

"Oh, forgive me, I didn't realize I'm permitted to speak now. Yes, I do, sir."

If she wasn't careful, she was going to choke on those canary feathers!

"Dammit, woman, will you stop addressing me as if you're a trooper in my regiment! My name is Clayton, or Clay, if you prefer."

"Very well, Clayton. As you know, it's my intention to leave with the wagon train, too."

"Under the circumstances, I think it's best you return to your home in Vermont."

"What circumstances, Clayton?"

"This ridiculous marriage. It would be too awkward for us to travel together. As long as you're my wife, I will not consider allowing you to make this trek to California. It's as dangerous as it is arduous."

She clutched her chest dramatically. "Your consideration for me warms the cockles of my heart, Clayton."

"Your mockery, madam, merely confirms what a cold-hearted little conniver you are. Are you totally conscienceless?"

"I do have a conscience, Clayton, and I'm not proud of what I've done. I acted out of desperation. I have no home to go back to in Vermont. I couldn't go back there even if I did; I spent all of my money getting here."

"I intend to sell the ring and give you the money. If you're frugal, there should be enough to provide for you quite comfortably until you can find employment wherever you decide to settle down. You're clearly educated and have a pleasing appearance, Rebecca. You should have no trouble securing a job as a teacher or clerk."

"Rebecca," Garth said gently, "why don't you want to return to Vermont?"

"I have no family back there. My parents are dead, but I have a brother in Sacramento. I intend to join him."

"Would you consider going to Virginia?" Garth asked. "Our family has a plantation and there is plenty of room."

She looked at him, appalled. "My husband was killed during the war. I hate the South and all that you Rebels represent. I could never live among you."

"Then why did you marry my brother, Rebecca?" Garth asked. "Clay and you are obviously not in love. You're an attractive woman; I'm sure you could have found a husband who shared your sentiments about the war. There's plenty of Bluecoats heading west, too."

She sighed deeply and lowered her gaze. "I needed a husband before that wagon train pulled out. Single women aren't allowed, unless accompanied by a male member of her family."

"So why me?" Clay demanded. "You just said you hate Southerners."

She raised her eyes and glared at him. "It certainly wasn't due to your charm. If you want to know the truth, for a time I did consider that perverted little desk clerk."

Garth chuckled. "We saw how that ended."

"When I saw that you and Garth were the cleanest looking of the—"

"You chose me because I looked clean!" Clay threw up his hands in frustration.

"It's not necessary to shout, Clayton," she said.

"So you admit you planned it all! The seduction. The marriage."

"I said that I'm not proud of what I did."

"Hear that, Garth? She's not proud of being low-down and conniving. You're breaking my heart, sweetheart." In his frustration Clay slammed his fist into the wall.

"Cool down, Clay," Garth said. "Let her finish. Whatever she's done, anger won't solve this."

"*Et tu*, Brother Garth? Maybe if it happened to you,

you'd sing a different tune." Clay turned his wrath on Rebecca again. "And you expect me to believe that stealing the ring was only an afterthought?"

She pulled the ring off her finger and flung it at him. It bounced off his chest and flew onto the bed. "I don't want your damn ring; I never did. Despite what you think, I'm neither a whore nor a thief. I told you I only took it to reinforce my story. If you'll just listen without shouting or trying to punch holes in the wall, I'll explain. I've thought this all out."

Clay snorted. "What a surprise. You figure out something else to your advantage?"

Her eyes pleaded with him. "Clayton, I don't want your money and I never had any intention of making husbandly demands on you. I'm quite capable of taking care of myself, no matter what Mr. Scott thinks. I just need your name so I can leave with that wagon train tomorrow. Once we get to California, I'll have the marriage annulled."

Clay snapped up his head. "Annulled? How is that possible, after we—"

"We never consummated the marriage, Clayton. You passed out and slept through the night. I simply lay down in the bed next to you."

Clay started to laugh, relief flooding him. "Then I'll apply for an annulment right here before we even leave Independence."

"I'll deny it if you do—and Judge Wilkins will believe me because he saw us in a very compromising position. All I ask for is your cooperation, Clay. We don't even have to speak to each other on the trip, and I swear to

God that I'll give you that annulment as soon as we reach California. You've got nothing to lose, meanwhile."

It was probably a mistake, but despite his anger, he was beginning to believe her. And hell, if it was so important for her to get to California, there'd be no satisfaction in his trying to prevent it. Besides, that way he could keep an eye on her to make sure she lived up to her promise. And she was right: What difference would a few months make?

But he still couldn't excuse the tactics she'd used; she should have been truthful with him from the start.

Clay walked to the bed and picked up the ring. "What about the theft of my name? Did you even think of anything but your own interests?"

"And I suppose you had my welfare in mind when you came into my room in the first place?" she snapped. "I don't think so, Clayton."

"Okay, I admit that was stupidity on my part. You were offering—I reached for it. But you've made a mockery of the sanctity of marriage, Rebecca, and no matter what *your* opinion of southerners may be, our parents taught us the meaning of marriage by the example they set, as well as the honor they instilled in us."

"I'm sorry," she repeated.

"Not as much as I am. But you carry the name Fraser now, so I'll honor this farce of a marriage whether I like it or not."

He strode to the door, then spun on his heel. "But hear me, and hear me good, *Mrs. Fraser.* As long as you are my wife, you had better honor the name you carry, too—because I'll kill any man you try to go near."

"If you're quite through, I have something more to say," Rebecca said.

"I'm not interested in listening to any more of your excuses, so save your breath. Garth, let's get the hell out of here. We'll have to find a buyer for the ring, so we can dredge up a wagon and team for my *wife*." He frowned. "Just how *did* you expect to travel if Scott had permitted you to join?"

"That's what I'm trying to tell you," Rebecca said patiently. "I already have a wagon and team."

The two men exchanged startled glances, then Garth grabbed her by the hand and pulled her out of the chair. "If it wouldn't be too much trouble, Miz Becky, will you show them to us?"

Scowling, Clay followed them out.

5

Rebecca studied Clay's face as he looked over the wagon she'd purchased. It wasn't one of the larger Conestoga wagons, but a farm wagon about five feet wide and ten feet long that had been converted to a covered wagon with treated cloth strung over hickory bows.

"Who sold you this?" Clay asked.

"A couple from Michigan. They decided they couldn't afford the cost of the food and supplies for the trip, so they're going back where they came from."

"They have a damn sight more common sense than you have." Clay hopped up into the wagon bed. He had to stoop, since the headroom was only about five feet high in the center. The wagon was empty except for a rocking chair and a rectangular box about six feet long attached to one side of the wagon. The box opened from the top for storage, and at night would serve as a bed. Clay pulled out the fur pallet that was rolled up inside of the box and spread it out on top of the box lid.

"Pretty narrow, isn't it?" he said critically.

"It's wide enough for me, and that's who I bought it for."

"But now there's two of us. Looks like it's going to be a pretty tight squeeze." He looked her over appraisingly.

She blushed. "That's not very funny, Clayton."

He grinned. "Maybe not. But fun? Oh, yeah. What did this rig cost you?"

"Seven hundred dollars for the wagon and team."

"What did you get to pull it? Oxen or mules?"

"Six mules."

"Hah," he said with a shrug.

"What does that mean?" The man had a way of putting her on the defensive, and she didn't intend to let him get away with it. "I was told mules are faster than oxen and can eat the prairie grass and sage along the way."

"That's true, and you should get along fine with them—they're as ornery as you are."

"I'm not the ornery one, sir. You're the most cantankerous individual it's been my misfortune to encounter."

"Does that mean the marriage is off?" He hopped out, knelt down, and peered under the wagon. "How does the underside look, Garth?"

Garth crawled out from under the wagon and brushed himself off. "I'd say it's built pretty sturdily. There are hardwood brakes and the underside's in good condition, except for the front axle. Looks like it won't take too much rough travel, so it'll have to be reinforced before we leave. All in all, it's well equipped. A spare wheel, a water barrel, and attached storage boxes on three sides. Who could ask for more?" He grinned at Rebecca. "You made a pretty good buy here, Miz Becky."

Before she could reply, Clay said, "No doubt. Speaking from experience, the lady looks out for herself. The poor couple from Michigan probably came out on the short end of the bargain."

Rebecca gritted her teeth. Oh, the man was deplorable! But if she responded, it would only encourage him to be more disagreeable.

"Mr. Scott has called a ten o'clock meeting for those of us leaving with the train," Clay said. "We'd better get going or we'll be late."

Garth nodded. "As soon as that's over, I'll work on that axle, and you and Becky can round up the supplies."

By the time they arrived, the warehouse was filled. They managed to squeeze inside just as Scott climbed up on a makeshift podium and held up a form.

"I think I've met each of you personally, but I want the head of each family to sign this form, on which you swear that you will abide by my orders and decisions. Get a copy from Jim Peterson, sitting over there at that table, and hand it back to him after you sign it. The moment we depart, I, and I alone, will be the only one to issue orders. I know there are some former Union and Confederate officers among you men, but think of me as your commanding general now, gentlemen—because your days of issuing orders are over for as long as it takes us to get to California. And while we're on that subject, let me remind all of you that the war *is* over. Whatever your past grievances, you leave them behind when we pull out of here. As of tomorrow, we are a united unit, and cooperation and goodwill toward one another is the only chance we have of reaching our destination. Anyone who's not willing to accept this should not join us, because I will not tolerate any violation of this order. You will be ejected at once from the train and not permitted to return. And if anyone commits a crime, the punishment will be as severe as the law would dole out. I will not jeopardize the safety of those in my charge. Does anyone have any questions or problems with what I just said?"

"Mr. Scott, if something happens to you, who's in charge?" one of the men asked.

"Jim Peterson. Jim and I have made three trips together, and he knows the route as well as I. As does our scout, Joseph Hawkins here," Scott said, nodding toward the man standing a few steps behind him on the podium. "He doesn't answer to anything but Hawk."

Hawk was the personification of how Rebecca anticipated a western scout would appear. Clad in buckskins, he was lean and grizzled, his face leathery and windburned from long hours spent in the outdoors.

"They are both good men and can answer any question you might have once we're underway," Scott continued. "But I'll warn you in advance that Hawk here isn't too talkative, so don't expect any long answers."

"What hostiles will we encounter, Mr. Scott?" a man near the rear yelled out.

"You talking about human ones or nature's?" Scott asked. "I doubt any Indians or bushwhackers will take on a train this size. But size doesn't mean a hill of beans to Ole Mother Nature. Between here and California you'll have to cope with lightning and rain, drought, cold, mountains, desert, and maybe even snow. As for

Indians, there's the possibility of Cheyenne, Pawnee, Sioux, and Ute. Any of them can be trouble if provoked, but in most cases they'll leave us alone. Don't go looking for trouble; it'll find you soon enough.

"Once we're under way, I'll draw up a schedule. Every man will be expected to stand night guard unless his wife gets sick. And that's another thing, folks. I can tell you right now, disease and accidents will claim some of you: Not everyone will make it to California."

Another question came from the crowd. "Mr. Scott, how do we dress?"

"It'll probably be warm between here and Fort Laramie, but from there on, you'll need warm clothing—especially in the mountains at night. If the trip's smooth, we could hit them as early as the middle of August, but if we hit them much later than that, we could be in for some rough going. We leave the Oregon Trail in southern Idaho, then we hit the desert, with intense heat during the day and cold at night. Figure on four to six months at least. On a really good day we can cover as much as fifteen or twenty miles; on a bad day, none.

"Anyone I haven't met, please come up and introduce yourself now or later tonight. The first wagon pulls out at six o'clock tomorrow morning. I don't want a stampede of wagons jockeying for a place in line, so after you've signed the agreement form, draw a number from the pot on Jim's table, and that'll be your wagon position. Those who draw the low numbers should position themselves near the western end of town, so there's no delay in starting off.

"Good luck to you all, and we'll kick off the trip with

a dance tonight right here in the warehouse. The grub and drinks are on me, so enjoy the evening. And then, California, here we come!"

His outcry was met with whistles and shouts. Rebecca couldn't help wondering if they'd all have that same enthusiasm in three months.

As she and Clay signed the form, the wagon master came up to her. "Mrs. Elliott, I made it clear there can be no single women on the train."

She smiled. "I'm no longer single, Mr. Scott. Clayton and I are married."

"Is that true, Fraser?" Scott asked.

She prayed Clay wouldn't reveal how she had manipulated him into marrying her. If the truth got out, she'd be mortified.

To her surprise, Clay slipped an arm around her shoulder.

"Yes, sir. We were married last night. Rebecca and I are old friends. It was my surprise and pleasure to run into her here, of all places."

"You and your brother signed on as part of my crew, Fraser."

"I still intend to be, sir. Rebecca understands that."

"All right. Sure isn't any way to spend a honeymoon, but congratulations. And I hope the two of you will be very happy."

As soon as they were outside, Rebecca said, "Thank you for not telling Mr. Scott the truth about our marriage."

"Well, it would have been just as embarrassing for me," he muttered. "Let's get those supplies."

Garth left to repair the front axle, while she and Clay purchased supplies. Rebecca had already prepared a long list and now increased the amount of several of the items, due to the addition of the two men, even though Clay informed her that the wagon master provided the food for his crewmembers.

He also insisted upon looking over her list. "Do you have a warm coat?"

"Of course. We have cold winters in Vermont, Clayton."

He gave her shoes a disdainful glance. "What about a sturdy pair of boots? The shoes you're wearing are useless. There'll be mud, mountains, and rivers to contend with."

"Mr. Fraser, it is not necessary for you to concern yourself about my wardrobe. I am quite capable of making those determinations myself. I have been doing so for most of my life." Rebecca made a mental note to buy a pair of boots.

By the time Garth finished the repair on the axle, they had accumulated the needed supplies. Then the three of them set to work loading the wagon with a camp stool and table, two hundred pounds of flour, a barrel of bacon packed in bran to prevent it from spoiling, one hundred and fifty pounds of coffee, twenty pounds of sugar, fifteen of salt, ten pounds of dried beans, and five pounds of hardtack. In addition, she'd bought ten jars of canned tomatoes, a gallon of molasses, a bushel of potatoes, a peck of onions, a bushel of apples, five pounds of dried peaches, baking soda, cornmeal, vinegar, rice, assorted spices, and a box of tea. Then there were the necessary items of soap, a few medicinal products, towels, dishcloths, bedding, a washbowl, chamber pot, wash boiler, a large kettle, a Dutch oven, a reflector oven, a coffeepot, teapot, a frying pan, a three-legged spider skillet, tin tableware, candles and molds, two lanterns, and cooking and eating utensils. At the last moment Rebecca had remembered to buy a mirror, a clock, pins, needles, thread, and a pair of scissors.

While she concentrated on the stores and cookware, Clay took care of the hatchet, some standard hand tools, a couple of buckets, rope, and extra harness and rein. By the time they finished loading it all, the wagon and storage boxes were filled to capacity, with just enough room remaining for their clothing to be put into the inside box. One final but critical purchase remained—a rifle and ammunition.

"Can you fire a rifle?" Clay asked Rebecca.

"No," she said.

"I should have guessed." He walked away, disgusted.

Garth grinned at her. "I'm afraid to ask, Becky. Have you ever driven a mule team?"

She shook her head.

He shoved his hat up on his forehead. "How in the world did you expect to make this trip alone?"

"I've driven a team of horses before," she said. "Mules can't be much different."

"Becky, mules are nothing like horses. They're about the most stubborn animal you can encounter."

"Worse than your brother?"

Garth grinned. "You have no idea. If they don't want to move, they won't. And they're mean as hell."

"Worse than your brother?" she repeated, tongue in cheek, and broke into laughter.

"You have the wrong impression about Clay, Becky," he said, turning serious. "I love him dearly and I'm proud to call him brother. He's a little down on women right now, but he's not unreasonable. He's always been fair-minded, understanding, and I've never known him to bear grudges, no matter what he might say or how it appears to the contrary. My sister and brothers and I have always looked to Clay for advice whenever we've had a problem. He's a good listener, and he puts the interests of the people he loves above his own. So I'm hoping the two of you can work out this situation enough to make the trip bearable. It's going to be hard enough, without the two of you at each other's throats. I'll do my best to try and ease the strain, but you've got to do your part, too, Becky." Then he grinned. "Now, let's get back to the problem of those damn mules."

"I know I can handle them, Garth. I've always been quick to learn, and there isn't anything I can't do once I put my mind to it," she said confidently.

"I don't doubt that, judging by how you roped Clay into marriage, honey. You might be wiser not mentioning this to him, so sit down, and I'll start you out with the basics."

Rebecca smiled at him. She'd found an ally in Garth Fraser—even if he was a Johnny Reb. It was hard to remember her hatred for them when she was with him. He was patient and understanding—too nice to dislike. But no matter what Garth said, his brother was just the opposite. It was going to be a long few months.

By the time Garth left, Clay had not returned from purchasing the rifle and ammunition, so Becky went to the cobbler shop and bought a pair of boots.

Returning to her hotel room, she sat down on the bed and counted her money. She had just over a hundred dollars remaining. Rebecca lay back on the pillow. She hoped it would last through the rest of the trip.

Awakened by a tapping on the door, she bolted to a sitting position. The room was in darkness, and it took her several seconds to get oriented before she realized the tapping was coming from the connecting door between the rooms.

"Who is it?"

"Clay."

"Just a moment."

Rebecca got up and lit the lamp. It was dark outside, and she realized that she must have slept for hours. She unlocked the door and Clay came into the room.

"Aren't you going to the dance?"

"The dance! Oh, my, I'd forgotten all about it. Maybe you and Garth should go on without me."

"Garth isn't going. He said he has no intentions of spending his last night in town with the same people he'll be with for the next few months," Clay said.

"He has a good point." But it had been years since she'd been to anything that remotely resembled a party, and the thought of the music and gaiety seemed appealing.

"I have to change my dress. If you want to go ahead, I'll come later."

"I'll wait for you," he said. "Appearances, you know."

He handed her a pair of women's leather gloves. "I noticed you didn't buy any today. You'll need these when you drive that team."

"Thank you, Clayton." The thoughtful gesture took her by surprise. "Did you get a rifle?"

He nodded, then reached into his pocket and pulled out a plain gold band. "And I sold the other ring. This doesn't have diamonds, but I think it'll be better if you wear it. Ah . . . appearances, you know. I'll wait until you're ready." He handed her the ring, then stepped back into his room and closed the door.

Rebecca stared at the gold band for a long moment before she slipped it on her finger. Somehow the simple, inexpensive ring made her feel more conscious of being his wife than the flashier, expensive diamond-studded band had. She raised her hand to her neck and pulled out the chain she had tucked under her bodice. She touched the gold band Charley had given her that now dangled from the chain, then stared at the ring on her finger, unaware of the tears sliding down her cheeks.

She couldn't do it. She knew she should, but she couldn't bring herself to put on the ring Clay gave her. Not when this marriage was just temporary. She quickly switched the rings and returned Charley's to her finger, then tucked Clay's in among the clothes in her bag. He would never notice.

Squaring her shoulders, Rebecca brushed away her tears and pulled a flowered chintz gown out of her trunk.

The ruffled flounce that ran down the front and circled the hem could have used a pressing, but there was no time for that and it was the only party gown she had. She changed into it quickly and combed out her hair, then retrieved the pair of red pumps from the bottom of the trunk. For a long moment she held them, gazing sadly at the slippers. Charley had bought them for her the Christmas after they were married. There'd been no occasion to wear them after he left for the war. With a deep sigh she removed her everyday black shoes and slipped on the red ones. Then she knocked on Clay's door.

The heated look in his eyes, as his gaze ran down her curves, made her forget about her gown's wrinkles, and awareness tingled through her as he took her arm.

The party was in full swing by the time they arrived, and hundreds of men, women, and children packed the room. As she and Clay ate the roasted chicken and savory potato salad, Rebecca looked around with interest. There was an excitement in the air.

Tomorrow was a new beginning, the hope for a fresh start from whatever desolation they all had left behind. Most of them were ex-Confederate soldiers, but there were many blue-trousered men among the crowd, as well. And as Mr. Scott had declared, from now on, there would not—and could not—be any division between them. They all had a common goal now: to start a new life in the land of milk and honey.

As soon as the orchestra struck an opening chord, Mike Scott quieted the crowd. "Folks, we've got a newlywed couple among us named Clay and Rebecca

Fraser, who were just married yesterday. With a little coaxing, maybe the new bride and groom will lead out the first waltz."

The building reverberated with applause and whistles from the crowd.

Good Lord! This can't be happening. Rebecca glanced at Clay, who looked as appalled as she was.

"Where is the happy couple?" Scott called. "Clay and Rebecca, come out, come out, wherever you are."

When the crowd picked up the chant, Clay grasped her hand. "I believe they're playing our wedding waltz, Mrs. Fraser."

She let him lead her to the center of the room. Surprisingly, his hand felt warm and strong, maybe because hers was so cold and trembling.

The orchestra struck up the strains of a Strauss waltz, and Clay took her into the circle of his arms. The warm pressure of his hand on the small of her back stirred awareness of his nearness, and made her more conscious than ever of the power contained within that tall body and the commanding set of those wide shoulders. As if his tantalizing scent of bay rum and pure male wasn't enough of a reminder.

She didn't know what made her more self-conscious: knowing how many eyes followed their movements, or her awareness of Clay's nearness. His steps were easy to match as he fluidly led her in the dance. Clearly he was no stranger to a Viennese waltz. But why would he be? Cotillions and balls were all part of that southern culture he'd fought to preserve.

To block out her growing awareness of him, Rebecca

closed her eyes. Imagining herself in Charley's arms, she tried to recall the last time they had waltzed together. To her dismay, she couldn't remember. The lack of memory was a painful stab at her heart. Daily, her memories of him were fading away. She wanted to cry.

As soon as the music ended, Rebecca stepped out of Clay's arms and quickly turned away. She couldn't get out of there fast enough. To her further distress, Clay followed her.

They walked in silence back to the hotel. He saw her to her room, and without a backward look she entered and locked the door. Within seconds a light appeared from under the connecting door.

Rebecca leaned back against her door and let her tears flow freely.

Clay shucked his gunbelt and boots, blew out the lamp, and stretched out on the bed. Alone in the dark, his thoughts immediately turned to Rebecca. He'd sensed she'd been on the verge of tears but was too plucky to let them flow in his presence. Since she had the gumption to head West alone, he doubted she'd been crying from fear of what tomorrow would bring. It took courage, and she sure as hell had enough of that.

As lowdown as it was, she'd taken a big chance in marrying a stranger. Another man might have beaten her—or even killed her—for pulling the trick she had on him. She had no idea how easily her scheme might have backfired on her. The West was too wild and uncertain for a woman on her own.

For that matter, it was no place for him, either. After four years he was finally able to go home—only to have to leave again to chase after Lissy. Unlike most of these people, he wasn't looking for a new beginning; he wanted to go back to the life he'd known before. Was it too late to recapture that, or could it be the same again? One thing was certain: Once they caught up with Lissy and were satisfied she was happy and that the Yankee had made an honest woman of her, he was making a beeline back to Virginia.

Clay yawned and closed his eyes. After his marriage was annulled, of course. If he took that delectable little termagant back to Virginia, she'd probably succeed in restarting the war.

But for now, it looked as if he was stuck with her.

6

Too excited to sleep a moment longer, Rebecca rose at four o'clock and peeked out the hotel window. Fires from a dozen blacksmiths' forges blazed brightly, and the clanging of their hammers had sounded day and night from the time she'd arrived in Independence. Due to the wagon train's departure, the hotel and general stores had remained open throughout the night for any necessary last-minute sales. She packed up her belongings and went down to the dining room.

She had just finished eating when Clay and Garth came in. "Good morning," she said pleasantly.

"Good morning, Becky," Garth replied, but Clay ignored her greeting. "All ready for the big day?"

She smiled excitedly. "I'm about ready to burst at the seams."

"I think we all are," he said. "Well, I promised to meet Scotty at the corral. I'll see you later."

"Why didn't you wake us when you got up?" Clay asked, as he sat down.

"I wasn't aware waking you was my responsibility. I'm quite willing to cook your and Garth's meals, but that's where it begins and ends."

"Your generosity is overwhelming, madam."

She also needed to lay down one very important ground rule before the journey began.

"Although it's necessary to keep up an appearance of being newlyweds, that does not extend to sharing a bed together."

Clay simply looked amused.

Oh, the man was exasperating, but she had looked forward to this day too long to let him ruin it for her. She smiled sweetly at him. "Just so you understand, Clayton."

He returned her false smile. "I think you're the one who doesn't understand, Rebecca. There are several obligations that go along with that marriage license you were so eager to . . . procure, one of which is conjugal rights. I intend to honor that obligation as well as my pledge to protect you."

She stiffened. "I don't require your protection any more than I need you in my bed."

"You should have considered that before you took an oath to become my *lawful* wife."

"Are you going back on your word, Clayton? We agreed to an annulment. If we become intimate that would be an impossibility, and you know it."

"The annulment was all your idea, Rebecca. I never agreed to any such arrangement. Through no desire on my part, we are lawfully husband and wife, and I honor any vow I make. So I intend to try and become a good husband to you, Rebecca, and I expect you to take your vow just as seriously. If you see that as a problem, I'd advise you to think twice before we start this journey— because you *will* have to honor *all* a wife's obligations."

He stood up to leave. "I thought about this for a long

time last night, Rebecca. I was damn angry over this trick you pulled, but after further thought, I came to the conclusion that this marriage might not be such a bad idea after all. A good-looking woman to cook my meals, wash my clothes, and warm my bed at night. Yep, it could make a long journey considerably more comfortable than I'd anticipated."

"You southerners just can't envision your lives without a slave, can you?" Rebecca was seething with anger, but she wouldn't give him the satisfaction of knowing how much his words disturbed her.

"You have about an hour to make up your mind, Mrs. Fraser."

Oh, what a blackguard! How could Garth claim his brother was a fair and compassionate man? Clayton Fraser was a smug, arrogant despot!

Well, he didn't intimidate her. *His* honor. *His* oaths. *His* obligations! The man's inflated opinion of himself was enough to turn her stomach. Well, he may have struck the first blow in this war between them, but the day hadn't dawned when any Rebel secessionist could outmaneuver a born-and-bred Yankee like her!

Rebecca had the team hitched to the wagon by the time Clay and Garth rode up.

"Drive carefully, Becky," Garth called out. He waved and rode by.

Clay dismounted and tied his horse to the rear, then climbed up on the wagon box and took the reins. "You have any problem with the mules?"

"Are you referring to the four-legged ones, or you and your brother?"

He cast an exasperated look at her. "Lady, you are such a shrew."

"You're right. My apologies to Garth; he doesn't deserve it."

Clay flicked the reins and began to move cautiously through the area, crowded with wagons piled high with supplies and people who were as eager as she to start the journey. Many had a horse or cow tethered to the rear of the wagon, and huge, lumbering oxen hitched to the front.

A white square painted with the number designating their position in line was pinned to the canvas side of each wagon. They were number fifteen.

The crowd stood hushed as the Reverend Kirkland called upon the Lord's blessing and guidance through the journey ahead, to guide them to a new land of hope and beginning, as He had Moses lead the Israelites to their Promised Land.

Then Hawk hopped into the saddle on a black gelding. "Stay safe, folks!" he shouted, and with a wave of his hat the scout galloped ahead.

A loud cheer rose from the throng as the first two wagons pulled out, carrying the supplies for the crew.

Many of the other drivers were inexperienced city dwellers who had never handled yoked oxen or a mule team, so there was a great deal of confusion and chaos when a team would balk or a wagon would bump into a tree or some other obstacle.

Clay sat shaking his head as he watched the confusion. "Are you sure you'll be able to handle this team?"

"Of course."

"Have you ever driven a mule team before?"

She'd be darned if she'd let him intimidate her into lying. "No, but I've driven a horse team enough times in my day."

"They're nothing alike."

"I"'ve always had a way with animals," Rebecca said airily.

She trembled with excitement as Number Fourteen was finally called. It actually had a horse-drawn carriage attached to the rear. Two women and a young girl and boy waved from it as they joined the line.

Rebecca waved back, and then Jim Peterson called out Number Fifteen. Her heart seemed to jump to her throat.

Clay leaned over to her. "This is it, Rebecca." To her shock, he placed a light kiss on her lips, then he smoothly maneuvered the wagon into the moving queue.

Her lips tingling, she turned her head and looked back for a final look. Behind lay the only kind of life she'd ever known. She turned ground and looked ahead. Ahead lay the future.

Rebecca stole a glance at the stranger sitting beside her. His light kiss had caught her by surprise. But in a way, it was kind of sweet. What part would he play in this future she looked toward?

By the time the ninety-eighth and final wagon had joined the line, the front of the train was over a mile ahead.

Garth rode up to them. "Clay, Scotty wants you to ride about a quarter of a mile off the right flank. See you later," he called as he rode away.

"It's all yours now," Clay said, handing the reins over to her. "Don't keep too loose a rein on them, or they might tend to stop on you. Same's true if you pull them tight." He jumped down from the slow-moving wagon, unhitched his horse, and rode off toward the north.

Rebecca had to admit that handling six mules was considerably different from driving a two-horse team. Even though the pace was much slower, there were more reins to hold and control. And Clay's gift of the gloves were a godsend; otherwise her hands would have been bruised and blistered from the reins. By the time they halted at noon for lunch, Rebecca was confident she had the situation well in hand.

There was no sign of Clay or Garth, so when Rebecca finished eating a sandwich and orange for lunch, she walked over and introduced herself to the family in the wagon ahead of her.

Howard and Helena Garson were a middle-aged couple from a small community in Ohio, heading to California to try their luck out West. Howard had served in the Union army during the war. A shy and soft-spoken man, he appeared to be carrying the weight of the world on his stooped shoulders, curved from long hours of planting and harvesting crops.

His wife was just the opposite. Stocky in stature, Helena was cheerfully outgoing, with a booming voice and laugh that seemed to resonate from the depth of her ample bosom.

The Garsons had three children: a sixteen-year-old daughter, Henrietta, fourteen-year-old Alden, and nine-year-old George. Howard's mother, Eleanor, was also accompanying them.

A much older couple, Otto and Blanche VonDieman, occupied the wagon behind Rebecca's. They had a cow attached to the rear of their wagon and some chickens in a coop. They were Dutch and, despite speaking halting English, were very friendly. They offered her milk and eggs whenever she needed them.

Blanche VonDieman suffered with a rasping cough, and they had sold their Pennsylvania farm to move to a drier, warmer climate in Southern California.

Thank goodness she wasn't surrounded by Rebels, Rebecca thought with satisfaction when the wagon train moved on after lunch.

By late afternoon she had begun to feel the effects from the pull of the reins in her arms and shoulders. She was glad when the wagon master called a halt at six o'clock. Since there was no threat of hostile Indians in the area, the train remained stretched out. The livestock was put out to graze and names were drawn to guard the herd. On the whole, though, the animals appeared as tired as the travelers and content to just graze and sleep.

Following the example of the others, Rebecca let her mules loose and gave them explicit instructions not to wander away from the rest of the herd. They looked at her calmly and then began to chew on the grass. She couldn't understand why mules had such a bad reputation. The darlings hadn't given her one bit of trouble all day.

Shortly after halting, the outriders rode in, and Clay and Garth joined her. Rebecca was glad when Clay took the hatchet and went out to get her some firewood.

Wood was already short in the area. Wagon trains had been passing through on their way West for over forty years, and the steady traffic following the Gold Rush in '49 had increased drastically in the closing days of the war. Now the wagon trains leaving Independence waited only long enough between departures to allow the grass to grow enough for the oxen and mules to graze on.

Since she was new to outdoor living, Rebecca didn't prepare anything difficult for the evening meal. Once Garth had the fire built, she made a pot of coffee, baked biscuits, and then fried bacon. When the bacon was done, she fried sliced potatoes with chopped onions in the bacon grease, and offered a fresh apple for dessert.

Pleased with herself, Rebecca thought the meal was very tasty. Clay must have thought so, too, since he didn't make any derogatory remarks. She was almost hoping he would, so that she could tell him to go eat with the rest of the crew.

After the meal was over, she set some dough to rise overnight so she could attempt to bake bread in the morning.

By eight o'clock the camp had settled in for the evening, and some had even started to prepare for bed. Garth had joined some folks down the line who were listening to a banjo player, fiddler, and several men with mouth organs play some familiar tunes. Clay had stretched out near the campfire with his eyes closed.

Rebecca lit a lantern and sat down in the rocking chair inside the wagon to read a cookbook that offered easy recipes for campfire cooking. If the bread turned out successfully tomorrow, she'd try a peach cobbler the day after. Having worked in a bakery, she looked forward to the challenge of baking in the small, three-sided reflector oven.

Unfortunately, the other challenge she had undertaken was not as satisfying. Her shoulders and arms were aching painfully, so she put the book aside and rubbed some unguent on her arms. Then she leaned back in the chair and closed her eyes. Oh, how she wished she could massage her shoulders! She was tempted to take the liniment over to the Garsons and ask one of the women to rub some across her back and shoulders, but they were sure to wonder why she didn't ask her husband to do it.

Rebecca opened her eyes and discovered Clay was standing at the rear of the wagon, his probing gaze on her. "Looks like you're favoring your shoulders. Are they sore?"

What did he think? He knew she'd never driven a mule team before. And she doubted he really cared how much they ached, anyway. This was just another way of goading her.

"Just tired," she said. "I'm going to bed." She stood up and blew out the lantern. As he stepped away, she closed the flaps and stripped down to her petticoat and drawers. Unfortunately, the fur pelt did little to make the wooden box any softer or the pain in her shoulders any less.

In a short time she heard Garth return. For a while, the two men talked together in low tones, then they got their sleeping rolls out of the storage box and settled down by the fire. She sighed in relief that Clay didn't go through with his threat to sleep with her. Of course, this was just the first night, and there were many more ahead of them.

The wagon was stuffy and smelled of the fruit and vegetables stored there. She got up and raised the front and rear flaps of the wagon, in the hope of catching a breeze. She envied the men sleeping outside. The ground would be softer than the box she was on, and it would be so pleasant to count the twinkling stars overhead, instead of imaginary sheep to try to get to sleep.

But other than her aches and pains, the day had gone well. Maybe the trip wouldn't be as hard as she'd been led to believe. And maybe—just maybe—Clay wasn't as much of an ogre she believed him to be.

Clay folded his hands under his head and thought about the woman in the wagon. He was responsible for her protection and welfare, which meant he now had two women to worry about. If they were lucky, maybe they'd overtake the wagon train Melissa was on. He should have anticipated that she'd take off with this Berg fellow after she told him about her condition. Sure, his mind had been cluttered with Ellie's perfidy, and he hadn't been thinking straight—but a little common sense then would have prevented this trip.

He also blamed himself for taking that first drink from the Yankee conniver in the wagon. She really was something else. He'd probably applaud her resourcefulness—if only she hadn't made him her target.

Women! They were nothing but trouble. Why couldn't they be honest and straightforward, like men? Ellie's betrayal of him, Lissy running off with a Yankee, Rebecca Elliott manipulating him into marriage . . . a sisterhood of Jezebels that had begun with that damn apple in Eden. That should have been a warning to all men. *Instead, we keep reaching out for the fruit.*

Well, not anymore. He had learned his lesson the hard way. And, like it or not, he was stuck with the Jezebel in the wagon.

"But I'm sure as hell not going to make the mistake of trusting her," he said, with a punch to his pillow.

"You still got Ellie on your mind?" Garth asked drowsily.

"No. Go to sleep." Clay rolled over and closed his eyes.

Much of the camp was still asleep as Rebecca struggled to get the fire started the next morning. The wood just wouldn't take to the match. The small loaf she had prepared had risen beautifully during the night, and she was determined to bake it this morning, but she couldn't spend the next hour just getting the darn fire going. After wasting two more matches in the effort, she was on the verge of giving up.

"What are you doing?" Clay asked groggily.

"What does it look like?" she said, exasperated by her failed effort. She turned and looked at him. He was sitting up in his bedroll, scratching at his head. "I'm building a fire."

"*Trying* to build a fire," he corrected. He pulled on his boots, then stood up and tucked his shirt into his trousers, and came over and knelt beside her. "Give me those matches before you use them all up. What time is it, anyway?"

"Four o'clock."

"Four o'clock! What in hell are you doing up this early? We're not pulling out until seven."

"I'm going to bake bread."

He shook his head. "Rebecca, what are you doing on a wagon train? You've never handled a mule team, you don't know how to use a rifle, you can't even build a campfire. You should have baked the bread last night when you had a fire, instead of trying to do it at four o'clock the next morning. A few more hours wouldn't turn the bread stale, you know."

Drat, he was right! She could have set the dough yesterday morning and baked the bread last night. But he was the last one she'd ever admit that to.

Within minutes he had a fire going and had lain down again. Rebecca got her bread baking, and then put a pot of coffee on to brew. She still had plenty of time to cook breakfast.

When she saw the VonDiemans were up and about, she went over to their wagon and got a small pitcher of milk from them, then returned to cook oatmeal and fry bacon.

An hour later Rebecca and the two men sat down to a breakfast of hot oatmeal and milk, fried bacon, freshly baked bread, and mugs of hot coffee. The bread was a little well done on the outside, but it was only her first attempt to bake bread in a reflector oven. She was confident the next time it would be perfect.

All in all, her second meal was as delicious as the first one she had prepared, which bolstered her confidence. Rebecca was so proud of herself, she almost popped the buttons off her bodice.

Arms akimbo, she struck a pose. "So, Captain Fraser, what do you think?"

"You can call me Clay," he said, generously spreading orange marmalade over the last slice of bread.

"Of the breakfast?" she persisted.

"It wasn't bad."

"It was darn good, and you know it."

"The bread was a little overdone."

"Yes, I noticed you actually had to chew it, instead of inhaling it like you did the rest of the food."

Garth snorted with laughter, and Clay reluctantly grinned. "It was good," he allowed.

"We'll just see how well I can do on this journey, Clayton Fraser," Rebecca murmured as she watched him ride away. "And I hope you like the taste of crow, because you'll be eating a lot more of it before this is over."

7

Promptly at seven the wagons up front began moving on. Rebecca finished hitching up the team and climbed up on the box.

Once again she had no trouble with the mules. She had given each one a name, and talked to it sweetly as she fed the animal a slice of apple before she harnessed it to the wagon. None of them had balked or tried to kick and bite, like some of the other mules were doing.

With a slight flick of the reins, they moved forward like trained trotters, following the Garson wagon. Rebecca couldn't help smiling, wondering if some sweet talk and a slice of apple would be as effective on Clay.

All along the line she could see women and children walking beside their wagons. As the hours wore on, she wished she could join them, just to have relief from the reins.

Mike Scott came riding down the line talking to each family, and when he reached her wagon, he greeted her warmly.

"Any problems here, Mrs. Fraser?"

"No, everything's just fine, Mr. Scott." She tried to sit up straight, and grimaced with pain.

"Are you okay, ma'am?"

"Yes, just a little stiff. I'll be glad when we rest for lunch."

He frowned. "I see." Then he glanced skyward. "Sky's clouding up. Hope we aren't in for rain."

"Do we stop if it does?" she asked hopefully.

"I'm afraid not. We'll be driving through thunderstorms, dust storms, sandstorms, and possibly even blizzards before we reach California. It takes some powerfully wicked weather to stop a wagon train, Mrs. Fraser. Lost time is our worst enemy." He nodded, and then rode on to the next wagon.

When they stopped for lunch, Rebecca didn't feel like eating. She drank a cup of water and ate an apple, then stretched out to try and relax her back. As she lay in the shade of the wagon, she wondered how long it would take for her body to adjust to the driving. All too soon it was time to get going again.

Shortly after they were under way, Henrietta Garson came back to her wagon and offered to drive it for a while.

"Have you driven mules before, Henrietta?"

"Oh, yes. On the farm." The girl climbed up beside her and took the reins. "And call me Etta, Mrs. Fraser. That's what my family does. Grandma says your shoulders and arms must be pretty sore by now."

"Your grandma is right, Etta. I can't tell you how good it feels to relax them. They hurt so bad, I could cry. And please, my name's Becky. That's what my . . ." She stopped. Charley had always called her Rebecca, and since her parents died, nobody had called her Becky except her brother and Garth Fraser. Yet the name had slipped out so naturally now.

Funny, she had never thought about that before. And she had always liked the nickname. Maybe, deep down, she was finally putting aside the sadness of the past years and carrying forward only pleasant memories into the new life she had chosen.

If that was the case, she sure had started out on the wrong foot by marrying Clay Fraser. It gave her a lot to think about as they rode along.

Hawk had chosen a pleasant area by a river for the campsite that evening. By the time Clay and Garth rode in, Rebecca had a fire built and had just finished rolling out the crust for the cobbler. She had soaked the dried peaches in a bowl of water all day to soften them, and now popped the finished product into the reflector oven.

She'd been around Clay long enough to realize that the first thing he always reached for was the coffeepot. He poured himself a cup of coffee, then without a hi or good-bye, he took the hatchet and disappeared.

So, he was angry again—there was no doubt about that. She glanced at Garth, who was sipping his coffee.

"What happened?" she asked.

"Scotty told Clay not to ride flank tomorrow, but to stay with you and drive the wagon."

"And that doesn't sit too well with Captain Cavalry, is that it?"

"Cut him some slack, Becky. He signed on as a rider. He didn't expect the responsibility of a wife and wagon." Garth walked away.

So now Garth was displeased with her, too. It wasn't

her idea to pull Clay away from his duties; she was much more comfortable when he was out of her sight. Surely it wouldn't take more than a day or two for her body to stop aching. Then she could convince Mr. Scott that she could handle the team herself, and Clay could go back to doing what he wanted to.

While the cobbler was baking, Rebecca rolled out some baking soda biscuits, and dinner was ready when Clay returned carrying some small limbs and twigs for firewood. "This is the best I can do. Everything's been pretty well picked clean."

"Thank you," she said.

"Where's Garth?"

"He's over helping Otto VonDieman tighten a wheel on his wagon. Dinner's ready whenever you are." She had mixed together a hash of dried beef, potatoes, and onions, and the aroma of it bubbling in the spider skillet was inviting.

"Give me a chance to wash up."

"I figured you would want to. There's hot water in the kettle."

Clay put the wood in the sling attached to the side of the wagon. Then he ladled some hot water into the wash-basin, set it on the wagon tongue, and began to shave.

End of conversation.

Garth returned and handed Rebecca a cup of butter. "Mrs. VonDieman churned some butter and sent this over for our use." He went over to the fire and sniffed the cooking food. "Hmmm, it should go well with that hash." It sounded as if he'd gotten over his disgruntlement, at least.

It was pretty obvious that Clay's displeasure was only directed at her; he seemed to get along pleasantly with all the others. *He* sure wasn't trying to make the best of a bad situation, she thought as she ladled some hash onto a plate. Smiling, she handed it to Garth.

"Grab a couple of those biscuits, Garth. That butter will taste good on them."

In Rebecca's unbiased opinion, the meal was once again a tasty success. Not a crumb remained when they finished, and Garth was his usual gracious self in letting her know how much he enjoyed it.

"That peach cobbler sure was good, Becky," he said again as he helped her clean up the dishes.

"Thank you. I figured you liked it, the way you and Clay finished it all off."

"Anything tastes better in the fresh air," Clay said. He settled down with a book, and once again had managed to have the last word.

Rebecca gritted her teeth and handed Garth a soapy plate.

"You sure have a hand with turning flour into something real tasty, Becky. Did your mother teach you how to bake?"

"No, both of my parents died from consumption when I was thirteen." Her forehead creased in a worried frown. "I'm afraid poor Blanche suffers with the same malady." She forced aside the painful thought.

"Actually, my husband taught me how to bake. I married Charley when I was eighteen, and we worked in the bakery of Charley's maiden aunt, his only living relative." She shook her head, recalling the woman.

"Aunt Charlotte was a bitter old woman who hated life as much as she did people. Charley and I lived in the two rooms over the bakery. We'd only been married for three years when he was conscripted into the army at the outbreak of the war, and he was killed shortly after. I've been a widow for four years. When Aunt Charlotte died two months ago, she willed her house and the bakery to an animal organization that will provide care and shelter for her six cats."

Garth shook his head in commiseration. "You mentioned you have a brother in California?"

"Yes. Matthew headed west after Charley and I were married. I got a letter from him last month, and he painted California as a land of milk and honey. I had nothing to keep me in Vermont, so here I am."

Garth chuckled. "Well, Becky, from what you can do with a little flour and water, there's no telling what you'll accomplish with all that milk and honey out there."

They broke into laughter.

"Why are you and Clay heading West?" she asked. "Looking for some of that milk and honey, too?"

"No, we're chasing our sister. Lissy ran off with a Yankee soldier who'd been quartered at Fraser's Keep during the war."

"Fraser's Keep? Is that the town you're from?"

He shook his head. "No, it's the name of our family's plantation."

She might have known they had a plantation; it was easy to tell they hadn't been raised in a backwoods cabin.

"We figure they'd have to be on the train that pulled out ahead of this one."

"So what do you intend to do when you catch up with them? Shoot the Yankee scoundrel?" she said lightly.

"We're hoping she'll return home with us."

"And what about this man she loved enough to run off with?"

"If she's happy and he's made an honest woman of her, then I guess we'll have no say in it."

She stopped what she was doing and looked at him intently. "And if he hasn't?"

"Like you said, we'll shoot the Yankee scoundrel. It's a question of honor, ma'am."

She couldn't help gasping. Garth always seemed so happy-go-lucky, but the grimness in his tone made it clear he'd do exactly what he said.

The dishes done, Garth put aside the towel and departed, drawn again to the music farther down the line.

As Rebecca repacked the dishes and utensils, she couldn't stop thinking about Garth's statement. So their code of honor had brought these Fraser brothers West—not the hope for a new life, like the rest of the desperate souls here. It was one more thing that she didn't have in common with the man she married.

Rebecca grimaced with pain as she picked up the heavy spider skillet.

"Let me do that." Clay put aside his book and hurried over to her.

"Thank you."

"How badly are you aching?" he asked, putting the skillet away in the storage box.

"I'm sure it will pass soon," she said, not about to

give him the satisfaction that maybe she'd bitten off more than she could chew.

She went into the wagon and changed into her nightgown and robe, but even with the flaps raised, it was too stifling inside to remain there. Rebecca lit a lantern and went outside, laid her pelt on the ground, and sat down. Clay had extinguished the fire for the night, and it was quite comfortable to lean back against the wagon wheel and feel the slight breeze as she listened to the strains of music coming from farther down the line.

With Clay's attention absorbed again in a book, Rebecca slipped off her robe. The neckline of her plain white nightdress was no more revealing than a ball gown, and she was able to rub more liniment into her aching arms.

Other than the nagging pain in her arms and shoulders, she felt contented. Strangely enough, more contented than she'd felt in years. Maybe because it was the first time in so long that she had something to look forward to.

"I'll do that."

Clay's voice jolted her out of her reverie. He knelt down and took the tin of liniment from her. "I think it will be easier if you lie on your stomach."

Rebecca felt torn. As much as she welcomed the help, he was the last person she would ever have asked. But, she'd be glad to be free of the pain. She turned over on her stomach.

"Slide the gown off your shoulders," Clay said.

"What!"

"I can't rub this into your shoulders if they're covered with your gown."

"But . . . but—"

"Don't tell me you're feeling modest, Rebecca. After all, unless my memory's failed me, you had on something much skimpier than this on the night you tricked me into marrying you."

If he thought his baiting would rile her, he was mistaken. "I only intended to say that slipping the gown off my shoulders is easier to do sitting up," Rebecca said. She sat up and unbuttoned the top of the gown and managed to get it off her shoulders while preserving her modesty. Then she lay down again, awaiting his touch.

The warmth of his hands on her bare shoulders sent involuntary shivers of delight through her as he worked the salve into her tense muscles.

"Relax, Rebecca," he said, in a mocking tone. "At the moment I'm not about to do anything that will jeopardize you getting your annulment."

His long fingers curled around the tendons at the back of her neck, working the taut cords until they relaxed. She laid her head on her crossed arms and closed her eyes, shivers of delight surging through her as his stroking fingers moved to her shoulders. The pressure was as stimulating as it was healing. It had been a long time since she'd felt a man's hands on her bare flesh, and her body responded with feelings she believed she'd buried when she lost Charley. It felt so good—too damn good to feel like a woman again.

Her last thought before she drifted into sleep was the

realization that Clay Fraser could be even more of a threat than she'd thought.

Her skin felt so soft and satiny. Under all that spit and vinegar, there was a soft, vulnerable woman, with a responsive body longing to be caressed and loved. He could tell that the moment she'd relaxed under his touch. Why hadn't she sought a lover after her husband was killed? Or maybe she had, for in truth, what did he actually know about Rebecca?

No, he doubted she had taken a lover. While he was massaging her arm, he'd observed that she still wore her old wedding ring, not the one he'd given her. Apparently she still cherished the memory of her dead husband. Charley Elliott must have been one hell of a man to win the heart and devotion of a woman as independent thinking as Rebecca.

But now she was his wife, and her wearing the ring of a dead husband was a slap in the face to him. A glaring testimony to the fact that she did not consider him her husband.

Well, she was mistaken. He was very much her husband. He'd signed that marriage license, so it didn't matter what she thought. He had his pride, too, and her walking around with another man's ring on her hand was an insult to his honor.

He had listened to the conversation between her and Garth. Orphaned young and then losing a husband in the war, Rebecca Elliott had had a pretty hard life. But while he sympathized with her desperation, he couldn't justify her fouling up his life. If she'd been honest and straightforward from the beginning, something might have been worked out between them.

Garth might even have been willing to marry her to get her out of her predicament. His brother currently had a greater appreciation of women than he did, and every woman in Virginia knew Garth could be hoodwinked into believing their tales of woe. Come to think of it, maybe the Widow Elliott had done just that. Garth was becoming very protective of her. Of course, he was that way with stray dogs, too.

Well, it was for damn sure he wasn't as trusting as his brother—even though her skin did feel like warm satin.

He had the urge to wrap himself around her and lose himself in her soft body. To forget the damn annulment she wanted, and satisfy his body—if not his soul.

Why did he let mistrust continue to tarnish his belief in the faithfulness of a woman's love? His mother had cherished his father. Emmaline certainly was a faithful and loving wife to Will. And as foolhardy as it was, Lissy must love that Yankee she ran off with. Why condemn all women because of a few like Ellie and Rebecca?

Because those two *had* betrayed him into believing one thing in order to get another.

When Clay realized Rebecca had fallen asleep, he reluctantly removed his hands. His gaze swept her body as he screwed the lid back on the tin. He was so tempted to turn her over. His groin knotted, remembering the brief glimpse he'd caught of the rounded fullness of her breasts. He wanted to fill his hands with them, taste the taut pink crests of them.

Garth was right. Four to six months would be a hell of a long time to go without a woman, even if that woman was Rebecca Elliott. But he had no intention of carrying out the threat he'd made in Independence; he'd never force himself on her, no matter how much he wanted her. And the Lord knew how much he wanted her.

She looked so sweet with her hands tucked under her cheek like that, and those green eyes of hers not flashing in anger, that kissable mouth not taunting him. She looked sweet and desirable, her honey-colored hair all brushed out and hanging past her shoulders. She really was a beautiful woman.

Get thee behind me, Satan.

Clay bolted to his feet and put the salve away. Then he climbed into the wagon and found her pillow and blanket. He tucked the pillow under her head and covered her with the blanket, then got out his sleeping roll, laid it a short distance away, and climbed in.

For a long time he thought about the woman lying so close. By the time he finally fell asleep, he'd resolved to keep a wide distance between them for a while. That seductive instrument of the Devil had done enough damage to him already.

8

The morning dawned gray and overcast, with low-hanging clouds that seemed to press the heat closer to the earth. Clay's massage appeared to have helped, or maybe it was not sleeping on top of that hard box in the wagon. Or maybe the combination of the two. Rebecca's arms and shoulders felt much better, and the feel of his hands last night kept creeping into her thoughts.

"How are the aching muscles this morning, Becky?" Garth asked as he saddled his mount, preparing to leave.

"Much better since Clay massaged them," she said.

"Massage them, did he?" Garth said, with a surprised glance at his brother. "Hmmm, that's interesting."

"Wipe the smirk off your face," Clay grumbled. "She was in pain. The sooner she feels better, the quicker I can get back to doing what I signed on for."

"Reckon so," Garth said, grinning. He swung into the saddle. "Have a good day, you two."

"I do thank you for what you did last night, Clay," she said.

"I'd do the same for an aching horse."

"Your humanity is only exceeded by your graciousness, sir."

When he began to hitch up the team, the mules balked and wouldn't budge. Clay cursed and jumped back when one of them tried to kick him.

"Let me do that," she said.

"My pleasure." He leaned back against the wagon, his arms folded across his chest. "Be careful the damn animals don't kick your head off."

She walked up to the first set of mules. "Shame on you, my darlings. Caesar, my love, I know you don't like the smell of Johnny Rebs, but mind your manners," she murmured, and fed the mule a slice of apple. She then slipped an apple slice into the mouth of the next one. "Mark Anthony, show the man how a real gentleman acts. You see, Captain Fraser was an officer in the Confederate army, and he's only used to those fancy Thoroughbred jumping horses they have when they chase little foxes. . . ." She cast a derogatory glance in Clay's direction. "Or runaway slaves."

She led the now-docile pair over to the rest of the team, greeted each of those with a slice of apple, and within a few minutes all six mules were hitched to the wagon.

"Your carriage awaits, my lord."

He snatched the reins from her. "Do you always resort to some form of manipulation to accomplish your purpose?"

"Whatever works," she replied with a sweet smile. "I far prefer it to pouting or scowling, which is your preferred approach, sir."

"I do *not* pout, madam." The forward wagons had begun moving out, and he climbed up on the box. "Do you intend to walk or ride?"

"Definitely walk," she said. "It will feel good to stretch my legs for a change."

"Well, since you've got about two thousand miles to *stretch* them, I reckon your legs will be a damn sight longer by the time we get there." Clay flicked the reins and the wagon rolled forward.

Had he actually attempted to joke with her? Rebecca shrugged off the unlikely thought and started off with a comfortable stride. Soon a steady drizzle began falling, which drove her inside the wagon. By the time they stopped for the noon meal, the drizzle had turned to a downpour. Fortunately the canvas on the wagon had been strung tightly, so it didn't leak, but that didn't help Rebecca's mood. Jostled and rocked from side to side, she tried to read her cookbook as the steady rain pelted the canvas. It sounded as if she were inside a drum.

The rain caused an added problem. Every rut and pothole became a muddy obstacle that each wagon carved deeper into the earth, resulting in constant delays as wagons got stuck in these ruts. The men had to dig and push the heavily loaded wagons to free them, and the side of the trail soon became cluttered as items were abandoned to lighten the loads. Progress was practically at a standstill, and when they finally reached the Kansas River, Mike Scott called an early stop. There were a few sod houses there and a ferry to cross the river, and he announced they would cross in the morning.

Garth stopped by to tell them he would spend the night in one of Scott's wagons to get dry. Rebecca and Clay shifted some of the stores around and made room for him to spread his bedroll on the floor of the wagon.

There was no hope of building a fire, so he went into one of the soddies and bought two cups of coffee. It was bitter tasting, but at least it was hot and helped to wash down the hardtack and jerky they ate for supper. They topped the meal off with apples for dessert.

Because of the cramped space, they couldn't move without bumping into each other. Clay made no attempt at conversation and settled down in his bedroll to read. Rebecca dug out her deck of cards and played solitaire.

"Do you play solitaire often?" he asked.

The unexpected question startled her out of her concentration. She hadn't realized he was even aware of what she was doing.

"It often helps to pass the time," she said.

"You know, if you win, you're only beating yourself."

"I figure I'm beating the odds," she said.

"Haven't you learned by now that you can't beat the odds, whatever you try? Lord knows, we tried hard enough during the war with the odds against us."

"By *we* am I to assume you mean the Confederacy?"

"That's right. You Yankees had all the advantages, with your industry, iron, steel, textiles, munitions, and medical supplies. You were the banking capital of this country, had all the railroads, and even a navy. The odds were all against us. But despite all that, for four years we put up one hell of a fight, thanks to the military genius of General Lee and his officers."

"But why did *you*?" Rebecca asked. "For someone who doesn't believe in bucking the odds, why did you continue to fight?"

His amazement was clear when he looked at her. "I was defending Virginia against invaders. The same way my ancestors did against the British in 1776 and 1812. It made no difference whether the invaders wore British or Yankee uniforms."

"But the Yankees weren't invaders—they were Americans."

"Rebecca, why did we fight the Revolutionary War?"

"Freedom, of course. Freedom from England's oppression."

"Exactly. Those early Americans did the *same* thing to England, what the Confederacy did to Washington— they seceded from it. The Confederacy freed itself from Washington's oppression when the principles of self-government were no longer important to Washington."

"To be a united country, the same laws must apply to all the states," she declared.

"But who determines those laws? Washington? Prior to the Revolutionary War, Virginia and Maryland each had the House of Burgesses—the first self-governing colonies in America. And when this country needed a leader in that freedom fight, Virginia gave it George Washington. Virginia gave America the wisdom of a

Thomas Jefferson, the inspiration of a Patrick Henry. And what of James Madison or Monroe? Why, four of the first six presidents of this country were Virginians. Four of the next six were Southerners, and three of those were Virginians. So where is the real seat of the government, or who has a better right to call themselves Americans, than Virginians?"

"How can you espouse the noble principles of these men when you Virginians advocate slavery?" she argued.

"And what of the young children working in factories and coal mines in the North? Are you an advocate of that abuse, Rebecca? Should we have invaded your state to put an end to that kind of slavery? Most of the people in the South didn't even own slaves—but there's not a family that didn't suffer or lose loved ones during the war. If it's any consolation to a true-blue Yankee like you, there are more white Southerners who perished because of slavery than blacks who died as abused slaves."

For the first time since the conversation began, Rebecca saw a look of despair in his eyes. "And the tragedy is that it wasn't even necessary," he continued. "You know as well as I that the issue of slavery should have continued to be fought in Congress. It would have eventually been resolved without bloodshed and stomping over the concept of states' rights."

"You truly believe that Virginia and the rest of the South would have willingly abolished slavery?"

"I do. After all, Virginia was rightfully considered the cradle of democracy. I take pride in my heritage,

Rebecca. My family landed in that wilderness in 1607. There was no government in Washington to tell them what to do or think. My great-great-great grandfather built Fraser Keep, and he defended it against the Indians, two English invasions, and any others who tried to take it away from him. He did it himself, with no slave labor. So when the time came for me to defend that home, I could do no less than those before me."

"I understand your pride, Clay. But you surely aren't blind to the contributions such great men as John Adams and Benjamin Franklin made to the birth of our nation. They were all Americans, no matter where they were from. And they were all patriots who put freedom's interest above their own."

"Perhaps we need such men now more than ever," he said sadly. "Those in Washington appear to be puppets whose strings are being pulled by the wealthy industrialists, whose purpose is to serve their own means."

She was surprised to see a sudden glint of amusement in his eyes. "But let me remind you, Rebecca, that there hasn't been a Southern president in Washington for over fifteen years. So that may be the reason this country's in the mess it's in—and why Rebs and Yankees alike are climbing on wagon trains by the thousands and heading as far west of Washington as they can."

He closed his book, put it aside, and rolled over.

Rebecca put the deck of cards away, then blew out the lantern and lay down.

The splatter of rain on the canvas suddenly had a

comforting sound to it, and the bed felt softer. She cuddled deeper into its furry folds and thought about the conversation with Clay.

As delicate as the subject matter was, she'd learned a little more about this man whose name she carried. Maybe she'd been mistaken about him—mistaken pride in his heritage for arrogance. He indisputably was a man of honor.

She grinned to herself. And at least he wasn't pouting any more.

Rebecca woke to daylight and a camp alive with activity. Peeking out the front flap, she saw that Scott had not waited until seven to move out. She quickly dressed and went outside.

Already too deep to ford, the river was swollen to a treacherous-looking torrent by yesterday's rain. Clay and Mike Scott were standing in ankle-deep mud on the bank watching the ferry bobbing in midstream, two wagons strapped to its deck.

"Good morning," she said.

"Morning, Mrs. Fraser," Scott said pleasantly.

"Why didn't you wake me, Clay?"

"No need to. There's still four wagons ahead of us that have to cross."

"What about breakfast? I imagine a hot meal would taste good right about now," she said.

"You'll have plenty of time to prepare food on the other side." Scott said. "This crossing will take most of the day."

"Then I'd better make sure everything is tied down

tightly." Rebecca slogged through the mud back to the wagon.

Determined not to track the mud inside, she pulled off her boots before climbing into the wagon bed, and then glanced at the sodden, mud-stained bottom of her skirt.

"Modesty be damned," she murmured. Releasing the skirt, she let it drop to her ankles. Her chemise was not as muddied, but would need a washing, too, once they were across. She changed and had everything folded and packed down tightly when Clay followed the Garson wagon onto the ferry.

"That's a dollar and ten cents," the ferry owner said when he strapped the wagon in place.

"A dollar and ten cents! That's outrageous!" Rebecca exclaimed.

"Fifty cents a wagon, and ten cents apiece for any livestock 'ceptin' dogs or cats, lady," the man said. "Take it or swim across."

Rebecca doled out a precious dollar and ten cents to the ferryman. At the price he was charging, the man could become a millionaire in one season.

Many on the train could not afford to pay the exorbitant fare and had removed the wheels on their wagons and were poling them across like rafts. Others had their teams swimming across the raging river pulling the wagons hitched to them.

It was a choppy ride. Even with the heavy wagons and livestock, the ferry bobbed in the water like a cork. Nearing midstream, they watched Howard Garson as he attempted to drive his buggy across the river. The poor horse was barely managing to keep its head above water as it struggled against the strong current.

To their horror, they saw a huge wooden crate, which had broken free from one of the wagons upstream, floating straight at the buggy. They shouted a warning to the unseeing Howard, but it was too late. The crate crashed into the lightweight buggy, tipping it over. Howard was tossed into the water and disappeared. Hitched to the buggy, the struggling horse could not maintain its balance and was dragged down and swept away with the carriage.

Helena and the children cried with relief when Howard's head appeared a few yards downstream, and he started to swim toward the opposite shore, where several rescuers waited to toss him a rope and pull him out of the water.

"Thank goodness no one else was in that buggy," Rebecca said.

"My little brother wanted to ride along," Henrietta said, "but Daddy wouldn't let him because Georgie doesn't know how to swim."

"Neither do I," Rebecca said. "I never had any reason to learn how."

A harsh bray erupted from one of the mules. The bouncing was making the livestock restless, and several more of the mules added their discordant protest. Clay went over to quiet them down, but the nervous mules started to stomp and tried to pull free from the ropes that were restraining them.

"Let me try," Rebecca said.

"Stay away from them, Rebecca," Clay warned.

Rebecca paid no attention to him. She went over to the one she'd named Brutus and started to unwind one of the restraining lines that had wrapped around the animal's leg.

"Rebecca, get away from that mule!" Clay shouted, just as she succeeded in freeing the mule's leg.

Braying loudly, the mule kicked out. Rebecca dodged the kick, but lost her balance when the ferry swerved. Arms flailing, she tottered like an acrobat on a high wire for several terrifying seconds. Then, with a terrified scream, she tumbled backward over the side.

Cold, watery blackness swirled around her, choking her with panic. When she surfaced, coughing, several of the crewmembers threw her ropes—but she couldn't swim, and made desperate grabs at them before the current seized her and carried her away.

Clay had already shucked his gunbelt and boots, and dived into the water. The cold shock took his breath away. When he broke the surface, he began to swim. Rebecca was already about fifteen yards ahead of him, floundering helplessly as the current carried her downstream.

The current aided his progress, and he rapidly gained on her and overtook her. She was still conscious, and as soon as he grabbed her, she clutched at him frantically. They both went under. When they resurfaced, she began choking and coughing, clinging to him with a stranglehold around his neck.

Now he was fighting not only the current, but also her, and his own waning strength. He had to pry her fingers away so he could breathe.

"Let go, Rebecca! I have you!"

His words must have cut through her panic, because she relaxed enough for him to grasp her under her arms and keep their heads above water.

"Hold on to my belt!" he shouted above the roar of the water.

Her hands groped at his waist. Then, still grasping her under the arms, he started to work his way toward the bank with a one-arm sidestroke.

It was a slow process. He was literally towing her and trying to keep her head above water at the same time—a process debilitating to both his breath and strength. At times he had to stop and tread water, allowing the current to carry them further downstream.

After what seemed like hours, they finally reached the riverbank.

Rebecca had swallowed a lot of water while being towed, and she was coughing and gasping for breath. Clay flipped her over on her stomach and began pumping the water out of her.

As soon as both had regained their breath, Clay stripped down to his drawers, then lay back, exhausted, and let the sun dry his shivering body. Rebecca's teeth were chattering, and she had her arms wrapped across her chest to try and stay warm. There was no dry wood to build a fire, and even if there were, he had no way to light it; his flint was in his pack on the wagon.

"Rebecca, you've got to get out of those wet clothes," he said. "You'll warm up a lot faster with them off, rather then waiting for them to dry on you."

"Are-aren't we head-heading ba-back?" she asked, unable to control her chattering teeth.

"Let them come find us." He pulled her dress off over her head. "Let's get some friction going to help dry off your skin."

"Bu-but wh-what if they don't try? They-they mi-might th-think we-we've dro-drowned," she said as he began to vigorously dry her shoulders and arms with his shirt.

"I know my brother—he'll show up. Now sit."

When she did as he said, Clay knelt down and pulled off her shoes and stockings, then pushed up the skirt of her chemise and rubbed her legs and feet.

He could tell when her body began to respond to his efforts. The shivering ceased, her flesh felt warmer, and her color gradually began to return.

Until then his actions had been reflexive; now he began to think about what had happened. She might easily have drowned—and regardless of how their marriage began, she was his wife. Clay felt an overwhelming relief that the life of this courageous, beautiful woman had not been swept away.

She still looked frightened—and so vulnerable. He wanted to take her in his arms and comfort her; he knew the crippling fear she had just experienced. He'd been in enough battles to know how terrifying the thought of dying was.

Rebecca looked down at the dark head bent over her. She had never known such fear before, and Clay had delivered her from it. Despite what she'd thought of him before, he had to have a great deal of character to have jumped into that river to save her.

He stood up and reached out a hand to pull her to her feet.

When the warm security of his hand closed around hers, the last vestiges of her fear and panic disappeared.

"Thank you, Clayton."

Clay lay with his hands tucked under his head and watched Rebecca spreading out their clothes to dry. He hadn't realized how petite she actually was. Less formidable, too, barefoot and stripped down to the bare necessities, her honey hair hanging down in sodden strands. By the time she had laid out all their clothing in the sun, her hair was almost dry. She pulled loose a couple of vines, then divided her hair into two long braids and tied the ends with them. She looked downright cute to him. Cute? Hell, with only those damp underclothes on, she looked downright bodacious! The way the clothing clung to her curves made his blood heat up.

But before long, Garth came galloping up.

"Thank God," he said when he saw both of them.

Dismounting, he grabbed a blanket from his saddle and wrapped it around Rebecca, then hunkered down next to Clay.

"You gave me a scare, Big Brother. I didn't think you cared for early-morning swims." The concern in his eyes belied the lightness of his tone. "What in hell happened?"

"It was an accident," Rebecca said. "One of the mules got frisky. I don't understand it; Brutus is always so docile."

As Clay rose to his feet, his exasperated look said more than his words. "Must be that you forget to bring your apple slices."

9

Their clothing was still damp when they dressed. Since Clay didn't have any boots, Garth gave him the horse. Rather than ride double with Clay, Rebecca chose to walk the five miles back to camp with Garth, so Clay rode ahead to get dry clothing for her. They had covered half the distance by the time he got back to them.

It was noon when they finally arrived at the camp. Rebecca was relieved to see both the Garson and VonDieman families had made it safely across, although Henrietta was mourning the loss of the horse.

Nearly half of the wagons still needed to cross, and since Scott had announced they would make camp there for the night, Rebecca decided it was a good opportunity to do the washing. Clay and Garth turned their dirty clothing over to her, then left to help with the crossing. When Rebecca and Henrietta went back to the riverbank, they found it was lined with women doing laundry.

Since the men were occupied with the wagons, several of the women decided it would be safe to take a bath. Rebecca had had enough of the river, so after warning them to stay near the bank because of the strong current, she remained as a lookout in the event any male strayed near.

The women and young children frolicked in the cold water, in a welcome respite from the heat, the mud, and the strain of the journey. Then they dressed and carried their wet laundry back to their wagons, to spread out to dry.

Rebecca and Henrietta remained. The young girl was still desolate, grieving the loss of the mare.

"Becky, do you think we'll all make it to California?"

"I don't know, Etta. Mr. Scott said it's very unlikely."

Henrietta's deep sigh bordered on a sob. "We've lost Callie. Both you and Daddy almost drowned. I hope it will all be worth it."

Rebecca slipped a comforting arm around the young girl. "It has to be, Etta. Anything is better than what we left behind, isn't it? We all have hopes of starting over, putting the past behind us. It would be too cruel to have it all be in vain."

"But I didn't think life was so bad back in Ohio. I don't think Momma or Grandma thought so, either. This was Daddy's idea when he came home from the war. He said he wanted to get as far away as he could, so he could forget it."

"I understand what he means, dear."

"Is that your reason, too?"

"My husband was killed in the war. I have a brother who lives in California. Since I had nothing to keep me in Vermont, I decided to take his advice and come West."

"I didn't know you were married before. I'm sorry to

hear about your loss," Henrietta said. "But you were very fortunate to find another husband as nice as Mr. Fraser. He's so handsome. You should have seen him, Becky, when you fell overboard. He didn't hesitate to jump in the river to save you. Oh, it was so heroic!"

With the amazing recovery of youth, Henrietta sighed deeply again, this time with wistfulness. "I hope one day a man will love me so much that he's willing to risk his life to save me."

Rebecca *was* grateful to Clay; he had saved her life. Not that she'd ever romanticize over him the way Etta was doing, but being fair-minded, she was willing to give credit where credit was due. He did have some redeeming qualities, besides handsomeness and cleanliness. He was a man of honor—and he gave a great massage.

"Etta dear, let's hope nobody will ever have to save your life. But speaking of one who would, look who's coming." Rebecca nodded toward a redheaded young man approaching them. "I think Mr. Thomas Jefferson Davis is quite smitten with you."

Henrietta giggled. "You really think so? Momma thinks so, too. Daddy says he don't want him coming around."

"How old is he?"

"He just turned seventeen. His family's from Tennessee. Tommy was about to join the Confederate army when the war ended."

"Oh, so it's Tommy, is it?" Rebecca teased. "Well, since your dad fought for the North, I can understand his objection."

"Oh, not because Tommy's from the South," Henrietta said. "Daddy said he respects any man who'd stand up and defend his home, no matter what side they fought for. But Daddy also says that by the time a fella reaches seventeen, they don't have anything but fornicating on their minds, so he doesn't want any of them sniffing around our wagon."

"It's a long way to California. I doubt Tommy or any of the other young men will be able to stay away from that pretty face of yours for that long." The young girl's long dark curls and flashing blue eyes, combined with a vivacious personality, would be too much for any young man to resist.

"How do, ma'am," Thomas Davis said, grinning widely. In all the times she had encountered the young man, Rebecca couldn't remember him not wearing a smile. "Miz Etta," he said, turning his blue-eyed gaze of worship on Henrietta.

Observing the love-struck glances between the two, Rebecca wondered if she'd ever been that young.

"Hello, Thomas," Rebecca said. "Did your family get across without any mishap?"

"Yes, ma'am. Heard about your accident. Sure glad to see you're okay, ma'am."

"Thank you," Rebecca said.

"I feel real bad about Callie, Miz Etta. Sure liked that mare." When Henrietta started to tear up, the young man blushed in distress. "I'm sorry. Please don't cry, Etta. I didn't mean to upset you more." He looked helplessly at Rebecca.

Henrietta dabbed at her tears. "It's not your fault, Tommy. I just have to get used to her being gone."

Rebecca rose to her feet. "Well, I'd better get back to camp and stir up some food." She left so the two of them could be alone.

After laying out the wet clothes to dry in the sunshine, Rebecca built a fire and then baked biscuits and an apple pandowdy. She had a pot of dried beef and beans stewing in a thick sauce of tomatoes when Clay returned that evening.

"Is everyone finally across?" she asked, handing him a cup of coffee.

"There are still about ten wagons to go. Scotty wants them to cross tonight in case it starts raining again. They should all be across by midnight." He plopped down and leaned back against the wagon. "It's been a long day."

"Is Garth going to join us for dinner?"

Clay yawned and closed his eyes. "No. He said as soon as they get the last wagon across, he's going to bed in one of Scott's wagons."

"Well, dinner's ready anytime you are."

But she was talking to herself; Clay had fallen asleep.

For a long moment Rebecca stared at his long, powerful body. Etta's words had played on her mind since she had returned to camp. She *was* fortunate to have Clay around, and there was no doubt that he had saved her life that morning. But if he hadn't been there, wouldn't one of the other men have jumped in to help her?

"I guess I'll never know, Clayton Fraser, because you were the one who did," she murmured softly.

He woke with a start. "I'm sorry, what did you say?"

"I said that dinner's ready."

They ate in silence. Clay was so exhausted that he barely touched his food, and Rebecca shooed him off to sleep in the wagon again. She looked at the big pot of beef and beans she'd prepared, picked up the pot and the pandowdy, and carried it down the line to a couple named Ryan who had just finished crossing and hadn't had time to start a fire.

Feeling better, she returned to her wagon and cleaned up the dishes. Clay never stirred when she climbed into the wagon, blew out the lantern, and then, exhausted, undressed and went to bed.

It had been a calamitous and long day. Despite the warm night, she snuggled deeper into the fur pelt, and then glanced at the sleeping figure on the floor. Thanks to him, she had survived it.

Several days later found them camped on the south side of the Platte River. Although a mile wide, the river was shallow and the crossing uneventful.

So far, the countryside had been pleasant but nothing spectacular; now they would begin the six-week trek across the plains. It was an unusual sight to those used to the forests or bustling cities of the East. High sandstone cliffs ran parallel to the river, and farther than the eye could see were the flat plains, totally treeless and covered with short grass.

As she prepared the meal that evening, Rebecca shifted her glance to Clay, who was tightening one of the wagon wheels. Something was bothering him. He'd barely spoken to her since the incident in the river, and when they did talk, it ended up in an argument, so they both avoided conversation whenever possible.

One good thing came out of it, though: they weren't sniping at each other anymore, so at least they had developed a fairly tolerant working relationship.

"Dinner's ready, Clay."

They ate in silence. He thanked her, and then went back to working on the wheel. Rebecca finished up the dishes, then hurried to the sutler store to look it over.

There was an unusual collection of merchandise in the store, mostly items abandoned or traded by people who had lightened their wagonloads. She had hoped to purchase some fresh vegetables or fruit, but there wasn't any. Instead, she bought a used game of backgammon. The game had always been a favorite of Charley's, and she hoped she could get Garth or Etta to join her in the evening to break up the boredom.

On her way back from the sutler, Rebecca paused by the river. The sweet smell of wildflowers permeated the air, and moonlight painted the countryside in ribbons of white. A light breeze rippled the shallow waters of the mile-wide river, and in the distance she could see the glow of campfires on the opposite bank.

The train was now down to seventy-four wagons. The other twenty-four had decided to turn back and had not crossed the Platte, some due to a change of heart, others to sickness. Dishearteningly, Mike Scott had said that by the time they reached California, they would lose a lot more. Well, come hell or high water, there'd be no turning back for her. She had chartered this course, and she would see it through to

the end, with the help of the Almighty—and Clay
Fraser.

Clay stopped abruptly and sucked in a breath, forgetting his purpose for being there. His gaze devoured the
vision of Rebecca standing alone on the riverbank, the
breeze ruffling her long hair and wrapping her dress
around her slender figure. Moonlight bathed her
golden loveliness in a shimmer that bordered on ethe-
real. Lord, she was a beautiful woman.

Since Scotty had pulled him off outriding, he and
Rebecca had been together constantly, and he'd had
plenty of time to observe her. True to her word, she had
an obsession for independence and never asked for
help, no matter how physically difficult the task might
be. And despite the hardships, she never complained.

He was the one struggling with the arrangement.
Since her near drowning, he'd become more physically
aware of her than ever. He wanted her—badly. She'd
been married before, so she knew the needs and de-
lights of sex. He could only hope that soon the same
physical cravings would surface with her.

When she had disappeared tonight without a word,
he had searched the campsite, but no one had seen her.
He'd made a damn fool of himself rushing from one
wagon to another. The woman did not belong out here
in this wilderness, if she wasn't going to obey the
warnings of those who knew the dangers.

He silently walked up behind her. "Scotty said not to
wander off alone."

Rebecca swung around in surprise, and her hand

fluttered to her breast. "My goodness, Clay! You startled me."

"You're lucky it was me, and not some Pawnee. We're in Indian territory now, and the Pawnee have been hostile lately."

Did he always have to put her on the defensive? "I hardly think they're going to attack a party this size, Clay. Besides, I was at the sutler's, and no one there appeared frightened of an Indian attack."

"Probably because the sutler most likely keeps them supplied with whiskey and ammunition. Come on, Rebecca, let's get back to camp."

The man was hopeless. From the time she had met him, he'd been issuing orders to her, trying to intimidate her with his scowls, and patronizing her with his superior attitude. She'd been on her own for four years and didn't need *any* man telling her what to do.

"I'll come when I'm ready. I can take care of myself, Clay. I've been doing so most of my life."

"And look where it's gotten us!"

Angry, she tried to brush past him, but her foot slipped on the moist grass. Clay grabbed her to help her retain her balance. For a long moment they stared at each other, their lips mere inches apart.

Call it anger, proximity, the passion of the moment—whatever the reason, she knew he was about to kiss her. And she wanted him to.

It wasn't a tender kiss; it wasn't a kiss to arouse or tantalize. The kiss was hungry, and dominating.

She bore it without a complaint—or a response.

When he stepped back, she met his gaze with defiance.

"Is that how you mete out discipline, *Captain* Fraser?" She turned away, and Clay followed her back to their wagon.

Garth was there waiting. He arched a brow when he saw the frowns on both their faces. "Did our honeymooners have a lovers' quarrel?"

The scowls turned to downright glares, and Rebecca stalked past him and climbed into the wagon.

"Look, Clay, you're both intelligent adults," Garth said. "This trip is going to start getting rougher, and we should all start working together. Can't you two declare a truce until we reach California?"

"Keep out of this, Garth." Clay lay down on his bedroll and turned his back to him.

"I'm already a part of it." Shaking his head in exasperation, Garth plopped down on his bedroll.

Long after Garth had fallen asleep, Clay lay awake damning himself for his stupidity. He had intended only to make sure she was safe. How could he have lost his control? Why hadn't he just walked away and ignored her taunt? The damn kiss had been instinctive. And her lack of response made it clear what she thought of it. What he should have done was kiss her until he broke through her resistance.

What I should have done was apologize.

Then he saw her. Clad in a white robe and nightgown, Rebecca stood with her head tipped heavenward as she gazed at the stars, her long hair a silky mantle across her shoulders—just as she'd been doing earlier at the riverbank. Moonlight bathed her figure in an aura more spectral than human, and once again he could only marvel at her beauty.

The wayward breeze rustled several of the strands across her cheek, and she lightly brushed them aside.

He felt—rather than heard—her sigh. Then she turned and went back into the wagon.

Clay cursed himself when he felt the start of an erection. Sitting up, he pulled on his boots to walk it off. A breeze had sprung up and it felt good on his heated body. He walked down to where the horses were tethered, made some small talk with Howard Garson, who was on guard duty, and then returned to the wagon.

He returned to his bedroll, but he didn't sleep.

10

As Rebecca was preparing breakfast the next morning, Mike Scott rode up. "Morning, Mrs. Fraser."

"Good morning, Mr. Scott. Have you eaten?"

"Yes, ma'am. I'll take a cup of that coffee, though. Hate to bother you so early, but I'm afraid you're going to lose your driver. I need a few more men to ride flank."

"I understand perfectly, Mr. Scott." And good riddance—it would be worth aching shoulders to not have Clay scowling down at her from the box.

"We're losing the horse-drawn wagons," Scott said. "They're going on ahead of us; said the going's too slow, traveling with oxen and mules. And counting those twenty-four wagons that pulled out already, we've lost a lot of able-bodied men."

"Are you expecting trouble, Scotty?" Clay asked.

The wagon master shrugged and took a sip of the hot coffee. "Hawk rode in and said he saw a lot of Indian sign ahead. The Pawnee have usually avoided a large party this size, but just the same, I'd like to increase the outriders during the day and guards at night. I need good riders as much as gun arms, and there's none better in a saddle than you Reb cavalrymen. I swear you're all part horse."

"Which part do you think Clay is?" Rebecca asked impishly, then regretted it. The last thing she wanted Scott to think was that she and Clay weren't loving newlyweds.

Clay picked up on it immediately. "It would have to be the head. How else would you have *roped* me into marrying you? Right, sweetheart?" He grabbed her and kissed her, then gave her a light swat on the butt as she ducked away.

Scott laughed. "I envy you, Clay. A beautiful wife with a sense of humor." Turning to Garth, he said, "Bet these two keep you amused all the time, don't they?"

"That's no lie," Garth said. "It's like being around a couple of kids when they're together."

"Ah, newlyweds. It's enough to make a man think about marriage himself."

"I'd think good and long about it, Scotty," Garth replied.

Rebecca lowered her head to hide her grin, but not before Clay saw it. Men actually believed that only they made the decision whether or not to wed, that women had no say in that matter. Ha! As if she needed any man to do her thinking for her. She needed a man for the same reason she needed a mule—the strength of his back. She sure as heck didn't need a man for his brain.

As soon as the three men rode off, Rebecca packed up and was ready when the train moved on. Shortly after, Etta came over and climbed up beside her. The companionship helped to pass the time.

Late in the afternoon Thomas Davis joined them and

offered to drive the team. Rebecca gladly accepted the offer, even though she suspected the young man had only done so to be with Etta. But that was fine with her. She enjoyed observing the course of true love.

And maybe, she thought, picking up a buffalo chip and putting it in the wood sling, deep down, she yearned for such a relationship.

Aches and pains accompanied her return to driving the team. By the second night the pain seemed even more severe than the first time she'd driven the team.

"What's wrong?" Clay asked after dinner when a groan slipped out as she bent down to pick up the heavy spider skillet.

"Nothing," she said.

Clay came over and packed the skillet away. "Where's the ointment?"

"I don't need any ointment."

"Dammit, Rebecca, you're not surrendering your independence by asking for a helping hand. I took an oath as your husband to take care of you. I can hardly sit on my ass reading a book while you hobble around in pain."

"I am not hobbling." She turned on her heel and strode away. When she started to climb into the wagon, though, she suddenly winced with pain.

"Okay, that's it." He swept her up in his arms and laid her on her pelt. "Where is it?"

She nodded toward a box in the corner. He was back in seconds with the tin of ointment.

"Let's get that dress off you," he said.

Rebecca unbuttoned the gingham gown and he helped get it over her head.

"Are you able to roll over?" Clay asked.

She shifted painfully onto her stomach. Then she closed her eyes and let those marvelous hands of his work their magic.

His hands felt warm and strong as they pressed into her flesh, seeking and soothing the aching tendons of her shoulders. As the pain disappeared, she became aware of his touch in a very different way, and a moan escaped her. Then he turned her over, and his long, tapered fingers caressed the taut muscles of her neck and hollow of her throat. A responsive quiver surged through her. Her breath quickened, and the ache in her body now had a far different cause.

Passion spiraled through her, arousing excitement she fought to restrain. She cast a wary glance at Clay; his eyes were hooded with arousal.

The divine pressure of his hands cupped her neck as he leaned forward, his voice a seductive murmur. "I'm sorry for kissing you the way I did at the river the other night, Rebecca. But I don't apologize for this one."

His mouth swallowed her gasp as his lips pressed to hers. Sweet ecstasy surged through her, and she gave herself up to it with a response as hungry as his.

He slipped the straps of her chemise off her shoulders and pushed it down to her waist. The cool air on her breasts was quickly replaced by the moist warmth of his mouth. She arched in response and pressed his head tighter to her breasts as his tongue teased the turgid peaks.

"Anybody home?" Etta called out.

With a shuddering breath, Clay raised his head and stood up as Rebecca quickly replaced the straps of her chemise.

He moved to the rear of the wagon and stepped down. "Hi, Etta."

"Is Becky here?" she asked.

"Yes, she'll be out in a moment. I was just putting some ointment on her. She's pretty sore again."

"I know," Becky said, her eyes warm with compassion. "Tommy said he'd drive the wagon for her tomorrow."

"Good," Clay said. "I appreciate that. I'll go and tell him so." He hurried away.

As soon as Etta left, Rebecca went to bed. This time she slept inside the wagon. She and Clay had come so close to making love—too close! Now the tension between them would be worse than ever. It had felt so wonderful . . . but she had to put it out of her mind. She wanted that annulment, and it would ruin everything if she gave in to a weak moment. Somehow, despite the growing desire between them, she had to resist him.

Clay stayed away as long as he could. By the time he returned, the fire had burned out and Garth was asleep. He peeked through the flaps of the wagon to make sure Rebecca was okay, then crawled into his own sleeping roll.

It had taken him a long time to get over that abrupt ending to their lovemaking. They had come so close. She had been so ready. And now he knew she was responsive.

Despite her resolve not to consumate their marriage, he had an ally in that delightful, quivering little body of hers. He tucked his arms under his head and gazed up at the starry sky.

An annulment? Never—he'd taken a vow, and Frasers always honored their vows.

You picked the wrong man to play games with, Rebecca Fraser.

Clay's mouth curved in a wry grin. But it was a damn sorry state of affairs when a man had to scheme how to get his wife into bed with him.

Scott had told them it would take six or seven weeks to reach Fort Laramie, but Rebecca had lost track of how long they'd been on the trail. The days passed slowly, one as uneventful as the other. She became stronger and very skilled at driving, and no longer ached as she had before.

And she loved testing her cooking skills. Game was plentiful, so there was always fresh meat to eat or trout in the streams.

And of course, buffalo! Thousands and thousands of buffalo. Big, lumbering, hairy, smelly buffalo—the *dumbest* dumb animals on God's earth. They had no instinct for self-preservation. A hunter could shoot one down and it wouldn't trouble the others next to it. They'd continue to graze or plod along, oblivious to what was going on around them. At least cattle had enough instinct to run when startled. But not buffalo!

Promptly at six, Scott called a stop. Rebecca reined up and climbed down from the box. She glanced in dismay at the buffalo herd that was grazing a short distance off the trail. There were thousands of the gargantuan creatures. The train had encountered the grazing herd early that morning and still hadn't left them behind. She saw Clay riding in, and knew he'd bring some buffalo chips with him, so she waited to start the fire. Their droppings were the only good things she could say about the beasts. Since the plains were treeless, the buffalo chips made a good source of fuel. And they were odorless.

"Pity the same can't be said about the beasts that dropped them, Cleopatra," she murmured to the mule she was unharnessing.

Since they were in Indian territory, Scott had ordered the wagons circled in the evening, with the tongue of each wagon shoved under the wagon next to it. The horses were corralled inside the circle. Since the Indians had no use for oxen or mules, they were set out to graze with guards riding nightherd. The arrangement made for very close quarters, but created a tight barricade in the event of an Indian attack.

Another good thing came out of the close quarters: It forced her and Clay to talk pleasantly to each other, despite the simmering sexual tension between them. There were too many ears within hearing distance for them to carry on their running argument, so they'd fallen into a forced truce. More often than not, the Garson family and the VonDiemans joined them in the evening meal, so the three families had become very attached to one another.

And with fresh meat and four females doing the

cooking, many of the bachelors and widowers on the train suddenly found reasons for dropping in around dinnertime.

Rebecca had the mules turned out to graze by the time Clay arrived. As she anticipated, he emptied a pouch of buffalo chips into the sling. In a short time the others joined them, and while a couple of the men built the fire, the women set to cooking. Rebecca had never had any close female relationships, and she got special pleasure out of these evenings, sharing laughter and jokes as the women prepared the meal.

Later, as Rebecca and Helena were finishing the dishes, her attention was drawn to the campfire, where a heated discussion had ensued among the men regarding guard duty.

"Ain't right we hav'ta stand guard at night," complained Jake Fallon, one of the bachelors who often joined them for supper. "It's Scott's problem," he continued. "He should have hired more riders."

"It's only fair that we do," Howard Garson said, drawing on his pipe. The scent of the pipe tobacco was a pleasant change from the pungent odor of the buffalo that carried downwind to them.

Unlike Howard, who took everything calmly in stride, Fallon constantly complained about one thing or another, and was considered by all to be a shirker who often came up with an excuse to get out of guard duty when it was his turn to serve.

"There's always the danger of an Indian attack," Otto VonDieman added.

"Bullshit!" Fallon said. "You seen any Indians? I ain't seen one redskin since we crossed the Kansas."

"Mike Scott knows what he's doing, Fallon," Clay said. "I trust his judgment."

He never tried to disguise his dislike for Fallon, and it was one of the few issues where Rebecca agreed wholeheartedly with her husband.

Fallon had served in the Union Army during the war and always wore a scabbard that almost touched the ground because he was so short. He claimed to be a carpenter by trade, but she'd never seen him raise a hammer or nail to help out when a wagon needed repairing.

She disliked him even more so from a female point of view.

Clay was always friendly and polite toward any woman he spoke to. Both Helena Garson and Blanche VonDieman clearly worshipped him. In fact, Rebecca was willing to bet that she was the only woman on the train who didn't think the sun rose and set on Clay Fraser.

But she never felt comfortable around Jake Fallon. His disrespect for women was evident, and his ferret eyes seemed to undress them when he looked at them.

When the little man stalked away in a huff, the conversation broke up and the others returned to their wagons early. Rebecca found herself alone with Clay for the first time since the night he'd kissed her.

An awkward silence developed between them. She couldn't concentrate on her cookbook, and he appeared to be having the same problem with the novel he was reading. Often, when she looked up, she found him staring at her.

She finally asked, "Do you think we could play a game of backgammon without arguing?"

Clay closed his book. "I suppose we could give it a try."

Rebecca got the board and box containing the dice and counters. "I hope you're a good loser, Clay, because I intend to beat the pants off you," she teased.

"Interesting choice of words, Rebecca. Any particular reason why you want my pants off?"

She blushed furiously. "It's just a phrase."

"Oh, really? Well, the prospect of beating the *pants* off you is becoming more appealing by the minute."

"You don't have a prayer, Clayton. I'm a master at this game."

"Time will tell, Becky."

She looked up, surprised. He rarely called her by name, much less a nickname. His gaze locked with hers, and she became aware of how beautiful his eyes were when he wasn't scowling. Their dark brown was rich with warmth and a gleam of deviltry that was dangerously seductive. She hadn't forgotten the thrill his kisses had generated, and it looked as if he hadn't, either.

Now, Clay's relaxed chuckles and impromptu comments brought her time and time again to laughter or giggles of delight. She soon discovered he was a good sport when he lost and a colossal tease when he won. And both of them were enjoying playing out their rivalry with a board and dice instead of nasty words. By the time they finally called a halt, no clear victor had materialized.

That night, after bedding down, Rebecca lay gazing contentedly at the stars. She had gotten into the habit of sleeping outside when there was no danger of rain. It was so much cooler than the stuffy wagon, and the stars seemed so close, she felt she could reach up and touch one.

"Clay, how long before we reach Fort Laramie?"

"Probably in another couple weeks," he said, climbing into his bedroll a few yards away.

"Is that the halfway mark?"

"Close to it, according to Scotty," he murmured in a voice husky with drowsiness. "Good night, Becky."

"Good night," she replied, and closed her eyes.

It was the first time they'd ever exchanged the felicitation.

The sandstone hills had gradually become higher, the terrain a little rougher, but the going still wasn't too difficult. They'd been following the south side of the Platte and had reached South Fork, where the river split and forked off south toward Colorado, or north toward Wyoming. In the morning they would cross back to the north side.

Rebecca and Henrietta were sitting side-by-side listening to several men who'd been entertaining them with songs, Thomas Davis among them. In a pleasing tenor voice he began singing the haunting ballad "Shenandoah." One didn't have to be from Virginia to feel the poignancy of the words.

Oh, Shenandoah, I long to see you,
Far away, you rolling river.
Oh, Shenandoah, I'll not deceive you,
Away, we're bound away,
Across the wide Missouri.

Rebecca stole a glance at Clay and Garth, and felt a stab of sympathy for them. Homesickness and heartache were written all over their faces as they listened to the moving words.

"Hey, don't you know somethin' different?" Jake Fallon yelled out. "I heard all I wanna hear of that Reb song. Do you know 'Marching Through Georgia,' boy?"

Thomas shook his head. "No, Mr. Fallon."

"You ought to: We Yankees sang it enough times as we whupped your asses, when we marched through the damn South. How about 'Rally 'Round the Flag?' Let's hear it, boy."

Fallon began singing, " 'The Union forever. Hurrah, boys. Hurrah.' " He paused when no one joined him, and his face twisted into a snarl. Drawing his sword out of its scabbard, he pointed the weapon threateningly at Thomas. "You heard me. Start singing, Reb."

"I like the song he was singing, Fallon."

Rebecca turned around in surprise at Clay's voice.

Etta gasped and clutched Rebecca's arm when Clay stepped forward. "Uh-oh, Becky. This looks like trouble," she whispered.

Fallon waved the weapon at Clay. "Then how about you volunteerin' to sing what I wanna hear, Fraser?"

Garth stepped up next to Clay. "My brother said he liked the song the boy was singing. So do I."

"Don't cut yourself in on this, Garth," Clay said. "I can handle this weasel alone."

Fallon snorted. "I killed enough of you Rebs during the war. A couple more of ya ain't gonna matter none."

"Must have been because their backs were to you, Fallon," Garth said.

Fallon's black eyes glowed with rage. "I'm gonna enjoy running this sword through that gut of yours, Fraser."

"Fallon, sheath that weapon at once," a stern voice demanded. All eyes turned to Mike Scott, who had arrived on the scene with several of his riders, rifles in hand.

With a glare at Garth, Fallon replaced the saber in the scabbard. "I wouldn't have hurt 'em," he grumbled.

"You've got that right," Clay said.

"What went on here, Clay?"

"Just a difference of opinion in the choice of music, Scotty."

"I made it clear in Independence that there was to be no refighting the war. And Fallon, if you ever draw that damn sword again on anyone here, you're off the train. Now get the hell back to your wagon." He turned to Rebecca and Henrietta. "My apologies, ladies." He gave Clay and Garth a stern look. "I'd appreciate you boys staying out of trouble." Then he and his entourage departed.

The scene had spoiled any further desire for entertainment, so everyone returned to their wagons and bedded down for the night.

Rebecca was too disturbed over the confrontation with Jake Fallon to fall asleep. If Mr. Scott hadn't shown up, that horrible man probably would have used that sword on Clay or Garth. The thought was horrifying. Despite their differences, she certainly didn't wish Clay—or Garth—any harm. Both of them put their lives on the line every day when they rode out alone, not knowing what they might encounter. Besides that, she owed Clay her gratitude for saving her life.

She sighed and rolled over. Even though she didn't understand it, she knew her feelings for Clay had nothing to do with gratitude. Despite all their posturing toward each other, there was something between them. And maybe, whether they admitted it or not, they'd begun to take their spouse roles to heart.

11

By the following morning, word of the incident between the Fraser brothers and Jake Fallon had spread through the camp. Until then there had been a feeling of cheerful camaraderie among them, but this morning everyone appeared more subdued.

Instead of starting the crossing bright and early, as they all anticipated, Mike Scott called them together for a meeting.

"You think he's going to talk about last night?" Etta whispered.

Rebecca nodded. "That's probably what he's got on his mind."

"Well, I sure hope he's not going to put any of the blame on Clay or Garth. That horrible Jake Fallon was responsible for what happened. He probably would have hurt Tommy if Clay hadn't interfered."

"I think so, too, Etta. Mr. Scott will probably give us all a lecture to avoid any further incidents."

"I don't know why he just doesn't make Mr. Fallon leave the wagon train. Daddy says it's a shame that some people won't put the war behind them. He said we've got to learn how to live together again."

Rebecca felt a sinking sickness in the pit of her stom-

ach as the truth hit her with a mortifying realization—
she was one of those people! Her resentment of Clay
was because he fought for the Confederacy, as if he
were responsible for Charley's death. But then she
frowned. She didn't resent Garth or Tom Davis, and
they were Southerners, too.

Was she solely to blame for the running battle between her and Clay? His bitterness toward her was not
because she was a Yankee; it was because she'd tricked
him into marrying her. Though he no longer threw
that up to her—so Garth had been right about Clay; he
didn't bear grudges.

In light of this new revelation, Rebecca hung her
head in shame. She *was* solely responsible.

"Folks," Mike Scott began, when all were assembled.
"I'm afraid I have some bad news for you. Last night—"

"Uh-oh! Here it comes," Etta whispered.

"—Hawk rode in with some very disturbing news."

Rebecca raised her head to listen more closely.

"You all know," Scott continued, "that ten wagons
had left the train and pulled ahead of us. Hawk came
upon them yesterday. The wagons were all burned, and
everyone was dead."

Gasps of shock and cries of disbelief circled the
crowd.

"You mean there weren't any survivors at all?" one
of the men asked.

"None."

"There had to have been at least fifty people with
that party," another said.

"Fifty-four to be exact," Scott said. "I looked up the

count from their registration forms. Trouble was, most of them were women and children. There were only twelve men toting rifles."

"Maybe the Indians took some prisoners," Howard said.

"No. Hawk said all the bodies were accounted for. He buried them in a common grave."

The sounds of steady sobbing could be heard as many in the crowd recalled those they'd known among the victims.

"Who did it?" Clay asked. "Pawnee or Cheyenne?"

Hawk held up an arrow. "Pawnee."

Scott raised his arms to quiet the rumble of shouts for revenge. "I wouldn't even have told you folks the bad news if I didn't think it was important for everyone to see the need for us to stay together," Scott said. "There are Sioux, Cheyenne, Arapaho, and Ute still ahead of us. This is no time for us to be pulling apart. We've got to put past grievances behind us and work together."

It was clearly a reference to last night, and many heads nodded in agreement.

"And don't any of you fellows start thinking of trying to track them. That raiding party is familiar with the land; you'll only get yourselves killed. I still figure the Indians won't attack a party this size. And most likely they were after the horses; they don't want mules or oxen. Now, Reverend Kirkland, will you lead us in a prayer for the dearly departed? Then we'll get to crossing that river."

After the crowd dispersed in silence or muffled sobs,

Rebecca remained motionless. It was difficult to accept how easily fifty-four lives could be extinguished.

"Are you okay, Rebecca?"

She looked up to find Clay at her side. She nodded. "It's all so brutal, Clay. Are these people so savage that they can slaughter babes in arms over a few horses?"

"There's no such thing as a humane war, Becky."

Angry words burst past her lips. "War! We're not at war with them. Was a child a threat to them?"

"They see us as a threat. We're invading their homeland."

She felt the rise of temper. "Good Lord, Clay, don't tell me you're justifying this savagery!"

"Don't put words in my mouth, Rebecca."

She watched him walk away. Obviously, she and Clay Fraser were not meant to ever reach an understanding. Returning to her wagon, she packed up to prepare for the crossing.

Hawk had picked out a spot where the river was only a half-mile wide. The problem was that the water was low, and bedded with quicksand. The first wagon that attempted the crossing got mired down in it. As the oxen strained at the harness, they only dug themselves in deeper.

Several of the men swam out with ropes and chains attached to six yoke of oxen on the shore. After tying the ropes to the wagon and oxen, they managed to free the trapped team and wagon from the sand. Scott had an eight yoke of oxen harnessed to the next wagon. With that pulling power, the wagon succeeded in crossing without getting stuck. It would be a slow process, but it would work.

Rebecca sighed. Slumping to the ground, she leaned against the wagon. It was going to be a long day.

Clay joined her a short time later and sat down beside her. "Becky, we have to talk."

"Clay, I really don't feel like arguing. The news about those poor people was so devastating."

"I'm sorry, but it's necessary."

Resigned, she sighed. "What is it?"

"Several of the wagons are turning back. I think it would be a good idea for you to join them."

"I'm sure you do. You'd like to get rid of me."

"Dammit, Becky, you heard Scotty. The worst is still ahead of us."

"Are the Garsons and VonDiemans among them?"

"Garsons definitely not. The VonDiemans are considering it. Otto's concerned about Blanche's health. He wants to get her back where she'll have a doctor's care. Look, Rebecca, I don't want to see that long blond hair of yours dangling from some Indian's coup stick. I have your welfare at heart."

"What about you and Garth? Are you considering turning back?"

"We came out here to find our sister. We aren't leaving until we do."

"I came out here for a purpose, too, Clay. New beginnings can be risky, but that's a chance I'm willing to take."

"If you hold off for a few years, there won't be a risk.

One day there'll probably be a railroad along this very trail and bridges to span these rivers."

"I've sat and waited my whole life for that 'one day,' Clay, but it was always just out of reach. But I didn't stop believing that it was just ahead of me, and that the next day, the next week, or the next year it would happen. If I give up now, I'd be giving up the hope that I've held on to, the hope that brought me here."

Clay sighed. "All right, Becky. God willing, you'll live to see the fulfillment of that dream." He stood up. "I'll tell the others you're going on."

The massacre had an alarming effect on everybody. Fourteen more wagons had decided to turn back, the VonDiemans among them. Clay bought their cow, several of their chickens, and some of their supplies. When it was time for the wagon to cross, Rebecca said a tearful good-bye to Blanche and Otto. She gave them her brother's address and promised to write them when she reached Sacramento. Then, dabbing at her eyes, she climbed up next to Clay on the box and waved farewell to the older couple.

Once across the river Clay went back to help with the crossings. Rebecca kept herself busy by unloading the wagon to dry out whatever got wet. It was exhausting moving everything around, but it helped to keep her mind off the sad events of that day.

The camp was quiet that night, and families stayed close to their own wagons. Clay had pulled a two-hour guard shift between ten and midnight. Garth was somewhere with Mike Scott. As exhausted as she was, Rebecca couldn't fall asleep until Clay returned.

"Everything quiet out there?" she asked when Clay crawled into his sleeping roll.

"Yeah. Don't worry, Becky. There are still fifty wagons in this train; Indians won't attack it. It would be suicidal for them."

"Yet Mr. Scott doubled the guard," she reminded him. Rolling over, she closed her eyes. Maybe the Indians wouldn't try an all-out attack on the train, but it wouldn't stop one from sneaking up in the dark and killing a guard, or crawling into a wagon and . . . She gulped, then got up and shifted her pallet closer to Clay.

Throughout the night she slipped in and out of sleep, and awoke to clucking chickens. It took her several seconds to realize the sound was coming from her wagon, then she remembered the VonDiemans were no longer with them.

Glancing at Clay, she saw he was sitting up in his bedroll. He looked dazed and disheveled.

In a voice rasped with drowsiness, he grumbled, "I hope you know how to fry chicken, because I'm about to wring the necks of those hens."

Rebecca got up and went over to the coop tied to the side of the wagon. "Aha!" She reached inside and pulled out two eggs. "Don't listen to him, ladies," she cooed to the penned fowl. "He doesn't appreciate how hard you labored to provide breakfast for him."

"I suppose you're going to name those damn chickens, like you did the mules."

"Of course. Who's your favorite Shakespearean female character?"

"Lady MacBeth. She was as crazy as the rest of you

females." He went off into the brush to seek some privacy.

By the time he returned, Rebecca had dressed. Clay built a fire while she rolled out the dough for biscuits. Since Scott had told them they'd be laying over there for an extra day in order to clean and dry out their wagons, Rebecca had great expectations of doing the laundry and baking an apple pie.

"Don't you have guard duty?" she asked when Clay sat down and began to clean his rifle after breakfast.

"Not until six o'clock," he said. "Why?"

"Would you mind milking Clementine?"

"You named that cow Clementine?"

"I didn't name her; the VonDiemans did. So, yes or no: Do you mind milking her?"

"I mind, but I'll do it, if that's what you're asking."

"Well, it's . . . ah . . ." She could see he wasn't in a good mood, so maybe she'd better not mention it at this time.

"What now, Rebecca?"

"Never mind, I can ask Garth."

Clay sighed deeply and gave her an exasperated look. "Garth rode out with Hawk and won't be around for a couple of days. What do you want?"

"I thought maybe you'd show me how to milk the cow."

"You've never milked a cow?" His look of reproach was as annoying as his exasperated one always was.

"No, I've never milked a cow, fed chickens, or ridden a horse. I was born and raised in the city, sir, and never had any reason to learn."

He snorted. "You can add unable to swim or shoot a rifle to that list. What in hell did you want with a cow, then?"

"Buying the cow was *your* idea." She slapped a pair of his soiled stockings into the wash boiler and began to scrub them vigorously on the washboard.

"I bought the cow because I thought you wanted milk and butter. Is there anything you *can* do?" he asked.

That did it! She had just made the ungrateful oaf a delicious breakfast of eggs, bacon, fried potatoes, hot biscuits, and coffee.

Did he tell her as much? No!

Did he appreciate it? No!

Did he give her one word of thanks? You can be sure not!

"Wash your own damn clothes!" She picked up one of the soapy stockings and let it fly. It hit him smack in the face. With a smile of satisfaction, she spun on her heel to walk away.

He was on her at once and turned her around. "That was a mistake."

Holding her firmly in place, he sloshed the stocking into the water with his other hand, then splashed it over her head. Squealing, Rebecca groped in the tub for the other stocking, pulled it out, and sloshed it over his head. Abandoning the stocking, Clay used his hand and splashed her with scoops of suds. Anger had been washed away with the suds, and, laughing, they circled the tub, each managing to splash the other.

When he dunked the stocking back into the tub to rewet it, Rebecca took off, but he chased after her and quickly caught up. He grabbed her, and they lost their balance and started to fall. Clay turned and took the brunt of the fall, then rolled over and straddled her. The way she squirmed beneath him aroused him, and he was instantly rock hard.

"Let me go," Rebecca squealed, still laughing.

"Oh, I don't think so." He pressed his arousal against her and she went still, her eyes widening.

"Please?" Her voice was breathless.

"As soon as you say you're sorry." Clay slowly leaned down as if about to kiss her, a mischievous gleam in his eyes, then he squeezed the wet stocking onto her face. "I'm tempted to use this wet stocking to wash out that smart mouth of yours, lady."

"Don't you dare, Clay Fraser!" Squealing and laughing, she managed to unseat him, rolled free, and raced to the wash boiler to rearm.

Wakened by the noise, Helena Garson sat up in alarm, fearing an Indian attack. Seeing her husband sitting calmly by the fire smoking his pipe, she asked, "What's happening over there?"

Howard Garson chuckled and winked at her. "Honeymooners, Lena. Just honeymooners."

"Where do they get the energy?" Yawning, Helena closed her eyes and settled back to bed to sleep.

Clay declared himself the unequivocal winner. Then, relaxing, he stretched out and closed his eyes.

Rebecca, however, wasn't ready to concede defeat. She grabbed the washbasin and scooped up more water. Sneaking up on him, she poured it over his head.

He raised an eyelid, water dripping down his face. "You're going to pay for that."

He got to his feet and picked up the tub.

"You wouldn't!" she cried, and backed away as he stalked her.

"Oh, yes I would, and with great pleasure."

"Okay, I'm sorry," she conceded, trying not to laugh.

"You will be when I get my hands on you."

"That's easier said than done." She shoved him, and he lost his balance and dropped the tub, spilling out the remaining water.

Giggling, she raced toward the river with Clay in pursuit. Without thinking, she ran into the shallow water. The quicksand sucked her feet into its depth. The more she struggled to free them, the more the sand clutched and held. She couldn't budge a foot.

"I'm stuck!"

Clay, who had halted on the bank, folded his arms across his chest. "Kind of looks that way."

"You'll have to get a rope and pull me out, Clay."

"More likely eight yoke of oxen. It'll take a while to round them up and get them harnessed, though. I'll be back in an hour or so." He turned to leave.

She felt a rising panic. "Clay, you aren't leaving me here, are you?"

He turned back. "Well, you see, Rebecca, my feelings are a little bruised. Maybe if I heard that apology again, I'd—"

"Okay, okay! I'm sorry. *Now* will you get me out of here?"

"Do you promise to behave yourself?"

"I promise. I *promise*." She tried to move, but her feet wouldn't budge, and she fell forward into the sand. "Oh, no!" She managed to free her hands as the sand tried to suck them in.

Clay started to laugh. "Lady, you're just digging yourself in deeper."

She put her hands on her hips. "Are you going to get me out of here, or do I have to start screaming for help?"

"What's it worth to you?"

"If you're suggesting that I let you sleep with—"

"Kiss. I'm suggesting my wife kiss me." He shook his head. "Tsk, tsk, Mrs. Fraser. Your remarks are very revealing. Well, stay where you are until I get back with a rope."

"Very funny, Clay. I'll wait."

Within minutes he returned with a rope and tossed the end to her. She grabbed it like a drowning person reaching for a lifeline.

"Hang on."

He began to tug on the rope and gradually freed her from the watery sand.

Once on the bank she sat down and shook off the quicksand that still clung to her hands and clothing. Then she looked up at Clay and grinned. "I sure could use some of that water and suds we wasted, now."

He grinned back, and they both broke into laughter.

"Come on, Trouble." He reached out a hand and pulled her to her feet.

12

The water fight between her and Clay broke the tension between them, and after cleaning herself up, Rebecca boiled more water and finished the laundry, while Clay milked the cow and then returned to cleaning his firearms.

Later they gave the wagon a good scrubbing together, and then reloaded the supplies. The remarkable thing about it was that they spent hours together and never exchanged a cross word between them. They even found things to laugh over as they worked side by side.

After eating an early dinner, Clay left to stand guard. When he returned at eight, he challenged her to another game of backgammon. Two hours later they settled down in their bedrolls.

Rebecca fell asleep instantly, her mouth curved in a contented smile.

Clay didn't understand why he couldn't sleep. The damn chickens had wakened him early, so he should be able to fall asleep easily. Instead, he was wide awake. Turning over on his side, he stared at Rebecca sleeping nearby. Try as he might, he just couldn't stay angry with her.

He had to give credit where it was due: She had a lot of grit.

And he grudgingly had to admit that it was no longer reasonable to put Rebecca in the same category as Ellie. They were complete opposites in every way: One had hair the color of sunshine, the other the darkness of night. Rebecca worked that trim little butt of hers off from sunrise to sunset. He'd never seen Ellie do a whit of work, and she'd go thirsty waiting for someone to bring her a drink before she'd get up and get it herself. Expecting someone to wait on her would never enter Becky's mind.

In retrospect he was damn lucky. He had thought the sky had fallen when Will told him Ellie had married another man. Now he'd come to realize Ellie's vanity. She was very aware of her physical beauty and used it on men to serve her interests. He doubted Becky was even aware of her beauty, and it puzzled him why some man had not convinced her into remarrying in the past four years. It must be that she didn't want to remarry.

His gaze rested again on Rebecca's sleeping figure. Lately, his thoughts dwelled more and more on the mysteries behind this woman—and that scared the hell out of him.

He closed his eyes and felt the welcoming lethargy of drowsiness. All things considered, he could put up with the arrangement between them, if they'd only share a bed. It was too bad she disliked him so much, because the truth of it was, he was beginning to enjoy having her around. He was ready to forgive and forget—but she wanted to hold on to that independence of hers. And she still wore Charley Elliott's wedding ring.

Well, before they reached California, that would change.

That and her idea of an annulment.

After a warning from the wagon master to make certain their water barrels were filled to capacity, the train pulled out promptly at seven the following morning. The landscape was gradually rising, with only an occasional buffalo in view.

Late in the day they reached a steep hill, and after cresting it, the terrain stretched out in a high, flat tableland. Even though there was no river or water hole, Scott called a halt for the night to rest the stock, with an added warning to go sparingly on their water since they would not encounter any the next day, either.

The following day the wagon train made the best progress thus far. After covering over twenty miles, they halted at a steep declivity where the tableland dropped suddenly into the North Platte Valley below. In the distance they glimpsed the leafy boughs of trees, something they hadn't seen in the weeks they'd crossed the plains. Everyone's spirits were renewed.

That evening, while the men were at a meeting organizing the following day's activity, Rebecca and Henrietta strolled over to the trail and gazed down the sharp slope into the valley.

"I can't see how it's possible to drive a wagon down that hill," Rebecca said.

Etta nodded in agreement. "Daddy said he figures they'll have to lower them some way."

"You got it all figured out, ladies?" Clay asked, joining them. Tom Davis was with him.

The young couple exchanged meaningful glances, then Etta said, "I'll see you later." The two departed.

Clay looked perplexed. "What got into her?"

Men were so dense when it came to matters of the heart. "I have no idea. So what was decided at the meeting?"

"We're going to skid the wagons down the hill."

"How do you do that?"

"By locking the wagon wheels to the box, and harnessing them to mule teams instead of oxen. The oxen are too slow and the wagons would probably overrun them."

"But wouldn't the wagons overrun mules, too? I can't believe the brakes will do any good at that sharp angle."

"We're using human brakes."

At her confused look, Clay grinned and said, "Men and ropes. Scotty said he'd probably need eight or ten men to a wagon to skid them down. The women, children, and rest of the livestock go down by foot. Unless you want to ride the wagon down, Becky." He grinned.

"I bet you'd like to see me try."

"I wouldn't let you try."

"Oh, I see. You're playing husband again."

"I'm not *playing*, Becky. You're the one who's tried to turn marriage into a game."

Even though there was no anger in his tone, there was no denying he was dead serious.

Her stomach suddenly felt tied in a knot and she forced a smile. "Well, at least you can look forward to the game coming to an end when we reach California. That should make you very happy. I never intended to be a problem for you."

"And what if Garth and I catch up with our sister before we reach California? We'd have no reason for continuing on with this wagon train."

"You have my word, Clay, that I would file for the annulment as soon as I reach California."

"Did it occur to you, Becky, that you wouldn't get to California if Scotty made you leave with us?" He walked away.

It certainly hadn't occurred to her! It was devastating to think that after coming so far, she might very well have to turn around and go back if Clay left the wagon train. She could only hope that Melissa stayed far ahead of them.

At dawn they prepared to lower one of Scott's wagons. The wheels were chained to the box to keep them from turning, and then, with a driver handling the reins, four men on each side, and two more at the rear manning ropes tied to the wagon, they began the descent. The mules struggled to keep their footing, and the men strained at the ropes to keep them taut and the wagon from sliding forward too rapidly. By the time they were halfway down, the dust cloud formed by their heels dug into the earth obliterated them from the anxious eyes of those watching from above.

The descent was as slow as the river crossings. There

were five teams of men, and once a team got a wagon down, they had to climb back up the hill, passing a team on their way down with another wagon.

Thus far all the wagons had made it down without a mishap. The Garson wagon was being lowered, and they were preparing Rebecca's wagon for the descent. She felt a pang in her chest when all was ready and Clay climbed up on the box and took the reins. After assuring her beloved mules that they could do it, she stepped away.

"Be careful, Clay," she called out.

"You, too. Take it easy going down that hill, and if that cow loses its footing, don't try to hold on to it. Do you hear me?"

"I'll take care of Clementine; you make sure you get my mules down there safely. And be careful with Katharina and Lady MacBeth. You know if Kate gets jarred around too much, she can't lay eggs."

"If those chickens weren't so dumb, they'd have figured out their wings are for flying down."

"Just be careful with them. See you below."

As soon as they started to lower the wagon, Rebecca tugged on Clementine's rope and began her own descent. The grade was steep, and she moved cautiously. Suddenly her foot slipped out from under her and she fell forward on her stomach, losing her grip on the cow's rope.

"Show off," she grumbled when, undisturbed, Clementine continued down the hillside.

Rebecca crawled to her knees and managed to sit up. Laughing gaily, several children passed her, skimming down on their butts. They appeared to be treating it all as a game, so why shouldn't she? She finished the descent on her rear end.

Clay was at the foot of the hill when she finally reached it. To her surprise, he looked concerned.

"What's wrong, did you hurt an ankle?"

Rebecca stood up and brushed off her skirt. "No, I'm fine. It was me or my dignity, so I let my dignity take the fall. Did the wagon and mules make it down okay?"

"No problem. I have to head back up. I parked the wagon over in that copse of trees. I saw Clementine and tied her to the rear. Drive about a mile down the trail, and you'll come to Ash Hollow. Becky, you're not going to believe the place. There are fresh pools of water everywhere! It'll take two or three more hours to get all the wagons and oxen down, so Scotty said we'll be laying over there for the night." He started to walk away, then turned back. "By the way, there's some Indians in camp, but don't be alarmed: They're Sioux, not Shawnee. They rode in with Hawk and Garth. Hawk said the Indian scare is behind us. We're in Sioux territory now, and they aren't hostile at this time." He grinned. "Of course, Hawk didn't warn them you were coming."

"That's very funny, Clay." Darn him, he always managed to have the last word.

For a long moment she watched him as he started up the hillside. He moved with a smooth stride and made climbing the steep hill look easy. She'd observed that he seemed to take everything in the same easy manner as that smooth, even stride of his. Well, maybe everything except getting tricked into marriage.

After complimenting the mules for the fine job they did, Rebecca apologized to Katharina and Lady Mac-Beth for the jolting ride they'd just had. Then she climbed into the box and headed down the trail. Occasionally she'd come upon one or two people walking. She offered a ride to any who were interested, but they just waved and shook their heads.

When Rebecca reached Ash Hollow, she couldn't believe her eyes. Surely she must have died and gone to Heaven. The mammoth meadow was abundant with tall ash trees, and leafy bushes ripe with grapevines, gooseberries, and currants. Trickling streams merged into translucent pools throughout the meadow. Countless wildflowers carpeted the ground in colorful splendor, and the sweet fragrance of wild roses and jasmine permeated the air.

She located the Garson wagon and parked nearby. There'd be no cramped circle of wagons that night; Scott had given the word they could spread out and enjoy the surroundings. Rebecca took the team to the distant grazing area that had been roped off for the livestock to eat and drink without dirtying the clear water in the pools.

Returning to her wagon, Rebecca saw that Helena and Eleanor Garson were already in the process of making currant jelly. She grabbed a pan to gather some fruit, and joined several other women who had the same idea. As soon as she finished, she hurried back to her wagon.

As she was rolling out a piecrust, five mounted Indians rode by on their way out of camp. This was her first glimpse of a mighty Sioux. Mr. Scott had praised the Sioux Nation at great length; he considered them the noblest warriors they'd encounter—and the deadliest, if they were on the warpath.

One in particular held her attention. He looked magnificent astride a black stallion, and held his head with the bearing of a crowned sovereign. Wearing only a flapped breechcloth over his loins and fringed moccasins on his feet, the Indian's muscled, bronzed chest and legs were free of body hair. A white feather dangled from the end of his coal black hair, which was woven into a single braid. But even more compelling were his black piercing eyes when he glanced at her as he rode past. His expression never altered as he continued on his way.

Somewhat awed, Rebecca returned to the task at hand. She had two gooseberry pies baked by the time Clay and Garth showed up, and a kettle of currants bubbling on the fire.

Later, needing a cup of milk, Rebecca glanced over to the wagon. Both men had dozed off, and she didn't want to disturb them. Going up and down that hillside all day must have been exhausting.

What the heck! She had seen a cow milked before; surely she could figure out how to do it herself. Grabbing the camp stool and milk bucket, she walked over to the cow, who was chewing on grass near the wagon.

"Clementine, I need a favor from you. I want to make a cream sauce and I need a cup of milk. I'd appreciate, my dear, if you'd let me have one. I'll tell you, now, I've never milked a cow before, so you'll have to be patient with me."

The cow raised her head, looked at Rebecca with its big round eyes, and then went back to chewing grass.

Rebecca sat down on the stool, put the bucket in place, and reached for the cow's teats. They felt like skin—hard skin. Clementine turned her head, a quizzical look in her eyes. Rebecca squeezed, but nothing happened. She tried again with the same result.

"You aren't cooperating, dear," Rebecca said. "Shall we try again?"

This time Rebecca squeezed a little harder. The cow switched its tail. Rebecca tried to dodge it but the tail caught her on the cheek, and she fell backward off the stool.

For a long moment she lay there, glaring at the animal. "That was not nice, Clementine. Not nice at all. I just want one little cup of milk." Rubbing her stinging cheek, she sat back down on the stool. "I'm not leaving without it."

Once again she reached for the teats and squeezed. No milk, but she succeeded in dodging the tail this time when it swung in her direction.

"Look, *dear*," Rebecca said, through gritted teeth. "I'm trying to be very patient about this."

"You probably aren't squeezing hard enough."

She jerked her head around. Clay was standing behind her. He knelt in back of her and enclosed her in the circle of his arms, cupping his hands over hers.

She was enveloped by the heat of his body, the power in the arms embracing her, the sensual huskiness of his voice at her ear. It made concentrating on a cow's udder most difficult.

"Now squeeze," he said, applying pressure to her hands.

She ducked the tail, and Clay caught the blow in the face.

"This is a mean cow," he pointed out.

He resumed his position. "The trick is to do it with rhythm. Squeeze, yank, squeeze, yank. Let's hear you say it."

"Squeeze, yank. Squeeze, yank," she muttered. She was sorry she had decided to cook the potatoes in cream sauce; beans would have been just as satisfactory. He never appeared to care one way or another what she cooked.

"Now try milking rhythmically," he said.

His closeness made it so hard for her to concentrate, she just wanted to get the whole thing over with. She shot to her feet. "Show me."

"Sure." Clay sat down on the stool. Matching the words of the song to his motions, he began to sing, "For I—wish I—was in—Dix-ie—Squeeze-yank—Squeeze-yank—In Dixie—land I'll—take my—stand to—live or—die in—Dix-ie—A-way,—a-way—"

He stopped singing and stared, dumbfounded, into the empty milk bucket. "That's sure odd."

"Maybe you yanked when you should have squeezed," she said. "But I think I understand. If you'll move aside, Maestro."

Rebecca sat down on the stool. She took a firm hold and began to sing, "The U-nion—for—ever—Hurrah

boys—hur-rah—Down with—the traitor—and up—
with the star—We will—ral-ly—round the—flag,
boys—ral-ly—round the flag.—Shout—ing—the battle—cry of—free—dom." Every squeeze-yank pro-
duced a solid squirt of milk.

Clay shoved his hat to the top of his forehead and
stared at the quarter-filled bucket. "I'll be damned! I
don't understand that."

Pleased as punch, Rebecca picked up the bucket and
camp stool. "I do. Admit you were an *udder* failure."
She broke into giggles.

Grinning, he said, "That is *udderly* the worst joke I've
ever heard."

"It's obvious to me, Captain Cavalry, what the real
problem is. The VonDiemans were from Pennsylvania.
Clementine's a Yankee." Rebecca walked away, swing-
ing the bucket.

Chuckling in amusement, Clay followed behind.

13

"Becky, this pie is delicious," Clay said.

Rebecca giggled. "Then I'd be *udderly* devastated if you didn't eat this last piece." She scooped the last slice of the berry pie onto his plate.

Garth looked from one to the other. " 'Udderly devastated?' Okay, what's the joke?"

"Just a private thing between me and my wife, Little Brother."

Clay went back to where he'd been sitting with his back against a tree. As he ate, he listened to Garth and Becky's good-humored bantering. Garth seemed to get a lot of pleasure out of teasing her, and Becky's spirits always perked up when he was around. This time his brother was accusing her of substituting flour for face powder. Clay, too, had noticed the flour smear on her nose; and he'd been tempted to wipe it off when he saw it. But it looked kind of cute, so he hadn't said anything. Leave it to Garth, though; he loved flirting with women.

Their conversation shifted to the dinner she had cooked, which once again had been exceptional. Give her a jar of tomatoes, an onion, and then a rabbit, a hunk of antelope, or a buffalo steak, and she could perform miracles. She also made the best cup of coffee he'd ever tasted. If the woman had any vanity, it was over her cooking. Clearly she embraced the task with passion—and she must have read the letters off the pages of that cookbook of hers, by now.

Her cooking ability was an unanticipated bonus on the trip. It was clear Garth held the same opinion, because he complimented her plenty on it.

Clay popped the last bite of pie into his mouth. He figured they had to be the best-fed men on the wagon train.

Etta came running over, her bright eyes glowing with excitement. Grabbing Becky by the hand, she cried, "Come on, you people, we're going to have a hoedown."

She didn't have to ask Garth twice. When Clay hesitated, Etta cajoled, "Come on, Mr. Fraser. Don't be a spoilsport."

Clay had been considering going to bed because he had guard duty later that night. But a spoilsport he wasn't, so he followed reluctantly.

The camp was in a jovial mood, the tragedies and hardships of the past six weeks put behind them. The makeshift band had already been formed by the time they joined the group. Clay was pleased to see there was no sign of Jake Fallon among the crowd. Since their confrontation, the shifty-eyed little weasel had avoided him, which was fine with Clay. He was glad the bastard wasn't there to spoil everybody's pleasure.

Fiddles sawed, banjos strummed, feet stomped, and hands clapped as the dancers do-si-doed and swung their partners to the lively music. Becky's smile was contagious as she weaved from partner to partner during the dance. Clay found himself partnered with her as the fiddler finished the call with "Now the dance is over and I insist, you fellas give them little gals a thank-you kiss."

For the briefest moment Clay hesitated, then he dipped his head and pressed a light kiss on her lips. They felt soft and tasted like sweet wine, and he would have liked a much longer drink from them.

Garth claimed Becky for the next dance, and Clay sat down to watch. He couldn't take his eyes off her. She had never looked lovelier. Her face was flushed with pleasure and her green eyes had an excited glow. She had tied back her hair, and the long blond strands bouncing bewitchingly on her shoulders glistened like gold in the glow from the campfire as she circled around. Her movements were unintentionally sensuous; she had no idea the effect they had on a male.

Howard Garson came over, sat down beside him, and lit his pipe. "Feels good to see people having fun," he said.

"Yeah, it's well earned."

"Long trail ahead yet. You figuring on going back to Virginia as soon as you find your sister?" he asked.

"Yeah. We no sooner got home than we headed out here. It will feel good when we finally get settled down."

"Ever think of staying in California?" Howard asked.

Clay chuckled. "Virginia's in my blood; I can't imagine living anywhere else. What got you to leave Ohio? War shouldn't have made any difference there."

"Been thinking about it ever since '62, when the government passed that Homestead Act. Finally made up my mind that if I made it through the war, I'd apply for a parcel of that free land. A hundred and sixty acres will set us up real fine. It's in a place called Napa Valley, a mite southeast of Sacramento. Supposed to be fine country. You ought to give it some thought, Clay. Supposed to be lots of land available. And we'd sure like to have you and Becky for neighbors."

"You know that those who fought for the Confederacy don't qualify for any free land, Howard," Clay said.

"Yeah, but I heard tell land's pretty cheap."

"Even so, I don't have money to buy land. And besides, Virginia's my home."

The dance ended, and Rebecca squealed with delighted laughter when Garth grasped her by the waist and swung her off her feet. Now, exhausted, the dancers collapsed around the fire.

The musicians began to play familiar songs, and the crowd raised their voices in an enthusiastic rendition of "The Old Gray Mare." Laughter reigned when they followed it with "Listen to the Mocking Bird."

Clay wasn't much of a singer, but his enthusiasm was as great as anyone's. He drew special enjoyment in watching Rebecca laughing and singing, her radiance an irresistible beacon to his gaze.

When the musicians had exhausted their repertoire of popular songs, they changed to patriotic songs and religious hymns. All were enjoying the fellowship too much to want to leave. The singers' voices rose in such songs as "America" and "Rock of Ages."

A cry went up for Tom Davis to sing a solo, and the young man's pleasing tenor began the romantic "Beautiful Dreamer," directed to a blushing Etta.

A few of the couples got up and began to dance or sway slowly to the nostalgic song. Helena Garson nudged Clay to do the same with Rebecca.

Clay would rather have walked barefoot on hot coals. He tried to ignore Helena, but the gregarious woman was persistent. Rather than make a scene, he took Becky's hand and they joined the other couples.

The feel of her in his arms was becoming a familiar warmth to him. The sweet fragrance of her was pleasing. He relaxed and let the music guide him. Funny, from the first time they'd waltzed together in Independence, their steps had flowed together as if they'd shared many dances before. And she moved as smoothly on this surface as she had on the wooden floor.

Day by day, he discovered more and more appealing qualities about her. Her compassion for others, a bright mind, and a sense of humor. And she sure wasn't a quitter. Under all that feistiness was steadfast courage and determination.

Deep in thought, he unconsciously drew her closer. Day by day, his physical desire for her was growing. She always maintained femininity, no matter what she was doing, smelled like an intoxicating combination of cinnamon and jasmine, and fit in his arms like she'd been made for them. And the feel of her was so damn good, too.

When the song ended, he discovered they were in

the shadows. Becky raised her head and smiled up at him. Stars gleamed in the emerald depths of her eyes. God knows he tried to resist the temptation, but his desire for her swirled through him in a floodtide, drowning out everything except his hunger for this woman.

He lowered his head to drink from the wine of her lips again.

For an instant he felt her stiffen with hesitation, and then she parted her lips and their mouths found a fit.

When she slid her arms around his neck, passion shattered the wall of reserve he had fought so long to maintain. He drew her closer, molding her soft curves to his angles, feeling the hammering of her heart against his chest.

Rebecca suddenly broke the kiss, and it took him several seconds to accept the loss of her lips. Then he became aware of the cheers and whistles. He opened his eyes.

The crowd was watching them, clapping their approval as jokes about newlyweds circled among them. Releasing her, Clay offered a stiff grin to the spectators. He felt like an ass.

Garth's look was as perplexed as it was amused when Clay sat down next to him. Leaning over, he whispered, "Isn't that overcorrecting, Brother Clay?"

The singing continued, but Clay didn't join in. He and Rebecca sat stiffly, avoiding any chance of contact with one another, yet he sensed she was as physically aware of him as he was of her. He stole a glance at her and saw she wasn't singing, either. As if sensing his gaze, she turned her head and looked at him. It was obvious that she was as shaken as he, and he wondered if she desired him as much as he did her. She had responded to his kiss, and he was still aroused.

Lately their waterfight, the backgammon games, and such had only heightened his growing desire for her.

He glanced at her again and met her confused stare. *What must she be thinking?*

What must he think of me?

Rebecca felt the hot flush creeping throughout her. He seemed to be able to probe her soul with that piercing gaze of his. Had she been so blatant that he'd guessed she wanted him to kiss her? Had she encouraged him to?

Surely he'd only intended to kiss her lightly, as he'd done during the dance. Why had he even kissed her in the first place? Maybe he didn't have as much aversion to her as she thought . . . or was he continuing to play the devoted husband because of the audience watching them?

Of course she had to go and throw her arms around his neck, encouraging the kiss to deepen. There was an undeniable excitement in being around Clay. Be it the thrill of his kiss, or the casual gesture of clasping her hand, she responded instantly to the masculinity. His kiss, his touch, the scent of him—the mere nearness of him. She loved the warmth that carried to his eyes when he laughed, and the delightful huskiness in his chuckle. They were such contradictions to those cold scowls he'd showered on her. Even the sparring between them was becoming more of an aphrodisiac than a deterrent.

When had she gone from abhorring the sight of him to missing him when he was gone? From loathing him for being a Rebel to admiring his sense of honor? Duty and honor were the tenets he lived by; deceit and treachery were abominations to him. Which was why they could never have a future together, why the marriage had to be annulled.

Once they reached California, they'd never see each other again.

When the crowd finally dispersed, Garth walked back with them to the wagon, enabling Clay and Rebecca to avoid talking to each other. It was just as well; she wouldn't have known what to say anyway.

Rebecca was laying out her fur pelt when Clay came up to her as he was leaving to stand guard.

"Becky, about tonight, I—"

"I had a good time, didn't you?" she said, hoping she sounded casual.

"Yes, I enjoyed myself. About the kiss—"

"Oh, that? I think we convinced everybody that we're a devoted couple, wouldn't you say? We're such good actors, we ought to go on the stage."

He was silent for a moment. "Yeah . . . a great acting job on both our parts. Good night."

"Good night." Rebecca sank down on the pallet and watched him walk away. She brushed aside the teardrop sliding down her cheek. *Why are you crying?*

*You're the one who set this whole thing in motion, Rebecca,
so stop feeling sorry for yourself.*

Rebecca had made up her mind earlier that the only
way to survive the hardships of this trip was to always
put the previous day's problems behind her. So today,
last night's kiss was ancient history.

Clay disappeared after breakfast and Etta had wandered off with Tom, so Rebecca cut up a couple apples
and headed for the meadow where the stock was corralled.

All except Brutus were together. After feeding them
the apple slices, she looked around for the missing
mule. She spied him in the shade of a tree and, as she
moved nearer, she was suprised to see that Brutus was
tethered there. And Clay was squatted down by the animal's front leg.

Strands of dark hair had tumbled over his forehead,
and he looked appealingly boyish. Perspiration dotted
his forehead, and he paused at his task to wipe his brow
on his shirtsleeve.

Rebecca hurried over to them. "What's wrong with
Brutus?" she asked worriedly.

"He must have scraped his leg. I noticed it was fester-
ing, so I've put a poultice on it. It should make him
more comfortable."

"I hadn't noticed it. Thank you, Clay, that's very
thoughtful of you. I didn't think you even liked Brutus."

"I don't. I just don't like to see a dumb animal in

pain." He finished tying a bandage around the mule's leg, and then stood and untethered him.

"Say thank you to the nice man, Brutus," Rebecca said, as she fed the mule the remaining apple slices. The mule swished its tail, then wandered toward its harness-mates.

Rebecca followed Clay away from the corral, and sat down in the shade of an ash tree while he washed off his hands in one of the many pools in the hollow.

He returned and sat beside her.

"It was very thoughtful, Clay. Thank you again."

"My preference would have been to shoot the damn mule."

"I swear you enjoy arguing. Just accept the compliment, and don't spoil it by being nasty."

"Nasty!" He chuckled. "Now, is that a nice thing for a woman to say to her husband? I thought you didn't want to argue."

"I don't. It's too lovely a day, and this place is so beautiful. It's like a Garden of Eden. I wish we could stay here forever."

"Speaking of Eden." He dug in his pocket and pulled out a couple of apples. "Here," he said, tossing her one. "I didn't have to use these after all."

They sat in silence as they ate the apples, then Clay stretched out with his hands tucked under his head. The distant lilt of Etta's laughter carried to their ears.

"What do you suppose those two are up to?" Clay said. "They're pretty smitten with each other, aren't they?"

Rebecca smiled. "Yes, I think so. I guess I was the same way at their age."

"And now?"

"I've learned you can't put your trust in love. I prefer my independence."

He sat up and gazed at her intently. "Are you saying you regret your marriage? I thought you loved your husband. You're wearing his ring instead of mine."

"I did love him. And I've learned that being in love makes you vulnerable. I don't ever want to put myself in that position again. I can take care of myself."

"Becky, you relinquished some of that independence when you married me. And as your husband, my honor dictates that I take care of you."

"But you know why I married you, Clay. You know I don't expect anything from you."

"Perhaps not, but the fact remains we *are* husband and wife. So we both have to take responsibility for our actions—and the obligations that come with those responsibilities."

"And I know you feel I'm not honoring my obligation to you by refusing to share your bed."

"We've been together every day and night for six weeks. You're a very desirable woman, and my wife, and I'm only human. It's becoming more and more difficult for me to keep my hands off you. And I can tell by your response when I kiss you that you want me as much as I want you."

"Please understand, Clay, whether I do want you or not, I can't let anything interfere with getting that annulment. If we become intimate, that will be impossible."

"So we stay married—I won't dishonor my vow," he said stubbornly.

"But I don't *want* to remain married. That's the point: I like my independence. I've been left destitute once, and I won't ever rely on someone else to take care of me again."

"And you don't think one day you'll need love in your life?"

"Definitely not." Her tone lightened. "And furthermore, Clay, aren't you the man who declared you'll never love or trust a woman again?"

"Did I say that?" He chuckled. "I must have been drunk."

"As a matter of fact, I think you were."

They both broke into laughter.

"I guess a man says a lot of stupid things when his pride's been hurt."

"Or his heart." The laughter left her eyes, and she said gently, "Did you love her very much, Clay?"

"I thought I did at the time. I realize now that I was more angry than heartbroken. But every man needs an Ellie in his life so he can recognize the merits in the next woman he meets."

Her eyes widened with surprise. "Why, Clay, since I'm that next woman, are you implying you think I have some merits?"

"Well, for one, you're a very hard worker."

"And Ellie wasn't?" she asked.

"The only thing Ellie knows about work is how it's spelled."

She grimaced with mock pain. "That sounds like sour grapes, and certainly not very gallant coming from a southern gentleman."

"Yes, you're right. That remark does sound like I'm bitter, and I won't deny I was at first. But I'm not anymore. I feel I'm damn lucky."

"So, what other virtues do you see in me that Ellie didn't have?"

"You make a great cup of coffee."

"Thank you. I have noticed you drink a lot of it."

"And you're a great cook."

"It took you six weeks to get around to telling me. But thank you."

His grin broadened in amusement. "I didn't want to add to your vanity."

"Are you implying I'm vain, Clay Fraser?"

"About your cooking? *Udderly*."

She grinned and gave him a shove. He rolled over and grabbed her, pinning her to the ground with his body.

Laughing, she cried, "Get off me, you ungrateful lout! I've cooked my last meal for you."

Suddenly cooking became the furthest thing on his mind as laughter turned to desire. The very air seemed charged with their awareness of each other. He could tell by the deepening in those gorgeous green eyes that she felt it, too.

"And what if I told you that I like the sound of your laughter, the smell of cinnamon on you from this morning's baking, the way your hair catches the sunshine. I like just looking at you—and I like the feel of you under me right now."

Clay lowered his head; she parted her lips. He kissed her with a fierce hunger, and his whole being flooded with desire when she responded with a hunger as great as his own.

She was breathless when he broke the kiss. "Let me up, Clay."

"You don't really mean that, Becky. That kiss belied every thing you've said. You want me as much as I want you."

"That's beside the point—I meant what I said. What you want from me, I won't give you."

The sound of laughter and voices caused him to glance up to see Etta and Tom approaching them hand in hand.

Clay gave Becky a quick kiss, then stood and pulled her to her feet. Slipping an arm around her waist, he headed toward the young couple. "Looks like you dodged the bullet again, Mrs. Fraser."

"And I'll do so all the way to California if I have to."

He chuckled. "You're sure about that?"

"Udderly sure," she replied confidently.

14

After two restful nights at Ash Hollow, they pulled out. There wasn't a person in the train who didn't cast a wistful backward glance at the wilderness oasis.

Once again, the land began a gradual but constant climb as they followed the waters of the North Platte River. Exotic rock formations began to dot the country-side, and despite the heat of the day, the nights began to turn cool due to the higher elevation. In the far horizon loomed the snowcapped peaks of the Laramie Mountains, so the party knew they were nearing Fort Laramie.

Occasionally they'd glimpse a band of Indians watching from the higher cliffs, but Hawk said to pay them no mind, because you wouldn't see a Sioux if he didn't want to be seen. Nevertheless, as a precaution-ary measure, Scott had returned to having them circle the wagons at night.

The landmarks were becoming extraordinary, with formations with such names as Courthouse Rock and Jailhouse Rock. One, a slim, stone shaft that stuck straight up in the air called Chimney Rock, held Re-becca's attention.

"How tall is it?" she asked Clay as they stood looking at it.

"They claim five hundred feet," he said.

"How do they know?"

"I imagine someone climbed up to measure it."

"Who would want to do that?" she exclaimed.

"Becky, some human beings feel compelled to climb anything—just because it's there."

She shook her head. "How silly. What can you do once you're at the top?"

"Climb back down, I imagine."

She leaned her head to the side and studied it. "You know, if you look at it from this angle, it looks like a long, inverted funnel."

"I might have known you'd figure out some cooking connection to it."

More followed, craggy shapes resembling parapets and towers, deep gulches, and rocky trails.

Three days later the wagon train arrived at the gates of Fort Laramie: the last bastion of civilization as they knew it, until they crossed the Rocky Mountains and reached California. Set in the foothills of the Rockies, the fort had originally been a fur-trading station, then converted to a United States army post.

Rebecca was delighted to reach the post at last. After traveling for six weeks and six hundred and forty miles, she could finally take a *hot* bath.

Mike Scott insisted the wagons form their usual circle outside the fort's gates. The army had constructed pens and grazing corrals for the stock, but informed them that they were not responsible for guarding them—which meant Clay and Garth would be pulling duty shifts.

Clay had hoped they might be lucky enough to find Melissa at the fort, but that hope was dashed when they found out their train was the only westbound one there. There were more than a dozen wagons heading back East, and in the remote possibility that Melissa was among them, he and Garth checked them out.

"Sure, I remember that gal," one of the men said when Clay showed him Melissa's picture. "Mighty pretty she was, too. Long dark hair and eyes the color of a Texas bluebonnet."

"That's Lissy, all right," Garth said. "Was she okay?"

He shrugged. "Never got more than a nod and a smile. Wife talked to her a time or two, though. Hey, Ma, you remember this gal, don't you?"

The woman came over carrying what appeared to be about a two-year-old girl in her arm, and holding the hand of another a year or so older.

"Ah, yes," she said, after glancing at the picture. "Melissa Berg. Sweet little thing she was, too." She shook her head sadly. "Poor little thing was sick most of the time."

"Sick?" Clay asked with rising panic. He'd heard horror stories about how often cholera occurred on these wagon trains.

"She's in a family way. Never saw anyone so sick in that condition. Hate to think of the poor dear crossin' 'em mountains, as sick as she is."

"What about her husband?" Garth asked.

"Fine young man. Fretted about her constantly and waited on her hand and foot, tryin' to make her more comfortable. I sure hope they make it safely to California. Me, I've had enough of it. I told Clem here that I ain't riskin' our children's lives anymore. We're gonna find us a spot right here near the fort."

"Thank you, ma'am. You, too, sir," Clay said.

"How does she figure raising a family right smack among the Sioux is safe?" Garth said, when they passed through the gates of the fort. "Those Indians can go on the warpath over a dead horse, if they've a mind to."

Clay had worried about Lissy's safety, but until now hadn't thought about her personal health. "That Yankee bastard should have turned back until Lissy was well enough to travel."

"Maybe he figured we'd be hot on his heels," Garth said.

"That's no excuse for him to let her make this trip when she's that ill."

"Yeah, but it sounds like Lissy. You know how we all spoiled her, so she's used to getting what she wants. The poor guy probably found it just as hard to say no to her as the rest of us always did. If Lissy thought there'd be a chance of us catching up and stopping her, she'd push on. The gal's got a lot of grit."

"Tell me something, Garth. Do you go through life making excuses for women who don't care how much their actions affect others, as long as they get what *they* want?"

Garth chuckled. "With one exception, Brother Clay—that female shark you intended to marry back in

Virginia. Ah . . . what was her name again?" he asked, tongue-in-cheek.

Clay couldn't help grinning. "Jezebel. Her name was Jezebel, Brother Garth."

Clay couldn't believe he was actually making jokes over losing Ellie. What a difference a couple of months made. Slapping Garth on the shoulder, he said, "I've thought of another angle. Let's try the post office."

After a lengthy discussion with the cigar-chewing postmaster, who lectured them on the sanctity of the United States mail and the integrity of his office in upholding that inviolability, they finally resorted to outright bribery with a bottle of whiskey. Then he let them look through the outgoing letters from people on last week's wagon. Clay found what he was hoping for—a letter home from Melissa Fraser Berg.

"At least he made an honest woman of her," Clay grumbled.

"Good, that means we won't have to shoot him after all," Garth said.

A box of cigars convinced the good postmaster to let them open the letter. The main body of it described how much she missed all of them, the attributes of her husband, her happiness, and how much she looked forward to having the baby; then she described the sights they had encountered thus far on the journey. In closing, she apologized if she'd caused them any concern and assured them how much she loved all of them.

In the last paragraph Clay struck gold. Melissa had written down the name of her husband's aunt, whom they would be staying with when they reached Sacramento. There was not one word about how sick she was.

"A real little trooper, isn't she?" Garth said.

Clay nodded, brimming with pride as much as Garth. "She sure is. But I still might strangle her when we find her."

Clay wrote Will a short letter to let him know where they were, and where they were heading from there. Then, under the watchful eye of the postmaster, he addressed a new envelope, enclosed his letter along with Lissy's, and gave it to the man to see that it was posted.

They had no sooner stepped outside when Garth asked, "Do you think there are any whores here?"

"I doubt they'd allow them inside the fort. But this fort's full of soldiers, so there's some whores around someplace. You'll probably find what you're looking for among the buildings and Indian teepees outside the gates," Clay said.

"Think I'll pursue that. See you later."

Clay watched Garth disappear through the gates of the fort. It wouldn't have been a bad idea to go with him. That near miss he'd had with Becky at Ash Hollow had stoked a fire that the dozen of dips he'd taken in cold pools since hadn't succeeded in squelching.

Thinking of that very issue, he spied Rebecca in the company of Etta and Tom. They'd arrived at Fort Laramie about an hour ago. If she was running true to form, it was plenty of time for her to have gotten into trouble.

"Oh, what a find!" Rebecca exclaimed, holding up the orange she just had the good fortune of purchasing. "The Good Lord has blessed the human race with many gifts, and two of the greatest are oranges and hot baths. I can't decide which of them is the most refreshing, but today, my dear friends, I shall have the pleasure of relishing both."

Etta giggled. "Oh, Becky, you're so funny."

"If you're hoping for a bath, you'd better go and sign up for one soon, ma'am," Tom said.

"You're right. What about you, Etta?"

"No. Mama said as long as we'll be here for another day, we should wait until tomorrow for the bath."

"I'm hoping I can take another one tomorrow, too. It's a long trip over those mountains. Who knows when the opportunity will present itself again? Clay said—"

"What did Clay say?" he asked, walking up and joining them. She'd been unaware of his approach.

"We were discussing the long journey, and that you told me we haven't even reached the halfway mark to California."

"Yeah, I guess so. Scotty said the worst is still ahead."

Suddenly Rebecca did a double-take. "I can't believe it! Etta, look." She pointed to several Indians who had just arrived at the fort. "See that Indian with the white feather in his hair? He's the same one I told you I saw at Ash Hollow."

"That's him!" Etta said in awe.

"Yes. Isn't he magnificent looking?"

"Oh, yes indeed! He's splendid looking," Etta said.

"I don't think he's so great," Tom said petulantly. "Do you, Mr. Fraser?"

"I remember him. He's a Sioux war chief named Eagle Claw. Scotty said at the time to give him a wide berth. He wields a lot of power and can be dangerous."

"But you said the Sioux weren't hostile," Rebecca said.

"Today they aren't. Who knows about tomorrow?"

"Just the same, he certainly is magnificent looking," Rebecca said. "Well, I'm going to reserve a bath for tonight. Then I'm going back to my wagon and eat my orange."

"I'll come with you." Clay followed her.

"You could save water and a tub if you shared the bath!" Tom yelled after them.

"The lad's growing up," Clay said with a grin as they headed for the bathhouse.

"Good Lord, he's only seventeen, Clay," Rebecca scolded. "Don't you remember when you were that young?"

Clay nodded. "Sure do. That's why I'd keep a closer eye on those two, if I were Howard and Helena."

The bathhouse was located outside the turreted ramparts of the fort. A painted sign saying: PUBLIC BATH, $1.00 PER PERSON. OPEN DAILY 5:00 A.M. TO 10.00 P.M. EXCEPT SUNDAYS, CHRISTMAS, AND THE 4TH OF JULY hung above the door of the building. Behind it was a cabin partitioned into two sections marked MEN and WOMEN.

They encountered Mike Scott leaving the bathhouse. He stopped Clay to give him some instruction, so Rebecca went ahead and entered the office.

The room smelled of soap, and a lingering odor of burnt wood that emanated from an unlit pot stove in the corner of the room. Stacks of towels and colorful jars of bath salts lined several shelves behind a long counter, which was encased behind a ceiling-high wire grid.

"I'd like to make a reservation, please," Rebecca said to the woman behind the counter. A young Indian boy sat beside her.

"Today or tomorrow?" the woman asked.

"Today."

"Only got one left at nine-thirty tonight. None left for tomorrow."

"That will be fine." Rebecca smiled at the young boy. He just stared at her.

"Cost is a dollar for thirty minutes, paid in advance. Includes a towel, washcloth, and soap. Bath salts are fifty cents extra."

"I'm not interested in bath salts," Rebecca said. She slipped the money through a coin slot in the grid.

"You with that wagon train that rolled in today?"

"Yes, I am. I can't tell you how much I'm looking forward to a hot bath."

"Well, be on time, honey," the woman said, " 'cause I close up promptly at ten."

"I certainly will."

There was no sign of Clay when Rebecca stepped outside, so she looked around for Etta and Tom. Having no success with that, either, she returned to her wagon, found a shady spot, and sat down to peel her orange. With most of the people shopping or plain gawking at the fort, it was peaceful and quiet at the wagons. It seemed like the first time in two months that she'd been entirely alone. As she savored the succulent sweetness of the fruit, she gazed at the looming peaks of the Rocky Mountains in the distance.

Clay left the meeting Scotty had called to inform his men the train would leave Fort Laramie the day after tomorrow. He wanted to make certain the train was out of the Rockies in the event of an early snowfall. When Clay went back to the bathhouse, there was no sign of Rebecca—not that he expected for her to still be there—and he registered for a bath.

He looked around the clearing, and then went into the fort, but there was no sign of her. He didn't want her wandering around alone, yet he knew she resented him watching over her like a hawk. Well, the woman needed watching over. And like it or not, he intended to do so until they reached their destination.

Upon seeing Etta and Tom, he hurried over to them, but they hadn't seen a sign of Rebecca. He encountered the rest of the Garsons and had no luck with them, either.

Clay rechecked the sutler's store in the event she was doing some more shopping. Now he was really worried. He couldn't believe she'd go back to the wagon so soon, when there was so much activity centered at the fort. But he'd give it a try.

The wagon area was deserted except for a few guards overseeing the grazing stock. Clay stopped in his track when he glimpsed Eagle Claw standing in some nearby trees, his gaze focused intently on something.

The Indian Chief had always appeared indifferent to those around him, but something clearly held his attention now. For some reason, it made Clay uneasy.

When Eagle Claw suddenly turned and strode away, Clay went over to discover what had held the war chief's attention.

Rebecca was sitting by her wagon in his direct line of vision.

15

There was no sign of Clay when Rebecca left for her bath. The woman in charge had just finished cleaning up the bathhouse after the previous occupant, and was refilling the tub. She handed Rebecca a towel, a washcloth, and bar of soap.

The small room was steamy and pleasantly warm. Rebecca found the bath mechanism quite inventive—and far more convenient than filling a tub with buckets of hot water, which she always had to do back East.

In the nearby corner was a sink containing a pump. Piping sent pumped cold water from the sink into either the bathtub or to a water back, a tank set in the firebox of a wood-burning stove at the foot of the tub. By opening a valve, the hot water from the water back was fed into the tub.

"My goodness, this is quite ingenious," Rebecca said.

"Yep," the woman said. "My husband used to be with the army engineers. He built it when he retired from the army. Sam died a short time after, but, God bless him, he left me with a means to make a living. With thousands of people coming through, now it's a gold mine."

"I suspect it would be," Rebecca said. "How do you dispose of the dirty water?"

"When you're through, just pull out the plug in the tub. The water drains through the hole and is carried by pipes to a ditch that flows into a nearby stream. As long as the well don't go dry, I'm in business."

"What's that cord for, that's hanging over the bathtub?"

"It's connected to that bell on the wall and in my office. Just yank on it if you need something or have a problem. I'll ring it five minutes before your time's up."

"And what's that other door for?" Rebecca asked.

"Separates the men's and women's rooms." She checked the handle. "Door's locked and the last customer is just finishin' up, so you've got the whole place to yourself, honey. There, that should do it," she said, closing the hot water valve.

"Now, when I leave, you lock this door so nobody can walk in on you. If you need anything else, or have a problem, just pull that cord. I'll be in the office."

"Thank you, Mrs. . . ."

"Crane. Maude Crane. Enjoy your bath, honey."

Rebecca couldn't wait to get into that bathtub. She quickly locked the door, then stripped off her clothes and climbed in. Sighing with bliss, she leaned back and felt the warm water close around her. She never had been one who yearned for luxuries, except for hot baths. Throughout her adulthood, she had gone to the trouble of hauling and boiling water to bathe every other night, instead of only the Saturday night ritual that most folks practiced.

Rebecca lathered and cleansed her body, then leaned back again and closed her eyes. She would savor every minute of it until the water turned tepid, or Maude rang the warning bell.

She woke with a start. She had no idea how long she'd been asleep but it couldn't have been long, although the water was no longer hot.

Reluctantly Rebecca stepped out of the tub and dried herself off. She felt like a new woman. After pulling on her gown, she gathered up her clothing. Her voice caught in a ragged gasp when a figure stepped out of the shadows in the corner.

"How long have you been there?" she asked.

"Long enough," Clay said. "I was next door in the men's bathroom."

"Maude checked that door! It was locked."

"From my side. I unlocked it."

"Then I'll thank you to go right back out that same door. You had no right to come in here, spying on me like a Peeping Tom."

"I wasn't spying on you. I was on the verge of leaving when I saw you come in, so I thought I'd wait. It's late, and I don't think it's safe for you to walk around this fort alone. No telling who you might encounter."

"Apparently. I've just discovered that."

"Becky, I knocked. You didn't answer. You were quiet for so long, I thought I'd better check to make sure you were okay."

The amber glow from the lantern flickered across his naked chest when he moved closer. She could see his face clearly now, and at the sight of the passion gleaming in his dark eyes, the pulse in her throat began throbbing, sending a warming shiver through her.

Why try to fool him, or herself? Since they kissed at Ash Hollow, she desired him with a passion as strong as the one she could see burning in his eyes—and she knew he was seeing the same in her eyes.

Clay reached out to her and she slipped her hand into his. The warmth of it closed around her trembling fingers as he drew her into his arms and covered her lips with his. The sweet heat of passion washed through her, and she responded to the persuasion of his moist, firm mouth. And as the kiss deepened, the slide of his tongue teased, mating with hers until she gasped for breath.

He finally broke the kiss, and she leaned into the hard wall of him. Burying her head against the bronzed muscles of his chest, she breathed in the tantalizing combination of soap and man.

"We both knew it would come to this eventually, didn't we, Becky? Why have you fought this for so long?" His voice was a husky seduction at her ear.

Oh, yes. How well she knew it would come to this. Lately, the thought of this moment had bedeviled her mind with erotic fantasies. She slid her hands to his shoulders and stroked their naked brawn. Trembling with excitement she felt the corded muscle, sensed the potent strength that lay beneath the warm flesh at her fingertips.

Raising her face to his, she parted her lips in invitation. His mouth claimed hers at once, and their combined passion fired an aching need for more—much more—until there was no thought, only sensation, a consuming mind-and-body sensation.

Clasping her tightly to him, Clay didn't release her mouth as he eased her to the floor. She thrilled to the feel of his long, hardened body pressed to her own. Heated kisses tantalized her neck and the hollow of her throat. Her body felt fevered with her need for him, as he pushed up her gown and began to paint electrifying tingles along her thighs and hips with his fingertips. Urgency turned to impatience, and he lifted her enough to pull the gown over her head.

For a long moment his hungry gaze worshipped her nakedness. Charley had always made love to her in total darkness, and she couldn't help feeling self-conscious, even as the approval in Clay's eyes fueled her arousal. Needing his touch, she reached for him, pulling him to her.

A groan of sheer ecstasy slipped past her lips when he cupped her breasts in his hands, turning her already sensitized nipples to hardened peaks. He teased them with his tongue, and then closed his mouth around one and then the other, sending sensual shivers streaking throughout her body. She arched up in ecstasy and clutched his head, pressing her breasts more fully against the warm, moist chamber of his mouth.

She didn't know how much longer she could bear the erotic torture as his hands and mouth continued down, exploring the curve of her waist, the flatness of her stomach, and at last, the hot intimacy of her womanly chamber, bringing her time and time again to a near climax. She knew when it came, she would be crying out for it—and his throbbing heat would be in her, linking them together forever.

As her hands roamed uninhibitedly across his muscled back and down to his buttocks, the solid strength of him felt so good. He was all male—hot lips, the graze of callused fingertips, and a tantalizing scent of musk.

How she had yearned for this moment, hungered for it. Not just these past weeks, but throughout her whole marriage. Her instincts told her that no matter how often he teasingly brought her near to plunging over that ecstatic precipice, Clay would not let her go unfulfilled; he was a lover who would give as much as he would demand.

Suddenly she felt the sinking distance of withdrawal. Why had she allowed the past to invade this moment? Charley's image brought a chilling sense of guilt, and as quickly as her passion had surfaced, it now cooled. Nearly in tears, she shoved Clay off her and sat up.

"I can't do this."

Clay sat up. Stunned, he stared with disbelief at her. "Why? Do you really want to live without love? Is independence so important to your peace of mind that you're willing to deny your body its needs?"

"I have to. As much as I want you, I must."

His face hardened with anger when he realized she meant it. "Is this your way of getting back at me, Rebecca?"

"I swear it's nothing like that." She felt sick with shame as she pulled the gown over her head. "It's nothing you've said or done. I'm sorry. I truly thought I could, but I can't."

"You sure could have fooled me. Lady, you were into this as much as I was, and you want it as much as I do."

"Don't you think I know what I've done to you? To myself? I'm not proud of it and I'm sorry. But something keeps me from—"

"Maybe you should try giving in to an honest feeling, for a change. You talk of starting a new life, Rebecca. Do you really think changing a location will make the difference? Not on your life, sweetheart."

He stood up, the contempt clear in his voice as he glared down at her. "The change has to come from within."

Rebecca cried out when he grabbed her hand and pulled off the wedding ring. "Start by getting rid of this," he said, tossing it away. "The man is gone. Are you going to mourn him forever?"

"My ring! Damn you, Clay." Sobbing, she began to crawl on her hands and knees looking for it.

The sudden tinkle of the bell was as harsh as his words had been. He strode to the connecting door and opened it. Then he halted in the doorway and looked back at her.

"The way I figure it, you've never been honest with yourself about anything." He slammed the door behind him.

Rebecca continued to sob as she crawled around looking for the ring. Finally she caught a glint of it in a darkened corner of the room. Snatching it up, she wiped it off on her gown. She couldn't stem her flow of tears as she put on her slippers to return to the wagon. She didn't want to be near Clay, but she had no other place to go. And she couldn't blame him for his anger; he was justified in thinking what he did.

By the time she drained the tub, her tears had subsided, but she remained motionless and stared pensively into space.

The situation between her and Clay had been difficult enough when there was mutual dislike—she could fight his cruel words with her own. But she'd grown to respect him, and with that change had come a greater threat—the physical need between them. It had been growing from the time they'd waltzed together, and the passion in their verbal spats had seemed to enhance that physical attraction.

She'd been lucky this time, but what if the same thing happened again? How much longer could she fight her desire for him? Somehow, she would have to.

As angry as he was with her, this was for the best. Making love would have been a huge mistake.

She glanced down at the ring clutched in her hand. What would Clay think if he knew the full truth about her marriage?

16

The next morning, things between her and Clay remained awkward. They avoided making eye contact and gave each other a wide berth to prevent the possibility of touching.

When Rebecca had returned to the wagon last night, Clay had been asleep—or appeared to be. After a restless night of feeling guilty, she was determined to apologize again for her actions. But every time she was on the verge of broaching the subject, someone would join them and prevent her from doing so.

Now Clay had left to stand guard, and Rebecca had made up her mind that when he returned, she would open the issue. He deserved an explanation, and as hard as it would be to do so, she was going to swallow her pride and admit the truth.

In the hours awaiting his return, she went over and over the best approach to the subject. Finally she decided she'd just blurt it all out. Clay was a good listener, and he could usually read between the lines, so there was no sense in trying to dance around what she had to tell him. She'd just get it out.

She busied herself by baking and doing the laundry,

and finally after dinner she found the opportunity to bring up the subject.

Taking a deep breath, she said, "Clay, about last night—"

"Yeah, it's been on my mind, too," he said quickly. "I shouldn't have said what I did, Becky. After all, I initiated it, and no matter what, a woman's got a right to change her mind."

"Or a man, for that matter," she said.

He gave a wry grin. "I'm not so sure about that. At that point it would never enter the minds of most men."

"Is that really true, Clay?"

He looked at her in surprise. "No doubt about it. What makes you think otherwise?"

He had opened the door; all she had to do was walk through it. But now that the time had presented itself, her courage was dwindling. Could she actually be that frank—especially with a man? This was an issue she had never discussed with another living soul; she'd carried the weight of that guilt for four years.

But she had to do it. As embarrassing as it would be to be truthful, she sensed Clay would never betray that trust.

"My first marriage. There's something you should know, Clay."

"Becky, I was just striking out in anger last night. Your first marriage is your private business."

"I still shouldn't have encouraged you. I know you thought I was trying to get even, but no one wanted it to happen more than I did last night. I wasn't lying when I said I desired you, Clay.

"The problem is . . . the problem is . . . it's me. You see, Charley never had strong sexual desires, and when . . ." She swallowed hard and tried again. "When he made love to me, he never fulfilled my needs."

Clay's expression never changed, so she couldn't tell what he was thinking—but it was important she finally get it all out. She'd carried the guilt within her for too long.

"He even questioned the decency of those needs," she continued, "and told me they were unnatural. It made me feel dirty—even depraved—so I struggled to repress those strong urges when we made love. And gradually I came to resent him for it. But marriage is a compromise, and I'm sure there were things about me that he resented, too.

"When he was killed, I felt so guilty for these selfish thoughts I'd harbored. He was a good man, Clay, and I'd resented him because I'd been thinking only of my desires. Now it's too late to tell him how ashamed I am of myself."

"For God's sake, Becky, he was your husband; he had a responsibility to you. What about another man, after your husband died? Did you attempt to . . . ah . . . I mean—"

"Of course not! I wasn't going to put myself through that embarrassment again; I'd learned my lesson. That's another reason why I felt it was safe to marry you: due to the circumstances, we wouldn't have to share a bed."

He gently took her by the shoulders. "Becky, look at me."

She was too mortified to do so, so he tipped up her chin with a finger until she met his gaze.

"Becky, you're a beautiful, wonderfully passionate woman. You carry that passion into everything you feel or do—joy, anger, your sense of humor, and your enthusiasm. You even carry it into your cooking, or working with those damn mules and chickens. Passion is as much a part of you as your blond hair or green eyes. It wouldn't be natural if you didn't bring it into making love, too.

"I don't mean to speak ill of the dead, Becky, but if there's any burden of guilt here, it lies with your husband. Since his needs weren't as strong, he chose to ignore yours entirely. Most men would welcome such passion from the woman they love—especially in lovemaking. It's as exciting to a man to make love to a passionate woman, as it is to her. There's no shame or disgrace to it. The sex act is so overpowering that it often blots out reasoning and inhibition.

"Frankly, I think that's why the Good Lord made the act so enjoyable—it was His way of guaranteeing immortality of the human race that He'd created." Then he grinned. "Of course, I guess you could say He did the same for any creature—human or animal. Because it sure comes naturally to man and beast alike."

Rebecca couldn't help smiling.

"I haven't quite figured out which species Garth is," he continued, "but he falls into one of those."

That brought an outright laugh from her.

Despite Clay's clear attempt to lighten her mood, she knew he was sincere. She had bared her soul to him, and he had shed a new light: Charley's guilt was no less than hers—if anything, it was greater. And his regrettable fate did not lessen that.

Clay's words had shown her that the passion within her was a good thing, which revealed itself in positive ways she had never considered. And that she should embrace it and never try to repress it again.

And from this moment on, she knew she never would.

She had just finished putting away the dinner dishes when the Garsons came over to visit, and it wasn't long before others strayed over to the campfire.

The wagon train would be pulling out in the morning. The fort had been a wonderful respite for the people, as well as the stock, and now the worst part of the journey lay ahead. The mood of the crowd was thoughtful and somewhat apprehensive.

A silence fell when Mike Scott and Garth suddenly appeared in the company of Eagle Claw and the other four Indians.

There was an air of danger about the war chief that struck a fear into people's hearts. Scotty motioned to Clay to join them, and the men began talking in low tones.

Rebecca could tell something was seriously wrong. Eagle Claw was doing most of the talking, gesturing and looking in her direction. She couldn't think of what she had done to cause a problem, but Clay was clearly angry, and even Garth was casting concerned glances in her direction. The conference broke up when Eagle Claw and the other Indians strode off angrily.

"What was that all about?" Rebecca asked, when the three men came over and joined them.

"Nothing," Clay snapped, and walked away.

"What does he mean by nothing? There was a lot of gesturing and looks in my direction. What did I do that upset everybody?"

"Eagle Claw made your husband an offer to buy you," Mike Scott said.

There were shocked gasps from many around the campfire.

"Buy me?" she said, horrified.

"I'm afraid so. He offered your husband five ponies."

"But he can't . . . I mean, Clay wouldn't . . . What did Clay say?"

"He refused, of course." Scott frowned. "But I'm afraid we haven't heard the end of this."

Etta and Helena rushed to her side at once and hugged her. "Don't worry, Becky," Etta said. "Mr. Fraser won't let anything happen to you."

"Oh, yeah? We all know how dangerous that Eagle Claw is," Jake Fallon said. "He ain't gonna stop till he gets what he wants."

"Oh, hush up, Jake Fallon," Helena Garson said. "Can't you see the poor thing is scared enough as it is?"

"We all oughta be scared," Fallon said. "If Fraser don't give her to that Injun, the whole wagon train's in danger. He's a war chief and he ain't—"

Garth took a threatening step toward him. "Damn

you, Fallon, if you don't shut up, I'm going to shove your rotten tongue down your throat."

Scott put a restraining hand on Garth's arm. "Steady, son. Fallon, I don't want to hear any more of that kind of talk. Get the hell back to your wagon and keep your mouth shut."

"Well, I say we turn her over now before he slaughters us all. Mark my words, that Injun's gonna round up the rest of his tribe and hit us when we least expect it." Fallon stomped away.

"Scott shook his head. All right, folks, I suggest you all get back to your wagons. We've got a rough trip ahead of us, so you all can use the sleep."

The people moved away, many of them whispering in hushed tones.

Rebecca looked at Garth. "He can't do that, can he, Garth?"

"Indians have a different culture than we do, Becky," Garth said. "But don't worry. Clay won't let anything happen to you."

"Eagle Claw is a very dangerous chief. What if he doesn't take no for an answer? Oh, Garth, what if he does attack the wagon train? There are children among us!" She turned away from him.

Garth came over and put his hands on her shoulders. "Hey, Little Sister, that's not going to happen. Eagle Claw's too smart to attack a train this size."

Rebecca dabbed at her eyes, then turned and faced him again. "Where did Clay go? Why is he so angry? Is he blaming me for this problem?"

"Of course not. He's as upset as you are. I know my

brother; he's probably just walking off his anger. I'll track him down. In the meantime, take Scotty's advice. There's still a hard trail ahead, so why don't you go to bed and get some rest." He kissed her on the forehead. "Don't worry, Becky, we won't let anything happen to you."

She watched Garth walk away, then sat down at the fire and stared out at the darkness beyond. Eagle Claw could be out there right now, lurking in the shadows, watching her—waiting for an opportunity to snatch her. A shiver rippled her spine and she suddenly felt cold. Why did he want her? When had he even noticed her? What if he succeeded in his attempt? What if Clay, Garth, or others were killed or wounded trying to protect her?

What if? What if? What if?

She buried her head in her hands and began sobbing. These thoughts were too horrifying for her even to imagine.

Garth found Clay at Scott's wagons, deep in discussion with Scotty, Hawk, and Jim Peterson.

"What if we pull out and head back to Independence with those wagons that are going east?" Clay said.

"Look, Clay, I'm not denying it would take a big load off everybody's mind if Rebecca was no longer with this train. But don't think Eagle Claw won't be watching her every move. You'd just be putting those other wagons in danger. You saw how easy it was for the Pawnees to wipe out those ten wagons of ours. You've got a much better chance staying with us. Eagle Claw won't attack a train this size."

"They wouldn't start a war over an incident like this, would they?"

"The fort's commander told me the Indians are riled up," Scott said. "Seems a couple months ago some stupid army captain named Chivington massacred over a hundred of them in Colorado at a place called Sand Creek. It was pretty atrocious; even babies and women were brutalized. It's got the whole Sioux, Cheyenne, and Arapaho Nations on the prod."

"So you outriders will hafta keep a sharper lookout fer Indian sign," Hawk added.

Scott nodded. "Once we're into Utah territory, we should be safe. I doubt that the Utes will give us trouble."

"And when will that be?" Clay asked.

"We've got the Rockies to cross first. But I'll be honest with you; if Eagle Claw decides he wants your wife, he'll try to get her. All we can do is try and prevent it from happening." Scotty slapped Clay on the shoulder. "Go back to your wagon, son, hold that pretty wife of yours in your arms, and get a good night's sleep."

Garth chuckled. "Now, which do you want him to do, Scotty? Hold his wife in his arms or get a good night's sleep?"

"Reckon the sleep would do him the most good," Scott said.

"You're getting old, Scotty. You're getting old," Garth said.

"What in hell's wrong with you, Clay?" Garth said as they walked back to the wagon. "Walking off and leaving Becky on her own like you did."

"I was so damn mad, I wasn't thinking straight."

"You sure as hell weren't. Dad and Mom are probably turning over in their graves."

"I wanted to strangle that damn arrogant Indian," Clay said. "Imagine coming in here and offering to buy my wife!"

"How do you think Becky feels? She's scared half to death, and on top of that, she thinks you're mad at her as if it were her fault."

"Why would I be mad at her?"

"Maybe because you're so damn worried about her, you have to take your frustration out on *some*body."

"What are you getting at, Garth?"

"I think you care for her more than you're willing to admit."

"I just don't like the idea of any woman being bought and sold."

"According to Becky, we Southerners are no better. We did that to the Negroes."

"That woman will still be fighting the war fifty years from now. Damn it, Garth, you know as well as I that a Fraser hasn't bought or sold a Negro in the past fifty years. Fraser Keep is home to them as much as it is to us. When any wanted to leave, Granddad and Dad gave them the papers that made them free men and enough money for them to get up North. Miss Yankee Doodle has no idea how many of those same people came back to Fraser Keep."

"So that's why you're mad at her."

Clay looked at the amusement in his brother's eyes and shook his head. "You did it to me again, didn't you,

Brother Garth? Okay, so maybe I did take my frustration out on her. I sure as hell don't want to see anything happen to the little minx."

"We won't let it happen, Clay. We'll just have to keep
a closer eye on her. Right now she's scared."

When they reached the wagon, Rebecca was lying
outside on her fur pallet. Either she was asleep or pretended to be, because she didn't say anything. Clay put
his bedroll down within a few feet of her, and Garth put
his on the other side of her. Then they lay down and
went to sleep.

17

Low-slung clouds added to the pall that hung over the wagon train as it departed Fort Laramie. With the threat of an Indian attack foremost on all their minds, there was a sense of security when they were surrounded by the United States Army at Fort Laramie, and a smaller garrison of soldiers at Fort Casper later down the trail. But from there on, all knew they'd be on their own.

Rebecca felt like a marked woman. There were small clusters of women talking in whispered tones as her wagon passed. Some of the looks were sympathetic, but the majority were resentful glares. As if it were her fault the train had been put into peril.

Fortunately, Clay was driving. Mike Scott had pulled him away from duty and told him to stay close to her. Last night she had slept in isolated stretches of ten or fifteen minutes, afraid to close her eyes lest she awake to finding Eagle Claw hovering above her. Now she climbed back into the wagon bed to avoid the stares and curled up on her fur pallet, hoping the motion would lull her to sleep, but the wagon bounced too much, making sleep impossible.

They were approaching the Rockies now. The land

was barren except for patches of sagebrush and occasional greasewood, and most of the water was putrid and had to be boiled. The only good thing was that Hawk and the outriders reported no sign of Indians. Rebecca could only hope Eagle Claw had accepted Clay's refusal.

The same was true for the next few days. They spent one night under the protection of the army at Fort Casper, where they crossed a bridge to the opposite side of the Platte. Four days and fifty miles after leaving Fort Laramie, they arrived at Independence Rock on the third of July.

Scott said they would lay over the following day to celebrate the Fourth of July holiday.

The wagon train camped by the river under tall cedars and pines, their pleasing fragrance permeating the air. For the first time since leaving the fort, Rebecca left the security of the wagon circle and joined the many others climbing the landmark to carve their initials among the hundreds who had gone before them. Tom and Etta had preceded them, and the lovestruck young man had engraved a heart around his and Etta's initials. Although the likelihood of an Indian attack diminished with every passing day, Clay and Garth never left her side.

Rebecca gazed with rapt wonder at the Sweetwater River flowing below. In the distance loomed the majestic peaks of the mountains they would have to crest. It was all so peaceful; and she finally relaxed and enjoyed the serene beauty.

If anyone still held any resentment toward her, it wasn't in evidence that day. Game was plentiful and there were several spits with roasting rabbits and venison. The women had baked cakes and pies, or cooked whatever food they had in excess.

A carnival atmosphere prevailed, with several games to test one's skills. Rebecca applauded Clay's sure eye and steady hand as he tossed rings over bottle tops.

Later she found herself partnered with Clay in a three-legged sack race. Garth and Georgie Garson were lined up on Clay's left, and Etta and Tom were on Rebecca's right.

Gripping each other firmly around their waists, Clay put his right leg in the sack and Rebecca her left leg. Then, each holding the open side of the sack, they hopped and scrambled toward the finish line.

The spectators clapped and cheered on the contenders. Clay and Rebecca had a narrow lead, with Clay and Garth naturally goading each other. With the finish line only a few yards away, Garth and Georgie tripped and fell sprawling into them. All four of them went down, and Etta and Tom crossed the finish line victorious.

"Becky, I hope you observed that my brother fell on purpose," Clay said good-naturedly. "He never could stand me beating him in any competition."

"Don't listen to him, Becky," Garth replied. "He's never won a shooting competition against me yet."

"And you've never won one against Colt," Clay retorted.

"And who's Colt?" Rebecca asked, brushing the dust off her dress.

Garth laughed. "He's one of our younger brothers. He could shoot the eye out of a gnat if he had to."

"I don't imagine there's much call for that," Becky said. "I've had enough competition for one day. You two can go ahead, but I'm relaxing." She sat down and leaned back against a tree.

"Same here," Clay said, and sat down beside her.

"Not me. That weasel Fallon has a shell game going. He's charging ten cents a try. See you later."

"What's a shell game?" Rebecca asked, after Garth left.

"It's a sleight of hand, done with a pea and three half shells of a nut. You put a pea under one of the shells, and then shift them around. The other person has to guess which shell the pea is under."

"And you have to pay ten cents to guess?" she asked. "What if you guess right?"

"Then he pays you ten cents."

"Why would anyone make a wager with that unpleasant Jake Fallon?"

"Becky, my brother can't resist being hoodwinked. I think he truly believes there's a pot of gold at the end of a rainbow. He always talks about chasing off to find a gold mine."

"Do you think he ever will?"

"Find one, or try to find one?" Clay asked.

"Try to find one," she said, laughing.

"No doubt, Becky. No doubt. One thing I know for sure: Garth would never settle down on Fraser Keep and raise cotton."

"But you would?"

"I don't love raising crops like my brother Will does, but Fraser Keep's in my blood. It would take something exceptional to draw me away from it."

That evening they had another hoedown, singing and dancing in celebration of the birth of the nation. A nation once again united—in body, if not in spirit.

Eventually, too exhausted to dance another step, Rebecca collapsed and sat down. Garth had gone off to refill his and Clay's plates, but Rebecca settled for just a cup of coffee and piece of pie. She was sipping the hot coffee when Garth returned.

"Becky, you should put something in your stomach besides coffee and pie," Clay said.

"I'm fine, Clay. I sampled the potato salad when I made it," she said.

"Aha!" Garth said. "That explains why it's so good."

"Garth, when you settle down and get married, you're going to make some woman very happy."

His teeth flashed white against the deep tan he'd acquired in the last couple of months. "Little Sister, I'd like to think I've made more than my share happy already."

"You have no idea how a woman appreciates a husband who enjoys her cooking."

"How could one not enjoy yours, Becky?" Clay asked.

"You're spoiling me, Clay. Other than your remarks about my cooking at Ash Hollow, you've never said what you like or dislike that I cook."

"I like it all," he said.

"Well, I can't make any promises about my future cooking since that little shrew Kate stopped laying," Rebecca said.

Garth choked on the food he'd just put into his

mouth. "Kate?" he gasped. "Laying who?" he managed to get out between coughs.

Becky quickly handed him her coffee, and Garth took several swallows to clear his throat.

"Don't get your hopes up, Brother Garth. Kate is a chicken," Clay said in a droll tone.

Rebecca nodded. "Yes, it must be this mountain air that's causing it, or the bouncing around. I barely had enough eggs for the potato salad. Poor Lady MacBeth can't keep up with the demand."

She sighed and leaned back again, feeling quite contented as she listened to a favorite folk song being sung from the nearby campfire. For the first time in almost a week, she wasn't obsessed with the fear of Eagle Claw lurking nearby. She realized that much of her contentment was due to the two men who were sitting at her side. Funny, how much they had come to mean to her in the last couple of months. For four years she had carried a hatred for Southerners in her heart; now, except for her brother Matthew, these two men meant more to her than any others on earth.

Garth finished eating and excused himself. As she watched him walk away, she thought about the rest of Clay's family. Were they all as nice as Garth?

"You're really homesick, aren't you, Clay?"

"Oh, yeah. Seems like the farther away I get from home, the more I miss it."

"What is it that you miss about it? The plantation itself, or the people you love?"

"That's a good question. It's kind of like that chicken and egg question, isn't it? Maybe they're one and the same in my mind. Yet we lost so many loved ones during the war, I guess it can never be the same—even if Fraser Keep is restored to what it once was."

"But can one really restore what is lost from the past? The fact that it was lost and cannot be restored is what makes it significant. Isn't that what all these people are trying to escape from?"

"You can't escape from the past. You have to come to terms with it, that's all. Pluck the good out of it and let the bad wither." He stood up. "I don't know about you, but I'm ready to go to bed."

"Yes, I'm overdue for a good night's sleep." They gathered up their cups and plates and returned to their wagon.

Rebecca fell asleep the instant she laid down, but Clay lay thinking about their conversation. He missed his home, missed the rolling hills of Virginia and the gentle flow of the James River. He couldn't wait to get back to it.

He rolled over, and his gaze fell on Rebecca. Could he ever love a woman enough to give up his home for her? He'd like to think he could; that he'd give up anything or anyone for the woman he loved. To keep her only unto him till death do them part.

He closed his eyes. Though he wanted to think that one day he could know such a love, he doubted he ever would.

In the next week they followed the Sweetwater River deeper into the Rockies. The higher they climbed, the more spectacular the scenery became—but the travel became harder and slower. Many trails were barely wide enough for a wagon, and dropped off sharply into ravines hundreds of feet deep. Other times they would come upon stretches of flat, grassy meadowland.

The weather had been better than they could hope for. Sunny and warm during the day, with cool evenings at night; neither rain nor snow had been a problem.

They were a few days away from reaching South Pass and the Continental Divide when they awoke to gray clouds and distant flashes of lightning in the sky. By the time they got underway, the first raindrops had started to fall. Within an hour the full fury of the storm was upon them.

Pelted by sheets of water, the wagons creaked and swayed under the force of the turbulent wind that threatened to overturn them.

Progress was slow on the steep ascent. Often a half dozen men would have to get out to push the wagons on the rain-slickened granite underfoot. Braying mules and oxen alike fought the reins as jagged bolts of lightning, accompanied by roaring booms of thunder, streaked from the sky, and the wail of frightened children rose above the continual chorus of shouts and cracks of whips.

Clay was maneuvering their wagon up a narrow trail to a tableland above. They were only ten feet from the top when a brilliant bolt of lightning struck the face of the ledge overhead and sheered away part of the edge. Rebecca screamed as fragments of granite flew past and dropped into the deep ravine below. The nervous mules shied in fright and tried to bolt, and for several seconds the wagon rocked dangerously close to the edge before Clay was able to get them under control and reach the flat surface above. Scott called a halt there to rest the animals.

While they waited for the rear wagons to reach the top, Clay loosened the reins on the mules. Now, with their number cut in half, it only took half as long for the wagons to join up. Garth got a small fire started under a tarp, and Rebecca put on a pot of coffee.

By the time the coffee was brewed, the thunderstorm had moved on and a bright sun burned away the dark clouds. Cup in hand, Rebecca strayed to the edge and gazed out at the magnificent beauty of the mountain range. A rainbow had appeared, and she felt she could reach out and touch it.

"Don't go too near that edge," Clay warned. "It's a straight drop to the bottom.

"Oh, Clay, the view is spectacular."

Rebecca turned to step back when she heard screams coming from the wagon that was about to crest the trail. A wheel had rolled off, and she watched in horror as the wagon flipped over. The axle snapped and the team broke loose. For several seconds the wagon tottered on the brim, then toppled over the edge. The screams of the occupants faded as the wagon plunged deep into the ravine.

"Oh, Dear God," Rebecca murmured, and sank to her knees.

"Get back to the wagon, Becky," Clay said, and followed Scott, who had already started down the trail as

Peterson and Garth caught the team and brought it under control.

"Keep moving!" Scott shouted to the next wagon when the driver reined up. "Keep those wagons moving. This is no time to jam up on that trail."

Rebecca waited anxiously for Clay's return. The last arrivals were grim-faced as the wagons rode past, and Clay and Mike Scott followed the last wagon up.

"Who was it?" she asked.

"The Ryan wagon," Scott said soberly.

"Don and Caroline Ryan?"

Scott nodded. "Jim," he said to his second in command, "let's get this train moving out of here as quickly as we can. I'll get the first half moving, and you start the rear moving about thirty minutes after. That'll give them time to rest their teams. The sooner we're out of here, the better it'll be for everybody."

"You aren't just going to move out and leave them?" Rebecca said.

"Mrs. Fraser, there's nothing anyone can do for them now," Scott said.

"You don't know that," Rebecca lashed out.

"My God, woman, that's at least a thousand-foot drop. No one would have survived that fall."

"The least we can do is give them a decent burial!"

Scott looked at her with disbelief. "There wouldn't be enough left of any of them to bury, even if we could get to them. And I'm sure as hell not risking anyone's life trying to." He strode away angrily.

Dabbing at her tears, Rebecca ran back to her wagon.

Clay looked helplessly at Garth. "Scotty could have

been a little kinder. Help me out here, Garth. I don't know what to say to her."

"Ask the Reverend. You know it rips me apart inside to see a woman cry."

"Thanks a lot, Brother Garth," Clay said sarcastically. "You're a big help."

"She's your wife, Clay. I suggest you think of some comforting words to say to her."

Clay paced back and forth for several moments, and then he went back to the wagon. Her eyes were swollen from crying, and her movements were slow as she packed up by rote.

"Are you feeling better, Becky?" Clay asked.

"I know Mr. Scott is disgusted with me. I let my emotions get out of hand, I guess."

"That's nothing to be ashamed of, Becky."

"It's just that it was so sudden, so tragic. Those two lives snuffed out so easily. Like blowing out a candle." She shook her head as if unable to accept the truth.

"Becky, you can't let your thoughts dwell on that."

"What Mr. Scott said was true, Clay."

"He didn't mean to sound so callous. Scotty's as shaken by the tragedy as you are. Everyone handles grief differently."

"I mean what he said in Independence. Many of us won't make it to California. We started out with ninety-eight wagons; now we're down to forty-nine. Who's going to be next, Clay?"

"Were you close to the Ryans?"

"Not overly. I've spoken to Caroline in passing. The night we crossed the Kansas River, I took a pot of beef and beans to them because they were one of the last to cross. I can still see the happy smile on Don's face when he saw the apple pandowdy." She started to tear up again. "They were such a nice couple."

"What would you think of putting up a marker?" Clay asked.

She jerked up her head. "Would you, Clay? At least it would show some respect for them."

"I'll get the ax and trim some wood."

"Do we have time? Mr. Scott said the first twenty-five wagons should get ready to move."

"We can catch up with them when the second group leaves. Finish packing up while I find some wood."

When others saw what Clay was doing, several of the men and women joined him, the minister among them. Soon they had a cross driven into the side of the trail where the Ryan wagon had collapsed.

They hauled a rock to the site and Rebecca painted the words RETURNED TO GOD on it, the date, and the names of the couple. The group huddled together as Reverend Kirkland led them in prayer, and then with bowed heads they listened to Tom Davis's voice raised in a solemn hymn.

Nearer, my God, to Thee, nearer to Thee!
E'en though it be a cross, that raiseth me,
Still all my song shall be, nearer, my God, To Thee.
Nearer, my God, to Thee, Nearer to Thee.

Later that evening a solemn camp bedded down for the night. Mothers hugged their children tighter, husbands their wives. All were gratefully aware that it could have been their splintered wagon lying on the bottom of that ravine.

The night was starry but cool at the higher altitude. Rebecca snuggled deeper into her fur pelt to ward off the chill. She still preferred sleeping outdoors, and hoped the snow would hold off.

She turned her head and looked at Clay, lying on his back close by. He had his hands tucked under his head and was gazing up at the stars. How mistaken she'd been about him. He was a good man—a compassionate man, a man of honor.

"Thank you, Clay," she said.

"For what?"

"For seeing the Ryans had a proper funeral. It meant a great deal to me."

"I did it for the Ryans, Becky," he quickly denied. "They deserved a decent funeral."

He always seemed embarrassed when she complimented him for doing something really nice for others. He'd make up excuses for his motives.

She rolled over on her side. Smiling tenderly, she whispered, "You can't fool me anymore, Clay Fraser. I think you did it for my sake, too."

18

A week had passed since they had left Independence Rock, and all were looking forward to camping at South Pass that evening. From there on, they would be starting down the mountains instead of climbing them.

As they rode along, Rebecca suddenly frowned and raised her head. "This mountain air must be affecting my hearing. I swear I hear a calliope."

Clay grinned at her. "It must be the atmosphere."

"Are you implying I'm light-headed, Clay Fraser?"

"That or the wind blowing through these ravines and peaks. You hear all kinds of crazy sounds."

Her head perked up again when a trumpeting sound pieced the air. "There it is again. Did you hear it? It sounds like . . . well, you'll think I'm crazy, but it sounds like an elephant."

"You know, I think I hear a calliope, too." Clay saw Garth come galloping hell bent down the line, and said, "Something's up."

Garth reined up at their wagon. "You two aren't going to believe what's ahead."

Clay winked at Rebecca. "A traveling circus."

"How'd you know?"

"Are you serious?" Clay asked. "I was only joking because Becky and I swear we hear trumpeting elephants and the music of a calliope."

"You're right about the music, but there's only one elephant," Garth said.

"Oh, you're such a tease, Garth," Rebecca said. "Is this more of your joking?"

"No, indeed, Little Sister. We have the pleasure of camping tonight with Professor Romano's Traveling Circus and Medicine Show."

As they got nearer, they could see several tents erected within a makeshift circle of a couple dozen wagons. A steam-operated calliope was playing a cheerful song of welcome. Chained to one of the tents was the huge bulk of an elephant, and two tigers paced back and forth in a brightly painted cage with iron bars. Not a mule or ox could be seen among the live-stock, but a black-and-white zebra amidst the horses caught Rebecca's attention. Many of the circus people came out and waved at them as the wagons passed.

Mike Scott was hurrying to direct their train into a circle before chaos reigned, because as soon as a wagon was properly parked, any children in it would jump out and chase over to the circus wagons.

Clay had no sooner put on the brake than Etta came running over to them. "Come on, Becky, let's go and talk to them."

Clay couldn't help smiling as the two hurried off arm in arm. They were as excited as two kids at . . . a circus! That brought a chuckle out of him. Who would ever have thought they'd encounter a circus on the crest of the Rocky Mountains?

Becky threw back her head in laughter. Her hair was tied back with a ribbon, and she looked as youthful as Etta.

He'd been worried about her. Being an eyewitness to the Ryan accident, she'd taken their deaths very hard. It had taken days for her to get a spring back into her step and that spunky gleam in her eyes. But it *was* back, and that's what mattered. Becky had an indomitable spirit that would ultimately prevail, no matter how severe the tragedy.

He admired her spirit. He also admired her body, and his physical need for her was becoming a problem. Somehow he had to get her to give up this obsession with an annulment.

They'd gotten along very compatibly since their talk at Ash Hollow. Every day they learned more and more about each other, and the only real issue between them was her independent streak. Every time he tried to help her, she considered it interference and resented him for it. But she was his wife, and he wasn't going to neglect his responsibilities.

Clay set the mules out to graze, then his curiosity drove him to go over to the circus camp. He spied the two women standing a safe distance away from the elephant, staring at it with curiosity.

"Huge, isn't it?" he said, walking up to them.

"I've only seen pictures of an elephant," Etta said. "I never realized how big they really are."

"I saw one once in a parade when I was very young," Rebecca said. "I'd forgotten how big they are. They're mammoth."

"Aha, I see you are admiring my lovely Sophia." The speaker was a short, rotund man with a tiny mustache that barely spanned the width of his nose. He spoke in a heavy accent as he swept off a stovepipe hat and bowed at the waist. "Permit me to introduce myself; I am Professor Angelo Romano."

Clay shook his hand. "How do you do, sir. I'm Clay Fraser, and this is my wife, Rebecca, and Miss Henrietta Garson."

Professor Romano clapped his hands together and stepped back. "Ah, two such lovely ladies to share your company. You are a fortunate man, Mr. Fraser."

"I won't deny that," Clay said. "I have to say, Professor Romano, the last thing I expected to encounter in these mountains was a traveling circus. Are you headed east or west?"

"We are headed east to Independence, Missouri. We intend to winter there and move on to St. Louis in the spring."

Etta's eyes were round with astonishment. "My goodness! How do you expect to cross these mountains with an elephant, Professor Romano?"

"Did not Hannibal cross the Alps with elephants?" His dark eyes rounded with merriment.

"Hannibal?" Etta asked, confused.

"The Punic Wars, Etta," Clay said. "He was a Carthaginian general who crossed the Italian Alps and defeated the Romans about two hundred years B.C."

"You know of him?" the professor said, pleased.

"We studied his military strategy at West Point. That's our military academy," he added for clarification.

"So you are a professional soldier, Mr. Fraser?"

"Not anymore. My soldiering days are over. You appear to be a fairly small party, Professor. That could be very dangerous. The Indians completely wiped out ten of our wagons that had left the train."

Professor Romano shook his head. "That is regrettable, Mr. Fraser, but I don't think they will bother us. Sophia is quite a . . . how do you say it—"

"Deterrent," Clay said.

"Yes. And if Sophia isn't enough, the roars and snarls of Romulus and Remus can discourage the stoutest of hearts," the professor added with a twinkle in his eyes. As if cued, a chilling roar emanated from the tiger cage.

Clay broke into laughter. "I can see, Professor Romano, you are a military strategist, too."

"Ah, yes. Now I must see what has aroused Remus's displeasure." He doffed his hat. "It is a pleasure to meet you lovely ladies. To honor this special occasion, we have decided to give a free performance tonight. I hope you will attend."

"A circus performance!" Etta exclaimed, when Professor Romano departed. "I've never seen one. I can't wait until tonight. I must go and tell Tommy." She ran off in delight.

Rebecca had trouble waiting for evening, too. The hours seemed to pass like days until the sound of the calliope heralded the official opening.

The people swarmed over to the other camp and spread out on the grass to watch the performers.

They held their breaths as a man and woman in colorful tights did amazing acrobatic feats on a tight rope strung on poles fifteen feet in the air.

Children cuddled closer to their parents when Romulus and Remus jumped through hoops in the center of a ring of fire; then they clapped in laughter at the sight of the organ grinder's monkey grabbing the hats off the heads of the male spectators.

Women in spangled tights stood on the backs of galloping horses, and clowns with painted faces handed out balloons to the children.

But the biggest thrill was when the trainers brought out Sophia. The audience gasped with amazement as the huge animal raised up on its hind legs, then balanced its front ones on a huge ball.

After the performance was over, everyone walked from wagon to wagon, where they were greeted by such unusual sights as a bearded woman, a man whose whole body was covered with colorful tattoos, and a midget man and woman who waved and talked to them.

A more exotic act was a woman dressed in a skimpy harem-type costume dancing with a huge snake draped around her neck. Clay and Garth were fascinated by the act, but Rebecca hated snakes and couldn't bear to watch it. She went over to a wagon brightly painted with eyes and tarot cards. The sign said that for twenty-five cents, Madam Angelina could predict your future. Rebecca couldn't resist it.

The woman within claimed to be a Gypsy and informed Rebecca that this rare gift of predicting the future had been passed down from generation to generation in her family.

"You vant za palm, za cards, or maybe you vant for Madam Angelina to call up za spirits of za dearly departed? So vat'll it be?"

"The palm will do fine," Rebecca said, handing her a quarter.

The Gypsy studied her hand and said it indicated a long life. Rebecca smiled in amusement when the woman predicated a lasting love and great wealth in her future.

Suddenly the Gypsy frowned. "Vat is dis? I zee you haf much zadness in your life, little von, and zer vill be more."

Rebecca's smile melted, and her skepticism changed into uncertainty.

"But only zhoze who know zorrow can rekonize true happinez," the Gypsy continued. "Do not let yezterday fill too much of today, en none of tomorrow, little one."

"So was it worth twenty-five cents?" Clay asked when Rebecca left the fortune-teller's wagon.

"I see you managed to drag yourself away from the entertainment. Tell me, Clay, was it the costume, the dance, or the snake that appealed to you the most?"

"Do I detect a bit of jealousy, dear wife, or did Madam Angelina warn you of a glum future?"

"I'm not sure. I can't figure out whether it was a message of hope or one of despair."

"Why? What did she say?"

"I guess that my life will get worse before it gets better."

"That's a pretty safe thing to say, considering we're still high in these mountains. You know it's all part of the act."

"Yes, I suppose so."

That night Rebecca lay awake, unable to shake the Gypsy's words from her mind. *Do not let yesterday fill too much of today and none of tomorrow.* Was she allowing the past to rule her life? Clay wanted to make the marriage a real one, but she was afraid. She'd been left alone too many times by those she loved, and she couldn't risk getting that close to someone again. It was better to depend only on herself, even if that meant a lonely life, than to be vulnerable to the pain of a loved one's death again.

The only part of the fortune that had a ring of reality to it was that she would know more sadness in her life.

She knew that was guaranteed.

The next morning Rebecca watched sadly as the circus train departed. It had been a magical break in the journey. But tomorrow it would be shoved to the back of all their minds, like anything else that has happened on the trek. If they were to believe Professor Romano, though, the rest of the trip wouldn't be as arduous. Once they were out of the mountains and across the Great Basin, they'd start to encounter homesteads and towns. Civilization was just ahead.

With breakfast out of the way, she decided to wash her hair. She put the wash boiler on to heat, and by the time she finished the dishes and had them packed away, the water was warm enough for a shampoo.

So as not to get her bodice wet, she removed it and had just dipped her head in a basin of the warm water when Clay came up behind her and grabbed her around the waist.

With a yelp of surprise she raised her head, water dripping down her forehead.

"Get away from here, Clay Fraser."

"You look like you could use some help."

"Yes, but you're a hindrance."

"We'll just see about that, if you'll give me that bottle."

"Okay, but don't waste it," she warned, handing him the bottle of the shampoo preparation. "It has to last the rest of the journey."

He read the label aloud. " 'Let Your Hair Smell Like A Summer Garden With Madam Celine's Lavender Shampoo.' No wonder you always smell so sweet."

He poured some of the liquid on her wet hair and worked it into suds, his fingers massaging her scalp.

"Oh, that feels so good, Clay."

Not half as much as it did to him. The wet strands curled around his fingers like a sensuous glove as he filled his hands with them.

"If you keep up those ecstatic moans and sighs, Mrs. Fraser, people are going to get the wrong idea."

She blushed. "Well then, you best hurry up and get this over with."

He slowly poured more of the heated water over her head, to rinse the suds. Unable to resist the temptation, he pressed a light kiss to the nape of her neck. Then he captured the sodden strands in a towel and rubbed them vigorously.

Clay bowed at the waist. "Can I be of any further use, *madame?*"

She curtsied demurely. "*Merci, Monsieur Coiffeur.* There are no limits to your talents."

He rolled his eyes mischievously as he curled an imaginary mustache. "Ah, *mon petite,* I am bursting at the seams to show you my best talent."

She grinned. "Then I suggest you wear a larger pair of pants."

His shoulders slumped in mock despair. "You have a hard heart, lady. Since you're refusing my offer, the least you could do is return the service. It would feel good to wash my hair in warm water for a change, instead of a cold stream. Though the truth is, I could use a haircut first."

"I offer an inch, you ask for a mile."

"No, an inch is fine," he said. "That should be short enough."

"Very well. Take off your shirt while I get my scissors."

When she returned, he was sitting bare-chested on an upended barrel. There'd been several occasions on the journey when he'd been shirtless, but she'd always kept her distance. The sight of his broad shoulders and muscular chest, with its dark hair that narrowed into a tantalizing trail to his pants, always stirred forbidden fires in her.

She put a towel around his shoulders and began the trim.

Rebecca loved Clay's hair. Despite the popularity of

long hair and mustaches, Clay was clean-shaven and wore his hair trimmed to his nape; its thickness clung to his head in soft waves.

She started at the nape, trimming the dark waves that felt like silk to her fingertips. Then, moving to the front, she stepped between his legs to get closer. She could feel the heat and male scent that emanated from his body, and she could feel his stare—but she dared not look into those compelling brown eyes, or she would be lost.

Her hair had begun to dry, and it glistened in the sun like gold. Silky strands brushed Clay's cheek as she bent over to clip the sides of his hair. It smelled like Madam Celine's country garden. But most of all it smelled like Becky.

Unable to keep his hands off her, he slipped then around her waist and pulled her closer. "Do you have any idea what you're doing to me right now?"

"Yes, cutting your hair," she said airily.

"You know damn well what I mean. How long do you expect me to go on like this?"

"How can you say that? You haven't even seen it yet. Besides, it will always grow back in," she teased.

Rebecca stepped back to make sure the sides were even. Pleased with the results, she added, "And it looks very good, if I do say so myself." She removed the towel and shook it out. "I'll wash it for you now."

Clay shook his head. "You are one stubborn female. But I'm a patient man, and I don't get discouraged easily."

"I'm told patience is a virtue. Lean over."

As she soaped his hair, he began to deliberately emit sighs of ecstasy as she had done. "Oh, baby, you're so good," he moaned. "That feels so wonderful. Who taught you how to do that?"

"Clay, if you don't shut up, I'm going to drown you," she hissed.

"Don't stop, baby. Don't stop," he groaned loudly.

"That's it!" She shoved his head under the water, and he came up sputtering.

"Now, did I do that to you?" he scolded.

"Hmph. All that wailing and mooing you were doing reminded me that Clementine needs milking." She picked up the stool and bucket, and strode away.

Clay chuckled as he watched her stomp off, that honey hair of hers bouncing as she walked. Then he reached for the towel and dried his hair.

Mike Scott had said they'd remain there another day to rest the stock, and it was a well-needed rest for all of them. Rebecca had washing to do, and enough dried peaches to bake a pie.

She had just put the pie in the oven when Etta came over. As always, the young girl was brimming with enthusiasm.

"I can't believe this place," Etta said, gesturing at the miles-wide expanse of grassy meadow. "Who would have thought there'd be a passage this huge at the top of these mountains?"

"According to Mr. Scott, South Fork is the most important spot on the trail." Rebecca said. "It spans the Continental Divide."

"Continental Divide?" Etta asked.

"Up to now, all the water flowed east toward the Atlantic. Now it will all flow west toward the Pacific."

"Who figured that out?" Etta said.

"Geologists and scientists, I imagine."

Etta looked at her with awe. "Becky, you and Clay are about the smartest man and woman I've ever known. I bet you know even more than my daddy. Where did you get all that learning?"

"My father was a teacher," Becky said.

"Well, I went to school, but no teacher ever taught me all you know."

"But, honey, you know a lot more about practical day-to-day things. I can't shoot a rifle, I still have trouble building a fire, and I can't swim or ride a horse. Clay even had to teach me how to milk a cow. Book learning is a fine thing to have, but it's worthless if you can't put it to use."

Etta giggled. "Well, that sure didn't stop Clay from wanting to marry you, did it?" Marriage was the main issue on her mind these days. "I'll see you later."

Rebecca smiled. "Where are you going?"

"Can't you guess?" Her blue eyes were as bright as the gown she wore.

"Just looking at that twinkle in your eyes tells me all I need to know, young lady. You're sneaking off to meet Tom again, aren't you? Didn't your mother tell you not to be running off alone?"

"Shhh, don't let Mother hear you. Besides, I'm not alone when I'm with Tommy." Bubbling with excitement, Etta stepped closer. "Becky, can you keep a secret?"

"Of course, if I'm asked to."

"Tommy kissed me yesterday. I'd never been kissed before." She clasped her hands together and sighed. "Oh, Becky, it was so wonderful."

"I'm sure it was, honey."

"And he asked me to marry him as soon as we reach California."

"Etta, dear, I'm so happy for you. But don't you think you and Tom are a little young to consider marriage right now?"

"I'm sure that's what my parents will say, too. But Mama was only seventeen when she married Daddy. And I know they would never really stand in the way of my happiness." She threw her arms around Rebecca and hugged her. "You're my dearest friend. Be happy for me, Becky."

Rebecca gave her an extra hug. "I am, honey."

"I must go now, or I'll be late. See you later," Etta said, and rushed away.

19

Etta hurried through the trees. She and Tommy had agreed to meet by a special little cove they'd discovered yesterday, about a half mile from camp and secluded enough so that no one was likely to stumble upon them. A place where just the two of them could be alone, hold hands, and confess their love to each other.

Her heart was pounding with excitement. She was so in love with Tommy. Yesterday, when he'd kissed her and asked her to marry him, she thought her heart would burst right out of her chest. She wondered if he would kiss her again today. She sure hoped so.

Of course, Becky was right: They were very young to get married. She wasn't quite sure how they would approach her parents about that. She could imagine her father calmly puffing on his pipe and shaking his head, but she knew that in the end he would give them his blessing. She was so fortunate to have the loving family that she did, to have someone as wonderful as Tommy in love with her, and to have a dear friend like Becky, the older sister she'd always yearned for.

Etta turned with expectation when she heard the approach of footsteps. "I've been waiting for you." The smile left her face when she recognized the arrival.

"Have you, now?" Jake Fallon asked.

"Oh, I thought you were somebody else."

"Would it be that lovesick beau of yours? 'Fraid you're gonna be disappointed, pretty girl. His pa's got him helpin' to fix a wheel on their wagon. Seems it came loose."

Etta frowned. "I saw Mr. Davis tightening those wheels just yesterday, after we got here."

"Is that so." He smiled wickedly. "Must be somebody loosened it later."

"Who would do such a foul . . . Oh, it was you, wasn't it?"

His laugh gave her goose flesh. "I've been watchin' the two of you, sneakin' off every chance you get."

"So what if we have? Tommy and I haven't done anything to be ashamed of."

"Seein' as how your beau ain't gonna show up, I thought I'd come and keep you company, pretty girl."

"No, thank you. I'm not interested in your company." She started to leave, but he grabbed her arm.

"But I'm interested in yours. How about givin' Jake here one of them kisses you gave that boyfriend of yours?"

"Let me go!" Etta struck out and hit him in the face.

Fallon's eyes glinted with malevolence. "You shouldn't have done that." He pushed her to the ground, then held her down with his body. "I ain't askin' for nothin' you ain't willin' to give him," Fallon snarled, and began to pull up her skirt.

"Stop it, let me go!" she cried. She tried to shove him off her, but he was too strong. "Stop it, I said!"

"Shut that wailin'. Ain't nobody gonna hear you, anyway. You be good to ole Jake, and he'll be good to you."

"Get off her!" Tom Davis pounded over and shoved Fallon off Etta.

Fallon sprang to his feet and drew his sword. "You've been a burr in my ass from the time we left Independence, boy. It's time I dig it out."

"Get out of here, Etta!" Tom shouted as Fallon approached him.

Tom glanced desperately around for a weapon and picked up a broken tree limb. "Hurry, Etta! Run back to the wagons and don't stop."

"I won't leave you!" Etta cried.

"Run, Etta, run!" He threw himself at Fallon. For a few seconds the two men scuffled as Tom tried to hold the man back. He managed to land a blow on the side of Fallon's head, and the decayed tree limb broke.

Etta screamed when Fallon thrust the sword into Tom and then pulled it out. For an instant Tom just stared at Fallon as a red stain began to darken his shirt. Then his eyes glazed and he slumped to his knees.

Shrieking for help, Etta sped toward the wagon train.

"Damn!" Fallon cursed. "Now she'll bring the whole camp here." He looked down at Tom's still body. "I'll settle up with you later."

Then he slunk away into the thick brush.

Etta's screams had brought people running, and as the women helped the sobbing girl back to camp, the men quickly created a stretcher from tree limbs and a blanket.

"My boy, where's my boy?" Tom's distraught father cried as he arrived in the clearing.

Scott put a restraining hand on his arm. "Sam, why don't you go back and let us take care of Tom?"

Davis shoved past them, dropped to his knees, and cradled his son in his arms. "Talk to me, Tommy," he murmured, rocking him in his arms. "Talk to me, son."

Scott said gently, "We've got to get the boy back to camp, Sam. He's lost a lost of blood."

Sam moved aside, then they carefully lifted Tom onto the makeshift stretcher and started back to camp.

Clara Davis rushed up to them the instant they arrived, and broke into tears.

Sam put his arms around his wife's shoulders. "Our boy's alive, Clara. And he needs you."

It was a rallying call to any mother. Clara squared her shoulders and turned to the task at hand. She and Sam stripped the bloodied clothes off their son, and cleansed his body. There was no doctor with the wagon train, so all they could do was cleanse the wounds in hope of preventing infection, and force an antipyretic down his throat to try and ward off a fever. Etta Carson hovered alongside the whole time, tears running down her face.

Becky was sitting by the Garson campfire, staring into space, and Clay went over to her. Howard Garson sat next to her with a glazed look of grief.

"How's the Davis boy?" he asked.

Clay shook his head. "Barely breathing. How's Etta?"

"She's still in shock, but tending Tom is helping her."

Garth came over and joined them, and gave Becky a sharp look. "She looks mighty peaked, Clay," he said quietly.

Clay hunkered down beside her. "How are you doing, Becky?"

"Okay. I should get back to help."

Clay helped her to her feet, and she hurried over to Etta to help the girl through the ordeal.

Pastor Kirkland called a prayer meeting that night, and everyone joined together in prayer that Tom's life would be spared.

People came by to offer assistance and support, but as the night grew long, only the Garson's, the Davises, Garth, Rebecca, Clay, and Pastor Kirkland remained at the campfire by Tom's side.

Clay glanced worriedly at Rebecca. She had remained stone-faced and not shed a tear throughout the whole horrible ordeal.

It was unnatural. Becky was driven by emotions—and her compassion for others was one of her beautiful qualities. She'd cried her heart out over the Ryan tragedy. She was keeping her grief bottled up inside now, and if she didn't let it out, she could become seriously ill.

Clay was about to suggest that they go to their wagon so Becky could try to get some sleep, when Mike Scott approached with Jim Peterson.

"Clay, Garth, I have to talk to you. Jim just told me we've got a missing horse. Could be it broke loose and strayed off, but I never did lean too heavily on coincidence. I'm figuring Fallon probably stole it."

"What do you want us to do, Scotty?" Garth asked.

"It's too dark to do anything tonight. In the morning you and Hawk can ride out and try and pick up the bastard's trail. In the meantime, I suggest we all try and get some sleep. This isn't over yet."

Clay nodded. As they returned to their wagon, he said, "I'm worried about you, Becky."

"Tom is the one you should be worrying about."

"Of course I'm concerned about him. But Tom is young and strong and he's held on this long, which is a hopeful sign."

"It's my fault." Her voice quivered.

"What are you talking about? Why would you blame yourself for what happened to them?"

"I could have stopped her from leaving today. I knew she was going to meet Tom." Her voice rose to near hysteria. "I should have stopped her Clay!"

He grasped her by the shoulders and looked down into her stricken face. Her anguish was so acute that his heart ached for her. "Becky, you can't keep piling guilt on yourself for the unfortunate courses of other people's lives," he said gently.

"They're so young, Clay. So unbelievably young and innocent."

"Tom's not dead, Becky. You have to have faith."

"Faith? How is a person supposed to hold on to faith when good people are hurt or dying, while that evil man continues to live?"

"I don't know. I've never understood the reasons for who lives and who dies. In war, I've had men next to me drop dead from a bullet or be blown apart by a cannon ball, yet I'd be unscathed. Why them and not me?" He shook his head. "I just don't have those answers. I don't think anyone does."

"No, nobody does. That's always the answer, isn't it?"

Clay stared at her. Grief had drained her energy. She needed sleep, but he knew it would be useless to suggest it.

Without another word, she went back to sit with the Garsons and Davises.

Clay lay down but could not sleep. He turned on his side and could see the figures sitting around the fire keeping vigil. He rejoined the others, sitting down by Becky, but he doubted she even realized he was there.

Drained emotionally, Rebecca gazed down at Etta, who sat by Tom's side. The thought that her vibrancy and trust had almost been destroyed by a madman was too heartrending to bear. And dear Tom, fighting to stay alive. The young couple's love was a joy to behold. Why was joy so fleeting—and pain so abiding? What was their crime—loving? Innocence? Hope? How often she had believed in the power of hope—but now she knew it was a fool's fantasy.

Rebecca dozed off sometime after midnight, and awoke with a start when Etta shouted, "He's conscious!" Tears of joy streaked her cheeks. "Tommy's conscious!"

The young man's eyes were open, and he was trying to smile at Etta despite his weakened condition.

"My boy's strong," Sam said. "He's gonna pull through this. I know he will."

The next morning, when word of Fallon's guilt got around the camp, it merely confirmed what all of them had suspected—Jake Fallon was an evil man who did not deserve to live. Not only had he attempted to molest Etta, but then had deliberately tried to murder Tom. His fate was sealed, as far as anyone on the wagon train was concerned.

Due to the extent of Tom's wounds, Mike Scott informed them that the train would remain there for another day.

Even though the crisis had passed, Rebecca didn't appear any better that morning. Her usual morning ritual was to greet Clementine and the two hens with a cheery good morning, but she didn't even go near them. She barely spoke to Clay or Garth, merely nodding or shaking her head as she prepared a simple breakfast of oatmeal and fried bacon. She hadn't gotten any sleep during the night, and she barely touched her food.

He wished she'd just open up and let the tears flow.

They'd just finished eating when Scott and Hawk rode up to get Garth.

"If we pick up a hot trail, we'll stay on it," Hawk told them as Garth mounted up. "So don't go worrying if we don't show up for a few days. If it's a cold trail, we might be back tonight."

"Watch your back," Clay warned as he shook

Garth's hand. "Fallon has a rifle and pistol, as well as that damn sword."

"And there's always Indians to look out for, too," Scott warned.

"Ain't seen no Injun sign since we left Fort Laramie," Hawk said. "You folks take care."

20

Rebecca awoke the next morning to the smell of coffee perking on a campfire. She sat up, surprised. Building the morning campfire and preparing breakfast were chores she'd grown accustomed to doing since the journey began. Then she overheard Clay speaking softly nearby.

"Please, ladies, you know how much she loves both of you. Is it too much to ask you to do this one favor for her?"

Rebecca frowned. Who could he be talking to? She began to get dressed.

"And if you do, I promise I won't complain about your annoying clucking any more," he said. "Just one egg, ladies. One little egg is all I'm asking for."

Rebecca couldn't help smiling. With all the grumbling he did about those chickens, she couldn't believe he was actually talking to them. She peeked outside and saw Clay staring earnestly into the chicken coop.

"Clementine has cooperated, didn't you, Clementine?" he said to the cow. "The least one of you can do is follow her example. I assure you; it's not for me. It's for her. So come on now—one of you lay an egg, or so help me, I'll wring your skinny necks!"

"Oh, you mustn't threaten them," Rebecca said, trying to keep a straight face as she climbed out and hurried over to them. "You can catch more bees with honey than you can with vinegar. Good morning, my darlings," she cooed. "I know I've been neglecting you, but I've really missed you."

The two chickens nestled down in their beds of hay, clucked, and each laid an egg. Rebecca reached in, patted each on the head and removed the eggs, then handed them to Clay.

He looked embarrassed. "How much did you hear?"

She grinned. "Enough."

"I wanted to surprise you and make you breakfast for a change. To try and bring a little sunshine into your life right now."

Her heart swelled with emotion as she smiled up at him. "You did, Clay."

The train moved out that morning. Scott had chosen a bypass to make up for the travel day they'd lost. Loose gravel underfoot, sharp ravines, narrow passages, and dried-up lakes made their progress slow on the tableland, but Scott said the bypass would save them fifty miles. They hadn't covered more than five miles by the time they stopped for lunch.

Rebecca showed little enthusiasm for cooking, and prepared a meal of two-day-old bread, venison jerky, and hot coffee. Once again, she barely touched her food.

"Becky, I know you're grieving," Clay said, "but you shouldn't hold it inside. Let it out, honey. The sooner you do, the quicker you'll feel better."

"How can I ever feel better after all these tragedies?"

"I didn't mean it that way. I meant you can't keep all that sadness bottled up inside of you. It will only make you ill."

"I'll be fine, Clay. I just need some time." She slipped back into silence.

A few hours later they came upon a site that had a few trees and a water hole that hadn't dried up yet, so Scott called a halt for the night. Garth and Hawk rode in a short time later.

"It's useless to pick up any trail," Garth said, disgusted. "There's no telling what direction the bastard rode off in."

"I reckon you're right," Scott said. "We'll have to abandon the search. All we can do when we reach a town is report the crime and give them Fallon's description," he said sadly.

"Well, I'll be damned!" Hawk exclaimed suddenly, looking past them. They turned around to see what had caught the scout's attention.

Eagle Claw strode toward them with a bound and badly bruised Jake Fallon stumbling behind him. The Indian gave Fallon a hard shove, and the villain fell at Clay's feet.

"Eagle Claw bring you man you seek. Now you give Eagle Claw the yellow-hair squaw?"

Clay heard Rebecca's shocked gasp, and she stepped behind him. He grasped her hand. "I won't do that, Eagle Claw."

Scott quickly intervened. "We are grateful to you, Eagle Claw, for bringing us this criminal, and we will gladly pay you in appreciation for what you've done."

Eagle Claw's stare remained fixed on Clay. "Eagle Claw give you ten ponies for your squaw, Fraser Man."

"No, Eagle Claw. You can have anything else I have—my rifle, my pistol—but not my wife. You would have to kill me if you try and take her away."

"Eagle Claw is a chief of his people. He has many warriors. Many times he could have struck you down and taken your squaw. But that is not his way. Eagle Claw is a man of honor. He offered you five ponies for your woman and you refused; he brought you this man you seek, and you refused. Now he offers you ten ponies. Still you refuse. You dishonor him."

"It is not my intent to dishonor you, Eagle Claw. But I would dishonor myself more if I didn't refuse," Clay said. "It is not the way of my people to trade our wives. I have taken an oath to protect her. The shame would be great if I did not honor that oath."

The Indian's unwavering gaze remained fixed on Clay, then, without another word, he turned and strode away.

"You figure that's the last we'll see of him, Hawk?" Scott asked.

Hawk shrugged. "Wouldn't want to say. You never know for sure what he might do."

By this time, most of the people in the camp had been drawn to the spot.

"Haul that bastard Fallon over to that tree," Scott ordered.

"What are you going to do?" Fallon cried out.

"You attempted murder, Fallon. We're going to hang you."

The announcement brought a cheer from the crowd.

"You can't do that," Fallon whined. "You ain't the law. I've got the right to a trial!" he shouted frantically as several men jerked him to his feet and dragged him over to a tree.

"Folks, let me have your attention!" Scott shouted to be heard above the murmuring. "This man attempted to ravage a young girl and kill the young man who stopped him. The punishment is hanging. If there is anyone present who wants to speak up in his defense, now's the time to do it."

"Hang him!" people shouted angrily, and several men threw a noose over the limb of a tree.

"You just had your trial, Fallon," Scott said. "The jury finds you guilty."

"You can't do this," Fallon whimpered, struggling as they lifted him onto the back of a horse. "If he ain't dead, I ain't no murderer, and I didn't rape the gal. If she said I did, she's lyin'. You can lock me up, but I ain't done any hangin' offense. You hang me, and you're the one guilty of murder."

"Did you forget you added horse theft to your crimes, Fallon?" Scott asked. "In the West, that's a hanging offense."

Fallon began sobbing openly. "You ain't the law, Scott."

"Yes, I am, Fallon," Scotty declared. "You signed an agreement in Independence to abide by my rules."

Then he addressed the crowd. "Ladies, hanging is no fit sight for children to see. I suggest you take them back to your wagons."

As several of the mothers hustled their children away, Scott said, "Howard Garson and Sam Davis, if you want to come forward and dispense justice, you may do so."

The two men stepped out of the crowd and each moved to the flank of the horse.

"Jacob Fallon," Scott said to the sobbing man, "we have evidence to prove you are guilty of the attempted rape of Henrietta Garson and the attempted murder of Thomas Davis, and stealing a horse. Therefore, you shall be hanged by the neck until you are dead."

Kicking out at his captors, Fallon tried to squirm off the horse, but several hands reached out to shove him back onto the saddle.

The shimmering glow of campfires cast eerie shadows on the scene enfolding under the barren limb of the gnarled oak.

"I don't want to die," Fallon blubbered as they put the noose around his neck. "I don't want to die. Please don't hang me. Don't hang me."

Shouts of "Hang him!" came from the crowd, and Rebecca looked around, appalled by the mercilessness on the faces of those around her.

Though Fallon deserved to die for the horrendous crime he'd committed, Rebecca felt as if she was part of a lynch mob.

She glanced up at Clay. He stood silent and grimfaced, Garth beside him looking the same. Neither man was encouraging the hanging, but they made no effort to halt it.

Rebecca pressed her hands to her head. Hapless victims struck down violently—the shouts of an avenging mob! The savagery of it all horrified her.

Unable to bear another minute, she put her hands over her ears and shouldered her way through the crowd. Her nerves were frayed, her ears sensitized to the slightest sound. She heard the whacks delivered by Howard Garson and Sam Davis to the horse's flanks, the gasp of the crowd, and then the silence. A silence so deafening that her internal screams threatened to burst her eardrums. She rushed into her wagon and threw herself on the fur pallet.

Clay had witnessed a hanging during the war, and it was a sight that you didn't forget. He turned his head to see how Becky had fared at the grim scene. Surprised to discover she was no longer at his side, he looked around, worried. He didn't want her wandering off alone in the emotional state she was in. And with everyone's attention on the hanging, it would be simple for Eagle Claw to snatch her away if he was inclined to do so.

He hurried back to the wagon, and heard the heart-racking sobs coming from within.

Becky was huddled on the pallet, her head bowed and her knees curled to her chest.

Thank God she's finally letting it out.

Kneeling down beside her, he gently put his hand on her shoulder. Her whole body was trembling.

"Becky," he said gently.

"No more," she whimpered pitifully through shuddering sobs. "Please, no more." She raised her head, and the naked anguish in her eyes made his heart ache.

"I never thought it would be like this. Indian massacres, others crashing to their deaths. People calling for hangings. And poor Etta and Tom . . . so sweet . . . so innocent . . .

"I can't bear anymore!" she cried. "Help me, Clay. Please, help me." She was crying so fiercely that she was choking on her own tears.

Clay lifted her huddled body into his arms and sat down on the rocking chair. Holding her close, he slowly rocked back and forth. What could he say—what could anyone say? The physical hardships of the journey were tough enough, but there'd been too many painful scenes for her compassionate heart to bear. He'd withstood the brutality and anguish of war, but Becky's heartache was tearing him apart.

Pressing a kiss to her forehead, he murmured tenderly, "Cry it out, baby. Cry it out." He continued to rock back and forth.

Gradually her intense crying was reduced to an occasional choked sob, and between the exhausting tears and the gentle motion of the rocking chair, she eventually cried herself to sleep.

Still, he continued to hold her and rock her throughout the night.

21

Clay awoke to clucking chickens, and bright sunlight streaming into the wagon. He bolted to his feet, and bumped his head on the overhead bow supporting the canvas.

Groaning, he slumped back down as the blood started to circulate through his numb arms and legs. It had been daylight when he dozed off, after holding Becky . . . Becky! Where was she?

He got carefully to his feet and felt the prick of a thousand needles as he shook the stiffness out of his legs, then jumped out of the wagon and glanced around. The campfire was already burning, and there were biscuits baking in the oven. But where was Becky?

For a moment he felt panic, his first thought being Eagle Claw. Then he saw her and Helena coming from the river carrying buckets of water.

He hurried up to them. Their exhaustion showed on the drawn faces of both of them. Reaching for the buckets, he said, "Here, let me do that, ladies." Both relinquished them without an argument.

"You should have woken me, Becky," Clay said, once they were alone. "I would have gotten the water for you."

"I needed the exercise, and you needed the sleep. I'm sorry you had to sit up all night."

"How are you feeling?"

"I'm the one who got the sleep," she said lightly, but her smile didn't carry to her eyes. He worried if it ever would again.

"See any sign of Garth?"

"He stopped by earlier, then he rode out with Hawk. You'd better eat, because we'll be pulling out soon."

They ate in silence and packed up to leave. Throughout the day Clay watched her closely, and that night as she prepared dinner, he could see that it was mostly still by habit.

The following day she was a little better. Oh, she still rarely spoke, her smile wasn't as bright or her step as light, but she had shed a lot of her tension. Clay felt better knowing that she was on the road to recovery.

Further good news was that they'd be out of the mountains in another week, and the threat of Eagle Claw no longer dominated their concern. According to Hawk, they'd be clean out of Sioux territory in another day. The Ute Nation lay ahead of them, but their threat lay more in what they would try to steal rather than the risk of human life. In truth, the greatest Indian danger was nearly passed.

That night Garth joined them for dinner. His concern over the change in Becky was evident, and he tried to draw her into a conversation with light teasing. But it wasn't until he mentioned her brother that she showed a spark of enthusiasm. Garth jumped on it at once.

"I imagine you're looking forward to seeing him again."

"Yes, I am. It's been seven years."

"Is he married?" Garth asked.

"I don't think so. At least he wasn't in the last letter I got from him, though he could be by now. Matt wrote it almost a year ago, and I received it last April."

"Were the two of you close?" Clay asked.

He saw a change in her eyes, and for a moment he thought she was going to cry. "If it weren't for Matt, I'd have ended up in an orphanage after our parents died. He was only sixteen then and I was thirteen, but Matt wanted us to stay together. We snuck away to a different town where nobody would know us, and he worked at two jobs each day, seven days a week, just to keep a roof over our heads and food in our stomachs. When I married Charley, Matt finally got the opportunity to live his own life and follow his dream."

"And what was that dream, Becky?" Garth asked.

"He used to talk about going to California and striking gold. That someday he'd be so wealthy, he would build me the biggest house in California, and I could dress in satins and furs."

This was the most interest she'd had in any conversation in days, and Clay wanted to keep it going.

"That sounds like you, Garth. You always had a fixation for that old gold mine map that Uncle Henry sent Dad."

"Still do," Garth said. "I studied that map so often, I can draw it from memory."

"Uncle Henry never took to life on the ole plantation," Clay drawled humorously. "He was always off on some endless search for the pot of gold at the end of the rainbow. I think Brother Garth here has been taking puffs from that same pipe that old Uncle Henry did."

"We all have dreams, Clay," Rebecca said.

There was an encouraging spark of contrariness in her voice.

"Striking gold is a fantasy, Becky," Clay declared firmly, hoping to get a further rise out of her. He forced back a grin when her eyes flared in response.

"Well, you just tell that to those forty-niners who fulfilled their fantasies, Clay Fraser." She turned her head and looked at Garth. "Tell me more about your uncle, Garth."

"Well, every time Uncle Henry came back to Fraser Keep, he'd tell us kids stories of how the West was just a big gold mine waiting to be discovered."

"Was he speaking figuratively, or actually referring to gold itself?" she asked.

"I think both. He never held the same regard for Fraser Keep that the rest of us did. Claimed that it was a great-great granddaddy's dream, not his, and a man shouldn't live to fulfill others' dreams at the cost of not pursuing his own."

"I think I would have liked your uncle Henry."

"I know you would have, Becky. I loved that old man. He marveled at the splendor of this land west of the Mississippi. Said the East was too full of skittish people who looked at a clock for the time, instead of the serenity of a sunrise or the beauty of a sunset. People with the jingle of coins in their pockets instead of the roar of a waterfall cascading down a mountainside."

"It sounds as if he were more of a poet than a miner."

"I think he was, at heart," Garth said.

"If so, why did he keep seeking that pot of gold at the end of the rainbow?"

Garth chuckled. "Tell her why, Clay."

"Uncle Henry said the pleasure was in keeping the hope alive, even if he never found it."

"So he wasn't really searching for wealth, he was following a dream," Rebecca said. "Did he ever actually strike any gold?"

"Nothing big. Just always enough to keep him staked and able to move on to the next site. Then in the fifties, he sent Dad a letter with the map enclosed. He said he was dying, but that he'd really found a bonanza this time. Dad figured it was more of Uncle Henry's wishful thinking, and he put the map aside. A year later Dad got a letter from a doctor in Sacramento who said Uncle Henry had died.

"You know, when we reach California and find Lissy, I might consider searching out that mine of his."

"Are you serious, Garth?" Clay asked. "You wouldn't go back to Virginia?"

"It's something for my mind to chew on." Garth stood up. "It's getting late; I better get back before Scotty comes looking for me. Thanks for dinner, Becky." He kissed her on the cheek and left.

"I hope Garth gets that crazy notion out of his head," Clay said.

"You know, Clay, Garth's entitled to pursue his dreams, too," Rebecca said with a sniff. She stood and climbed into the wagon.

Clay smiled. She sounded as spunky as ever. Why had he ever doubted her ability to pull herself out of her sadness? Becky's fortitude was one of the qualities he admired the most about her. Grieving just required time to heal.

"Becky, do you remember when I said I hoped that some day a man would love me so much that he'd be willing to risk his life to save me?" Etta said as Rebecca brushed the young girl's hair the next day.

"Yes, I remember. It was the day I fell in the river and Clay jumped in and saved me."

"Well, I was wrong, Becky. That was a childish romantic notion. And so selfish. When I saw Tom trying to fight Fallon with practically his bare hands to try and save me, and thought Fallon had killed him . . ." Tears glistened in her eyes. "I wished Tom had never come along, then. I would rather have died than have him die saving me. I love him so much, Becky."

Rebecca hugged her. She could only hope that one day she would understand the real depth of love as well as this sixteen-year-old girl did. Rebecca had suffered a lot in her life, but now realized she still had a lot to learn.

That evening they had just finished dinner when Scott, Peterson, Hawk, and Garth approached their campfire.

"Clay, we've got a decision to make," Scott said, "and I'd like to hear your opinion. Hawk and Garth have scouted the trail ahead. According to the boys here, there's a tableland a hundred feet below that eventually links up with the trail we're following, and would probably cut off seven days of traveling time. There's some decent graze for the stock and a couple of water holes."

Rebecca had no further desire in listening to the conversation, so she left the fire and climbed into the wagon.

She curled up on the pelt and closed her eyes as the low murmur of the men's voices carried to her ears. She had lost all interest in what lay ahead; she just wished the trip was over. But there were still six or eight weeks to go! Her last thought, before dozing off, was wondering if she could bear another two months of this.

She woke up with a start when she felt a tugging at her feet. Clay was removing her shoes.

"I'm sorry to wake you, Becky. I thought you'd be more comfortable with your shoes off. You should get into your nightgown, stretch out, and get a decent night's sleep. You'll be the better for it in the morning."

She sat up. "Is the meeting over?"

"Yeah, they just left."

"What's the problem now?" she asked.

"Getting about a hundred and fifty feet straight down the side of this mountain."

"I heard that part of it. So what did you all decide?"

"To try it. Hawk figures it should save about seven days."

"And how many people does he figure we'll lose trying it?" she asked.

She regretted the bitter remark as soon as she said it; none of these misfortunes were Clay's fault.

But he remained undisturbed. "We shouldn't lose any, using a windlass."

"What's that?"

"It's a simple mechanical device usually used for hoisting; we're simply going to reverse the process. Garth studied engineering in college, so he's figured out how to construct it. It will be crude, but sounds pretty safe." He turned away. "Well, I'll leave so you can go to sleep."

"Clay, it's chilly at night. Why don't you sleep inside the wagon?"

"We've got to construct this windlass through the night. And they figure the best spot to try it is right near us, so unfortunately you'll be hearing a lot of hammering."

He started to step out, then hesitated and turned his head to her. "And, Becky, don't worry—there'll be plenty of us right outside."

She'd forgotten all about the threat Eagle Claw still presented to her—but Clay hadn't. He always had her welfare in mind. That thought cut through the numbness she'd felt for the last few days, and brought a warm glow to her heart. She lay back and closed her eyes.

Soon the clang of hammers and screech of saws made sleep impossible, however, and Rebecca gave up trying, and went outside.

Campfires blazed everywhere, illuminating the men laboring in their light. A score of trees had been felled, and a half dozen men were trimming off the branches and binding the trunks together to form what looked like a scaffold. A short distance away, several others were driving stakes into the ground.

"Don't try to eyeball it, boys," Mike Scott ordered. "Use a level to make sure those stakes are even."

Others were occupied checking and linking lengths of chain together. She saw Clay and Garth working on two barrels. Thick pieces of wood had been hewn to form right angles, and they were attaching those through holes in the tops and bottoms of the barrels.

Seeing Helena moving among the men with a coffeepot, Rebecca realized she should do so, too. After putting a pot to brew on the fire, she went over to help Helena. The rest of the night passed swiftly.

By the time a rising sun streaked the sky with pink and gray, the mechanism had been completely assembled, and all that remained was to test it and string a guideline.

The barrel was placed horizontally on the two lateral posts. A chain running over a hundred feet in length was connected to the crank at one end of the barrel, and the same length of chain connected to the other end of the barrel. The free ends were attached to each side of the wooden platform, ready to be lowered. To lower the platform, one turned the crank and the barrel would spin on the makeshift axle, unwinding the chain as it did. To raise it, one would just have to reverse the cranking direction.

"So you think this will actually work," Rebecca said, stepping back to observe the finished product.

"Keep the faith, Little Sister. I know it will," Garth said. "All I need is a volunteer."

She glanced at Clay. "Don't even think it, Clay Fraser."

"Sounds like the little lady means it, Clay," Scott said.

"I'll take it down," Jim Peterson said.

"Good man," Garth said.

They loaded two stakes, guidelines, and a sledge-hammer on the platform.

"Don't try and stand up, Jim, until we get the guidelines anchored and the boys find their rhythm when they start cranking."

Jim stepped onto the platform.

"You men on those cranks, take it slow until you get the hang of it," Scott ordered. "And stay in rhythm. If you don't, that platform will tilt and . . . Well, just stay in rhythm," he said gruffly. He shook Jim's hand. "Good luck, Jim. I'll see you below."

Jim sat down in the middle of the platform and nodded to Garth. "Okay, let her go."

The men began to crank, and each turn of the barrel released some chain. Once the platform cleared the edge of the cliff, it began to sway. The pull on the chain became greater and it took two men on each crank to slow the descent.

Rebecca was almost afraid to draw a breath. In a matter of minutes the scaffold touched bottom. Jim jumped out and waved to them, then unloaded the ropes and stakes. He drove the stakes into the ground, attached a guideline to each stake, then tossed the lines back on the scaffold and signaled them to hoist it back up. The men reversed the crank and hoisted the scaffold.

As soon as it was up, they retrieved the guide ropes, pulled them taut, and tied them to the stakes. Now, everything was in place to start the move.

"Clay, your wagon's the closest so let's start with that," Scott said. "Mrs. Fraser, will you remove the chicken coop and take that down with you?"

"What about Clementine?" she asked.

"The cow," Clay offered in explanation to Scott's confused look.

"We'll send her down with your mules," Scott said.

"When will I be lowered?" she asked.

"Let's try your wagon first," he said.

Rebecca watched with trepidation as they pushed the wagon onto the scaffold and lashed it firmly in place. Then they lowered it, accompanied by a couple of men.

Rebecca heaved a sigh of relief when she looked down and saw the wagon being rolled onto firm ground.

"Well, Mrs. Fraser, are you ready to try it?" Scott asked.

"I guess now's as good a time as any," she said.

"I'll go with her," Clay said. "I'm sure Jim can use more men down there, too."

"All right, get on," he said.

"Can we take Clementine, too?" Rebecca asked.

Scott sighed deeply. "Okay, take the damn cow." He turned to Clay. "Shackle it so it doesn't shift around."

The descent went very smoothly, but Rebecca sighed with relief when her feet were back on terra firma.

Her wagon had been pushed out of the way, and it

would be hours before all the wagons and stock were lowered. To keep her mind from straying to sad thoughts, she decided to bake some sugar cookies. Clay seemed to enjoy them.

She got a fire started, then gathered fallen wood from the nearby trees. When she returned the men were all working furiously, unloading the platforms as quickly as it was lowered. Rebecca went back to the trees to gather more wood.

As she bent down, she was suddenly seized from behind. A hand clamped over her mouth and shut off her scream as the smell of bear grease assailed her nostrils. She struggled to free herself, but her assailant was too strong and held her tightly as he gagged her, then tied her wrists behind her back with a strip of rawhide.

He turned her around, and terrified, she stared into the black eyes of Eagle Claw, before he picked her up and flung her over his shoulder.

22

Clay glanced over to the wagon in time to see Becky dump an armload of wood into the sling, then he returned to helping to unload the next wagon. When he looked a few minutes later, Becky was gone. He wished she'd stay at the wagon, where he could keep an eye on her. It was a mistake to have brought her down so soon; she should have remained with the crowd above.

To his relief, the next wagon coming down was the Garson's, and the family was going to follow it. Knowing Becky, Helena, and Eleanor, they'd get a big meal started for everyone. That would keep her occupied for the next few hours.

There was still no sign of Becky when they finished unloading the Garson wagon, and Clay was getting worried. While they waited for the Garsons to be lowered, he went to see if she was inside the wagon.

There was no sign of her.

Cupping his hands to his mouth, he called out her name. When there was no reply, he tried again.

The hair prickled at the nape of his neck. Where was she?

He headed into the trees, calling out for her at the top of his lungs, fearing the worst but not wanting to admit it. When he found a pile of wood that had been abandoned, apprehension knotted his innards.

"Becky!" he shouted. "Becky, can you hear me?"

Consumed by a panic he'd never known before, he frantically searched the small wooded copse and was relieved when he didn't find her body or any sign of fresh blood. They were encouraging signs that she was still alive.

He caught the glint of sunlight on something lying on the ground a short distance from the treeline. Hurrying over to it, he picked up a ring and recognized it as Becky's wedding ring. Now he had no doubt that Eagle Claw had grabbed her.

Clay raced back to the clearing. "I need a horse!" he shouted up to Scott. "Becky's gone, and I figure Eagle Claw's got her."

"You can't go after her alone, Clay!" Scott yelled back.

"Tell Garth to get down here!"

"He and Hawk just rode off. I'll send a rider after them. Wait until they get back."

"There's no time to wait. If she's in the hands of that savage, Lord knows what he'll do to her. Get that horse down here!"

"I'll send mine down!" Scott yelled. "It's already saddled. You're a fool to take on that Indian alone. He probably has others with him, too."

As soon as they started to lower the horse, Clay ran to the wagon. From habit during the war, he always kept a change of clothing and a few useful items in his saddlebags. He added some cartridges, coffee, and several pieces of jerky. Then he grabbed his rifle, a jacket, and a rolled blanket.

By the time he raced back to the clearing, the horse was ready. Clay adjusted the stirrups and mounted.

"God be with you, Clay," Jim Peterson said, reaching up to shake his hand.

"Thanks, Jim. Tell Garth I'll try and leave him some kind of sign." He wheeled the horse and rode away.

Returning to the spot where he found the ring, Clay took a calming breath and analyzed the situation. Eagle Claw could hardly scale the mountainside, nor could he go in the opposite direction without being seen by them, so there were only two directions he could take: south or east. Logically, he'd head east to remain in Sioux territory. Dismounting, Clay checked the ground until he found what he hoped for—an unshod hoofprint. Indians didn't shoe their horses. Knowing Garth would follow, with or without Hawk, he made an arrow with pebbles, and then mounted and headed east.

Several miles later he found a muddy hoofprint by a water hole, where Eagle Claw must have stopped to rest the horse. When he found several more muddy prints leading away from the spot, he knew he was still on the right trail. There appeared to be only one horse, so if luck was with him, Eagle Claw had come alone.

A short time later Clay came across some horse spoor. He didn't know enough to be able to determine how fresh it was, but since it wasn't entirely dry he knew he wasn't that far behind them. The only thing that gave him food for thought was why Eagle Claw wasn't cutting off the trail. He seemed to be holding a steady course. Surely he knew he'd be followed, so why didn't he try to throw his pursuers off course?

The only explanation Clay could think of was that Eagle Claw, knowing he'd be pursued, was covering as much ground as possible while there was still daylight. That way, when he stopped for the night, he'd be deeper into his own territory, where there would be a better chance of meeting up with some of his own tribesmen.

Two hours later Clay passed a deserted cabin that clearly hadn't been used for years. He hadn't seen any sign for several miles, and he began to fear he had lost the trail. Cresting a rise, he had a good overview of what lay ahead and could see for miles. Clay pulled out the spyglass he had carried throughout the war and focused it on the meadow ahead. His heart leaped to his throat when he saw the faint figures in the distance, one of them a woman with blond hair. He spurred his horse forward.

Having to carry a double load, the Indian's horse would tire much more quickly than his own, but at sunset Clay pulled up for the night. He had to hold on to common sense. He had closed the gap between them, and would overtake them tomorrow for sure. He dare not go on in the dark, because he could easily lose the trail completely. Then Becky could be lost to him forever.

He put on his coat, covered himself with a blanket, and hunched down for the night. Despite the heat of the day, it turned cold once the sun went down. But a campfire would be a beacon to anyone in the area, and he didn't want to be spotted by other Indians.

Was Becky warm enough? She wasn't wearing a

coat the last time he saw her. A damn blanket wouldn't be enough to stay warm if Eagle Claw didn't build a fire, either.

Would the bastard rape her? It was unlikely, since Eagle Claw knew he'd be pursued. But God forbid if he did—it would sink her deeper into the troubled frame of mind she was suffering, and she might never recover.

He'd kill the son of a bitch when he caught up with them. The thought of what she was going through right now was tearing him apart.

Hold in there, Becky. Do what you have to do to stay alive. No matter what, stay alive. I'll find you wherever you are, no matter how long it takes.

Eagle Claw dismounted, then he lifted her off the horse. Rebecca limped over to a tree and sat down. She was stiff and aching. When they had stopped to water the horse, he had removed the gag, but had kept her wrists bound. Her arms and hands were numb, and she wanted to scream.

"Will you please untie my wrists?" she asked.

For a long moment his obsidian gaze fixed on her. If he intended to kill her, he certainly would have done so by now, but she still drew back in alarm when he approached her with knife in hand.

Eagle Claw slashed the rawhide, and as her arms dropped down, thousands of needle pricks raced up them. Rebecca shook them vigorously to get the circulation flowing.

Impervious to her pain, he said, "You get wood, Yellow Hair Woman."

Too frightened to challenge him, she got up and began to gather pieces of fallen wood. Glancing back at Eagle Claw, she saw he had started to build a fire and seemed entirely oblivious to her. She watched him for a long moment, and he didn't even glance in her direction. Dare she try to escape? The sun had set, and if she could elude him until it got pitch dark, she might be able to get away.

But she had no idea where she was, or even which direction to head in if she did succeed in evading him. Once there was broad daylight, he'd probably have no problem in tracking her down. But why he felt she was worth it was beyond her comprehension.

Rebecca started to inch farther away. She stole another quick glance behind her; there was no sign of him. She was about to dump the wood and run when he suddenly stepped out of the trees. When and how he got there so fast was a frightening mystery, and she glared at him defiantly. His expression remained inscrutable, but she knew he had guessed her intent. She spun on her heel, returned to the campsite, and dumped the wood. Then she sat down and tried to ignore him.

The thought of a life away from civilization and subjected to the whims of this savage was unbearable to her. He was the enemy of her people, and a war chief who advocated violence as a solution. She would never be able to endure a life with him.

Clearly he intended to use her physically. Would he kill her after he had his way with her? It would be a blessing if he did. She prayed that Clay and Garth wouldn't try to find her, for that would only get them killed, too. And neither deserved to die to try and save her. Etta had taught her that lesson.

Were it not for her scheming, they wouldn't even know she existed. Were it not for her scheming, she would still be back in Independence.

"What you sow, you reap, Rebecca."

"What?" Eagle Claw asked.

She hadn't realized she'd spoken the words aloud. "Nothing. I was talking to myself."

"Is that the way of Yellow Hair Woman?"

"Yes. I talk to myself all the time. You'll find that out for yourself, and it will serve you right for making me your prisoner."

If this Indian was going to harm her, she wasn't going to give him the satisfaction of seeing her sniveling and whining. It may be time to pay the piper for all her misdeeds, but she'd go down fighting.

He looked at her. "Eagle Claw does not understand the words of Yellow Hair Woman."

"Rebecca! My name's Rebecca. Stop calling me by that ridiculous name. Do I call you Feather In The Hair, or some such nonsense?"

His eyes darkened. "Silence, woman. You do not speak to a Sioux warrior with the bark of a jackal."

"Better than the way you bray like a jackass," she shot back.

"Eagle Claw does not know that word."

"That doesn't make you less of one."

He eyed her suspiciously, then returned to building a fire. She could tell he wasn't used to anyone talking back to him; he'd probably think anyone who did was crazy.

Crazy! That was the answer! Someone on the wagon train had said the Indians never harmed anyone whom they thought was mentally ill. They believed that person was possessed by a spirit that would be released if the person was harmed.

"Oh, now look what you've done. You woke the baby!" she cried out.

Rebecca pretended she was holding an infant in her arms, and began to rock and coo to it. Maybe she could plant doubts in his mind that he'd made a huge mistake.

She rocked and sang the "baby" to sleep, then carefully laid it aside and pretended to cover it up. She could feel his fixed stare on her.

Rebecca smiled and put a finger to her lips in a motion to be quiet. "We must speak softly so we don't wake him," she said in a low voice.

"Eagle Claw is a chief. He speaks with the roar of the mighty mato."

"What is the mighty mato?" she asked.

"Your people call it a bear."

"How did you learn to speak my language, Eagle Claw?"

At first he appeared to ignore the question. Then he said, "A holy man. He stayed many summers with my people."

"You let him remain, yet you kill others who come here?"

"He came in peace. Others come to drive away the

Sioux. They kill the buffalo and deer that feed us, they dirty our water holes with their animals, your soldiers rape our squaws and go unpunished. They tell us we must live by their laws, not the laws of the Sioux. This is our land; my people have lived here for moons too many to count. We do not go among your villages and tell you to live by the law of the Sioux. Why do you come to ours and say we must live by yours?"

"You sound like my husband," she said.

"Fraser Man has said this, too?"

"Yes. We just had a great war among my people."

"What is your tribe?"

She was about to say they didn't have tribes, and then thought differently. "We are all of the American tribe, but those in the South, were of the Confederacy and warred with those in the North called Yankees."

"There are many different Sioux tribes, too. Our brothers stretch far toward the rising sun."

"The Confederacy tribe felt that Washington was forcing them to live by laws they did not agree with."

"Washington is the village where the white man's great chief lives."

"Yes, that is right. That is where our tribe's laws are made for both North and South, East and West. For all the Americans to obey."

"But not the law of the Sioux, Arapaho, Cheyenne. We have our own tribal laws. Fraser Man was right to fight for the laws of his people. Did he win?"

"No. The South lost the war."

"That is bad to hear. Then they are still enemies with this Yankee tribe."

"No, we are all united Americans again."

Eagle Claw shook his head. "That is not the way of the Sioux. Your enemy is always your enemy."

He dug into a pouch and handed her a piece of jerky. "You eat."

Rebecca began to chew on the jerky. It tasted like buffalo and was very tough. She had to soften it with her teeth before attempting to even chew it well enough to swallow it.

His gaze never wavered. Fearing he might attempt to molest her now, she knew she had to do something more to try and convince him she was insane. She spied a grasshopper nearby.

Desperate times calls for desperate measures, Rebecca.

Rallying her courage, she spit out the jerky in a show of distaste and picked up the insect and put it into her mouth. Rebecca forced herself not to cringe when she crushed it between her teeth and swallowed it.

"You eat the creatures that crawl?" he asked scornfully.

"Of course. Don't you?"

"Eagle Claw is a Sioux warrior. He does not eat the dregs that crawl the earth. He hunts the mighty mato. Stalks the noble deer."

"And the frightened rabbit and tiny squirrel," she added.

"Do not scorn me, Yellow Hair Woman."

"Well, grasshoppers taste better than your buffalo jerky," she said. "I think you would like them. I'll catch you some for breakfast."

Rebecca started to crawl around on her hands and

knees searching for more. "I wish I could find some grubs. I know you would like them. They're delicious. They're easier to chew than your jerky, and taste much sweeter."

He strode over to her and tossed down a blanket. "You sleep now." Then he turned away in disgust.

Rebecca crossed her legs and sat down. In a singsong, childlike voice, she recited a bedtime prayer, bobbing her head back and forth with every word.

" 'Now I lay me down to sleep; I pray the Lord my soul to keep. If I should die before I wake, I pray the Lord my soul to take.' " Then she smiled at him and wiggled her fingers in a wave. "Nighty-night."

Eagle Claw's expression remained inscrutable.

Rebecca lay down as close to the fire as she could, in the hopes of staying warm. Her ploy had seemed to work, at least for that night. The Lord only knew what she'd have to come up with tomorrow.

As she feared what might lie ahead, she thought about Clay and wished she'd shown him more gratitude for all he'd done for her. Now it was too late.

Eagle Claw shook her awake. The sun had risen, but she could tell from the feel of it on her body that it was still early. "You come." He handed her the pouch to take a drink.

She gasped with alarm when three Sioux warriors suddenly appeared. The four men spoke together in low tones, then the three slipped back into the trees and Eagle Claw came over to her. "Come."

Unsuspecting, she stood up and was unprepared

when he suddenly put the gag around her mouth. After tying her hands behind her back again, he forced her to sit down by the campfire. Confused, she watched him build it up, and then stand up with his arms folded across his chest. Soon the reason became clear: she was a decoy.

Rebecca began to squirm, trying to loosen the gag or her hands, but to no avail. Her heart leaped to her throat in a silent scream of warning when Clay rode into sight.

He saw her at once and slowly rode up to the fire before dismounting. He made no attempt to reach for his rifle or the gun in his holster at his hip.

"I came for my wife, Eagle Claw."

"You know Eagle Claw can kill you, Fraser Man."

"Yes, I know that. You or those three bucks among the trees. You might as well tell them to come out, because I know they are there."

"And still you come with your weapon sheathed."

"I don't think you'll shoot me in the back, Eagle Claw. I think you are one who faces your enemy and doesn't have others do it for you."

"You speak the words of a warrior, Fraser Man."

"I have been," Clay said. "In the recent war."

"Yellow Hair Woman told me your tribe is like the Sioux; they do not want to live by the laws of your great chief in Washington."

"That is true, Eagle Claw."

"You are a brave man, Fraser Man. And you have much courage and much heart. It was Eagle Claw's intent to kill you, but he has changed his mind. Eagle

Claw holds great respect for you. Give me your hand, Fraser Man."

Thinking Eagle Claw intended to shake it, Clay extended his hand. The Indian drew his knife, nipped Clay in the thumb, and then cut his own. He rubbed their two thumbs together.

"We are now blood brothers, and you shall be known as Gray Pants, blood brother of Eagle Claw. From this day on you and members of your gray pants tribe can pass safely through the land of the Sioux."

"And what about my wife, Eagle Claw?"

"Eagle Claw would not dishonor his blood brother. Yellow Hair Woman may leave with you. Eagle Claw fears that his brother's squaw has tasted too much juice of the mescal." He made a circling motion with his finger and pointed to her head. "Eagle Claw will now go to the mountain and thank the Great Spirit for his deliverance."

Mescal juice? Deliverance? Eagle Claw had been obsessed with Becky; now he appeared to be relieved at getting rid of her. But Clay wasn't going to argue, he just wanted to get out of there before the Indian had a change of heart.

Clay cut Rebecca's bonds and removed the gag. Unable to resist, he took her in his arms and just held her, needing to feel her safely in his arms. She clung to him and he held her closely until she ceased to tremble, then he lifted her onto his saddle and climbed up behind her. Enfolding her in his arms, Clay reached for the reins and they rode away.

What had made the Indian chief give her up without one shot being fired? Those questions and the answers could come later; for now he just held her.

A few hours later the sky opened up with a downfall. Streaks of lightning in the distance indicated the storm was approaching fast and would get a lot worse before it got better. Clay goaded the horse to a faster gait, hoping to reach the abandoned cabin before the worst of it hit.

Rebecca was too relieved to let the rain bother her. Clay halted long enough to slip a poncho around her, then they continued on their way. She leaned back against him, and her tears of joy mingled with the raindrops running down her cheeks.

She had learned another lesson today, one she would carry with her as long as she lived. She snuggled deeper against Clay, and his arms tightened around her.

Life, miraculously, had become so good. So very good.

23

It was a miracle they even found the cabin, in the downpour and darkness. Clay dismounted, went inside to check it out, then came back to the horse and lifted her down.

"Get inside while I get the saddlebags," he said.

Rebecca stepped inside. It was too dark to see anything, but at least she was out of the storm. Within a minute Clay followed her inside, forced the door shut against the fury of the pelting rain, then tossed a blanket and his saddlebags on the floor.

"You'd better get those wet clothes off, while I get a fire going."

When the door suddenly swung open, Rebecca screamed and spun around in alarm.

Clay slammed it shut and slipped the bolt in place. "It's just the wind."

"I guess my nerves are on edge," she said.

"Rightly so, but you've got nothing to worry about now. Eagle Claw won't go back on his word."

She picked up the blanket and moved to a dark corner. By the time she'd undressed, he had a fire started.

"In another half hour this place should be warmed up," he said, riffling through the saddlebags. "I've got jerky and the makings for coffee, so at least we won't go hungry tonight." He dug out a coffeepot. "I'm going out to take care of the horse."

The light from the fire gave her a chance to look around at the tiny, one-room cabin. The room had a sod floor and was bare except for a huge pile of wood stacked up against the wall. Rain dripped through a hole in a far corner.

Rebecca dried her dripping hair with her skirt and then spread out her clothing to dry in front of the fireplace. By the time Clay came back inside, the room had taken on a pleasant warmth. He handed her the coffeepot filled with rainwater, then shook out his dripping Stetson and hung it on a wall peg.

"Whoever built this shack had the good sense to put up a lean-to for stock. At least the horse will be out of the storm."

Rebecca added coffee to the water and put the pot on the hearth. "I wonder why anyone would build a cabin up here."

"Probably somebody who got caught in the snow, and put it up to sit out the winter." He glanced around. "All in all, he did a pretty good job; cabin's pretty airtight except for the leak in that far corner."

"It seems like a palace to me. It feels so good just to be under a roof again. Funny, what you take for granted when you live in a city."

"Yeah, I spent most of the war sleeping outside or in tents. Guess I've kind of gotten used to it."

"You'd better get out of your wet clothes, too, Clay. You're dripping all over the place."

He sat down, pulled off his wet boots, and poured

them out on the sod floor. His socks and shirt followed. Rebecca turned her head away while he shucked his pants and drawers, then slipped on a dry pair of pants he had in his saddlebags. He remained bare-chested.

She felt a flush of excitement as she waited for the coffee to perk. He has such a beautifully proportioned body, she thought, stealing glances at him. Broad shoulders, muscled chest, slim hips, and long legs. She'd noticed it before, but in the intimacy of the cabin, she was more aware of it than ever.

Later, as they sat by the fire eating jerky and sipping coffee from the same tin cup, Rebecca told him about the grasshopper incident and her pretended insanity. They shared their laughter.

"I can't believe you fooled that old war horse," Clay said. Then the laughter left his eyes, and he reached out and caressed her cheek. "It must have been hell for you," he said soberly. "You're a very courageous woman, Becky."

Rebecca suddenly felt very warm. She lowered the blanket off her shoulders and tucked in the edges at the cleavage of her breasts.

"If that blanket's too bulky, I can give you a shirt to put on," he said.

"No, the blanket's fine. Between the hot coffee and the fire, I was beginning to feel too warm."

He got up and moved to the fireplace. "And otherwise, are you fine?"

Surprised, she looked up at him. "Why do you ask?"

"I just wonder if Eagle Claw . . . I mean, did he harm you in any way?"

"No, Clay. He didn't harm me in *any* way."

Relief flashed in his eyes. "He's a strange man. I know he's probably killed his share of white settlers, and will continue to do so. But I'd trust his word over that of many who condemn him."

"Why did you do it, Clay?"

"Do what?" he asked, tossing another log on the fire.

"Risk your life to come after me."

"I think you know why. It's a question—"

"Of honor," she said. "And honor comes ahead of anything, doesn't it? Even risking your life." How she wished he'd said he'd done it because he loved her.

Whatever put such a ridiculous thought in her mind? She didn't want him to love her.

Clay raised his head and the intensity in his eyes matched that of his words. "There's a lot more between us than just honor, Becky."

"I know. I discovered something about myself in these past couple of days. When I thought Tom would die, I sank to the pit of despair. I didn't care whether *I* lived or died."

"That's a common reaction when you believe someone you care for is dying."

"But that wasn't the only reason for my despair. I felt life was hopeless—that no matter how you strive to accomplish a dream, the outcome is out of our hands. No one could have prevented the deaths of the Ryans or of those massacred, or saved Tom. And I knew that nothing you or the whole U.S. cavalry could have done would've prevented Eagle Claw from taking me, if it was meant to be."

"I believe that death is certainly inevitable, but what you make of your life is your own choosing. We don't all take the path of a Jake Fallon."

She raised her head and smiled. "I agree. But it doesn't change my belief in destiny."

"So what are you trying to say, Becky?"

"I realized that it's natural to grieve over the loss of those we love, but we can't feel guilty that we're alive and they aren't. Guilt was really what I've been feeling, Clay. I was well and alive; Etta and Tom were hurt. But nothing I thought or did caused it, or could have prevented it.

"And that's why I no longer carry guilt over Charley's death, either. No matter how much I resented him for what was between us, I wasn't responsible for his dying. In the total scheme of things, we play a very small part in the events surrounding us."

"And you came to this realization just because I caught up with you and Eagle Claw?"

"Yes. When you caught up with us and Eagle Claw didn't kill you—and he could have so easily—I knew it wasn't your destiny to die there. Any more than I was destined to live whatever life remained for me in an Indian camp."

"Sounds like you've got everything all figured out," he said.

"Not everything," she said.

"What's left," he asked, "*when* you meet your Maker?"

"No. The *why you?* of it. There were many available bachelors in Independence. I know *my* reason for choosing you, but what was destiny's reason?"

Clay broke into laughter. "I've asked myself that same question from the time I woke up with that marriage license."

Rebecca smiled and shrugged. *Destiny, Clay.*

Something in that mysterious smile made Clay burningly aware of the intimacy of the moment—the beauty of the woman across from him, and her nakedness beneath that blanket. He'd never wanted any other woman as much as he wanted her.

"Here we are, just the two of us in this remote cabin," he said huskily. "Reunited after a harrowing separation. Any other married couple would seize the moment."

"Surely every event of the past months has brought us to this time, this place. Do we seize the moment or let it slip away?" she sked softly.

Clay moved to her and lightly grazed her cheek with his knuckles, then gently tipped up her chin with a finger. "What do you think we should do with this moment, Becky?"

Their gazes met in man's message to woman, and woman's response, as ageless as Eden.

Shifting closer, she said, "Let's seize the moment."

Lowering his head, he drew her into his arms, claiming the lips she had parted in anticipation. Gentle at first, the kiss deepened until breathlessness forced them apart.

"Are you sure you're ready for this?" he murmured. "I don't want to stop this time, so be sure this is what you really want."

She slipped her arms around his neck and leaned

into him. "I do, Clay. I've never wanted anything so much in my life."

The throaty passion in her voice stoked the fire in his loins, and he flared to flame. Despite her reassurance, he vowed to raise her passion to a height beyond the point of no return.

The blanket slid off her as he lowered her on it to the floor. Under his hungry gaze, her naked flesh shimmered like ivory in the fire's glow.

As he quickly shed his pants, his gaze remained on the sensuous beauty of her body, stretched out in wanton anticipation. His hope of any sustained foreplay was diminishing as rapidly as his control; her body was a magnet that drew his to it.

Clay stretched out on top of her. Driven by the erotic feel of flesh against flesh, the peaks of her breasts pressing against his chest, he rubbed against her in a sensuous friction, drinking in her gasps of pleasure with drugging kisses.

Raising his head, he pressed a soft kiss to her lips. "Becky, what do you want me to do with you?"

Darkened with aroused passion, her eyes gleamed like emeralds. "Anything. Everything," she murmured in a throaty whisper, and squirmed against him.

"Isn't there one thing you've fantasized about more than any other?"

"It's happening right now."

"Oh, God, Becky!" He could feel her trembling, and knew it was from anticipation, not fear. She was so eager, so incredibly trusting.

"Don't stop, Clay. Please don't stop."

"I couldn't if I wanted to."

Crushing her lips in a soul-dredging kiss, he filled his hand with her breast and grazed the taut nipple with his thumb. The feel of it sent his passion soaring. He had to taste more of her. Shifting down the satin smoothness of her body, he tasted her nipple with his tongue. Her quick gasp spurred his hunger to greater heights, and he shifted to the other breast. Laving the peak with his tongue, he tugged it lightly between his teeth. Each pressed kiss or lick of his tongue elicited a responsive gasp or moan.

His name became ecstatic pleas from her—this time there would be no withdrawal on her part. No groin-aching, mind-shattering halt. She reached out for him, but he caught her hands and held them, linked with his, to the floor by her face. Mouthing one of her breasts, he began to suckle it voraciously as hot blood pounded at his temples. She arched against him, yearning for more. The thought of doing this had filled his mind for weeks, and he'd lost count of the number of times he'd dived into cold water for self-control.

"Now, Clay. Now. Please, please," she pleaded.

Raising his head, he looked into her eyes. They were glazed over with passion, and he couldn't hold out any longer.

Releasing her hands, he palmed the heated core of her need. She was moist and ready, and he intensified the pressure, reclaiming her lips and drinking in her gasping moans as her body imploded with tremors. It didn't come a minute too soon; he was near to losing it.

He mounted her swiftly and thrust into her. Her

chamber closed around him, tight and warm, and his body shuddered in the rapture of climax.

For a long moment he lay spent over her, only the rasp of their breathing and crackle of popping logs breaking the silence. Then he gently rolled off her so they lay side-by-side.

Rebecca finally opened her eyes and sat up. She gazed down with wonderment at Clay, whose eyes were closed. He was so unselfish in his lovemaking. She had never felt so alive, so uninhibited. Clay had seen to that, had made certain her passion would not be suppressed. It was so incredible, she wished it could go on forever.

As if sensing her gaze, he opened his eyes. "Hey what are you thinking?"

"How much I want to touch you." She reached out and lightly grazed his cheek. His flesh was warm, and her fingers tingled from the excitement of it's feel. She curved her palm around his shoulder and followed its slope to his chest. It felt firm . . . muscular—and so warm.

Her caressing fingers encountered the marbled pebble of his nipple, and she wondered if it was as sensitive as hers. Driven by curiosity, she lowered her head and licked it. She could feel the sudden surge of his heartbeat. She did the same to the other nipple, and his breathing intensified.

Although he remained motionless, she could see the arousal in his eyes. She lowered her head and took the nipple into her mouth, just as he had done to her. His quick gasp carried to her ears, encouraging her to bolder moves as her own arousal began to mount.

Recalling the erotic rasp of his chest hair against her naked flesh, she pressed a kiss to the dark patch, then began to trail kisses down its path. The clutch of his fingers stopped her descent, but she was far from done with her exploration, and began to taste and caress whatever fell under her roving hands and mouth.

His body was taut with tension, and a sheen of perspiration dotted his brow and shoulders. The taste of him, scent of him, the feel of his long, muscular body straining against her, drove her to a boldness too great to be thwarted.

Rebecca straddled him and then leaned down and kissed him, the darting forays of her tongue sweeping the chamber of his mouth. Divine sensation swelled her breasts and coiled around the hub between her legs.

Clay's restraint snapped.

With a feral growl he gripped her shoulders and rolled over, his mouth pillaging her senses as they rode together in a tumultuous release.

Afterward, too exhausted to move, Rebecca lay marveling at the heights of passion that Clay had raised her to. Even in the farthest stretches of her imagination, she had never believed it possible.

She turned her head and glanced at him as he lay beside her. Everything about the man was remarkable. How could she have once thought otherwise? He was the handsomest, noblest, most honorable man she had ever met—and surely the greatest lover in the world. And he was so protective of her and courageous. Were it not for Clay, she would still be a prisoner of Eagle Claw. How could she ever repay him?

"Deep in thought, aren't you?" He had shifted to his side and was gazing at her.

"I was just wondering how I can ever thank you."

He chuckled. "The pleasure was all mine."

"I don't mean for what we just did. I mean for everything, Clay. I'm so indebted to you, and ashamed for how I deceived you into marrying me."

"Which brings up another issue," he said in a hard voice. "Tonight has spoiled any chance for an annulment."

Was that all tonight meant to him? Just a physical release? The thought pained her unexpectedly, and she hardened her heart. Well, this would never happen again. And there was still the option of divorce.

Rebecca pulled the blanket over her shoulders and turned her back to him.

"Hello, inside. Clay, are you in there?"

The shout woke Clay and he sat up. Recognizing Garth's voice, he stood up and pulled on his Levi's as he went to the door and opened it to bright sunshine.

"Sure glad to see you," Garth said. He whistled, and Hawk came out of the trees. "We recognized Scotty's sorrel, but we weren't taking any chances." He glanced in Becky's direction. She was sitting up, looking confused. "Is she okay?"

"She's fine." He nudged Garth out of the doorway. "Let's give her a chance to get up and put some clothes on. We got soaked last night in that rainstorm." He went out and closed the door.

Once outside, the two men crowded around Clay. "Well, what in hell happened?" Garth asked.

"Eagle Claw gave her back to me."

Garth arched a brow. "Gave her back. Just like that."

"Yeah, I rode in, he had her tied up, and I told him I came to get my wife."

Hawk snorted. "And he handed her over."

"That's right."

"What did I miss here?" Garth asked.

"From his conversation, I gathered the Confederacy missed a chance to have a powerful ally in the Sioux Nation. Eagle Claw admires us because we don't want to live by Washington's rules." He shrugged.

"So this war chief of the Sioux—one of the most feared Indians in this territory—went to all the trouble of stealing your wife, then simply handed her over to you when you showed up, because you fought for the Confederacy."

"He also made me his blood brother. That's why he gave Becky back to me. He wouldn't dishonor himself by taking the wife of his blood brother."

Hawk shook his head. "If that don't beat all. Just let you ride away, did he?"

"Yep. Oh, yeah, and there was something else. I think he believes Becky is a little mentally unbalanced."

"That's the first thing you've said that makes any sense," Garth said. "And he could be right. She hasn't been herself lately, And having that Indian kidnap her couldn't have helped."

"She's fine, Garth." Recalling the passionate sex they had last night, Clay couldn't help smiling.

Becky came outside then, and Garth gave her a bear hug.

"Sure glad to see you, Little Sister."

Becky's emotions were written all over her face as she thanked them all for coming to her rescue. "I shall never forget that all of you put your lives at stake." Her chin was quivering and she looked on the verge of breaking down, but she got through it successfully.

They brewed a pot of coffee, ate some more jerky, and then rode back to rejoin the wagon train. They caught up with it at midday.

Rebecca was jubilant upon seeing her dear friends again. She also made a point of individually greeting her beloved Clementine, mules, and chickens.

By day's end her routine had returned to normal. But as she lay awake that night, gazing at the stars overhead, she thought of the past two incredible nights she had experienced: one of unbelievable fright, the other of ecstatic bliss.

What was next on this journey that destiny had charted for her?

24

Etta came over the next morning, excitement glowing in her eyes.

"Becky, I have the most exciting news to tell you. Our parents have given Tommy and me permission to wed! They all agreed that considering how close he came to dying, they wouldn't stand in the way of our happiness."

"Oh, honey, that's wonderful. I'm so happy for both of you. So when's it going to be? As soon as we reach California?"

"No, Tommy and I don't want to waste another moment being apart. We're going to wed tonight."

"Tonight! But, Becky, Tom is still bedridden. Don't you want to wait and get married in a lovely wedding gown when he's feeling better?"

"I have a white dress, that will do fine. And just because Tommy's still recovering is no reason why we can't be together. I spoke to Mr. Scott, and he said we can have one of his wagons. He'll transfer the supplies into Fallon's wagon."

"Who'll drive the wagon?" Rebecca asked. "It's for certain Tom can't."

Etta giggled. "We know that. But several of the men have offered to help drive, and we'll take our meals with our folks. I can take over nursing Tommy, then. He can sit up now, and he should be able to get out of bed in a couple of weeks."

"What do your parents think of this?"

"Oh, at first they had their doubts just like you, but Tommy and I convinced all four of them how important it is to us. Nothing would be gained by waiting. Becky, when you love someone, being together is the only thing that matters." She lowered her head in a blush. "Even if we won't be able to . . . you know . . . make love, at least we'll be together day and night, and know we belong to each other." She raised her head and looked directly into Rebecca's eyes. "You should know how we feel, Becky. Isn't that how you and Clay feel about each other?"

Rebecca couldn't look into Etta's trusting eyes and lie to her. She smiled and hugged the young girl to disguise her emotion.

"Well, if there's going to be a wedding tonight, I guess I better bake a cake right away."

"Oh, Mama, Grandma, and Mrs. Davis are already doing all that. Tommy and I want you and Clay to stand up as witnesses for us. Will you do that, Becky?"

Etta's happiness was contagious. Rebecca reached out and hugged her again. "We'd be delighted to stand up, honey." With a teasing grin, she added, "Since the groom can't, somebody has to." Slipping her arm around Etta's waist, she said, "Come on, darlin', we've got to go on a treasure hunt. How does that saying go? 'Something old, something new, something borrowed—' "

"Something blue!" Etta cried joyously.

That night the hushed pilgrims gathered in the flickering glow of campfires and listened as a hand-clasped Etta and Tom, whose young hearts were bonded in love, were now bonded in matrimony by the Reverend Kirkland.

As much as Rebecca loved the couple, she couldn't get into the spirit of the occasion. When the music and dancing began, she wandered away, seeking a quiet spot away from the celebrants, and leaned back against a tree.

"Why aren't you happy for them, Becky?"

She might have known Clay would follow. He propped an arm against the tree, enveloping her in his shadow.

"I am happy for them, Clay. I just don't feel this was the time for them to marry."

"There could never be a better time, Becky."

She looked up in surprise. "How can you say that, Clay? They're both still recovering from their near-tragedy."

"And there's no better medicine for either of them than each other. Becky, one of the things I've admired about you is your indomitable spirit. That's why it surprises me you don't recognize what's happened here. Those two young people both took devastating blows, and with the odds against them, they fought through it and showed everybody with this marriage that they're looking toward the future.

"At a time when everyone was weary and spirits were low, with the prospect of a damn desert still ahead to cross, those two kids have renewed everyone's faith in our ability to get through whatever lies ahead."

For a long moment, Rebecca stared into his eyes. If anything could give her the confidence to get through a crisis, it was the warmth and serenity of those brown eyes.

"You're right. I guess I was thinking so much of their hardships that I never thought beyond that. You know, Clay, sometimes you really surprise me."

The sound of Tom singing "Beautiful Dreamer" to his bride drifted on the air, as lightly as the breeze that ruffled her hair. Clay reached out and gently brushed the strands off her cheek. "I think I'm about to surprise you again," he murmured—and lowered his head.

The kiss was gentle—so incredibly tender, it soothed her soul, not aroused her passion.

Wordlessly he stepped back and opened his arms. She stepped into their circle. When she felt them close around her, she pressed her cheek against his chest, and they moved in rhythm to the beautiful music.

In the days that followed, they left the Rocky Mountains and headed into the Great Basin of the Utah Territory, with it's great Salt Lake—a caldron of white alkali sand that was roasted by the sun reflecting off the Wasatch Mountains surrounding it. The trail was marked by the bleached bones of oxen and mules, and water holes baked into dried clay.

Having made the trip several times, Scotty had ordered every empty space, barrel, pan, and bottle filled with water before they began the crossing. But still, water became more precious than gold. It was the greatest test of physical endurance they had to bear thus far.

What kept them going was pure grit and the promise of an easy passage through the Sierra Nevada mountain range ahead, knowing the Sacramento Valley was on the other side of it.

The end of the trail.

Throughout the ordeal, as one endless day passed into another, those ecstatic hours she had spent in Clay's arms became like a fading dream to Rebecca. They never spoke of it, and avoided any physical contact with each other.

The sound of distant laughter from the campsite carried to Rebecca's ears as she strolled along the riverbank. This was their final night together; tomorrow they would reach the city of Sacramento, and the weary travelers were celebrating the occasion.

She crested a rise and gazed with wonderment at this shrine of Nature. As far as the eye could see lay the verdant rolling hills of the Sacramento Valley. Masses of bright poppies, ferns, clover, thistle, and sage carpeted the grassland that stretched between towering woodlands of oak, maple, cypress, and Douglas fir. In the distance the graceful rise of willows and poplars framed the banks of the Sacramento River.

She couldn't believe they had done it. Exactly one

hundred and twenty-eight days ago, they had left Independence, Missouri, with a train of ninety-eight wagons. Forty-nine had finished the perilous journey.

They had anguished emotionally, pushed themselves physically, shed tears of joy and heartache. They'd thirsted and hungered, sweated in the heat of a blazing sun, huddled against the force of blustering winds, and shivered in chilling rains.

They swallowed the alkaline sand of the desert and drank from brackish streams on the prairie. They'd pushed wagons and stock over granite mountain passes, raging rivers, and ankle-deep mud, marking the trail with discarded family heirlooms—and the crosses of the loved ones left behind.

There were times they'd wished they were dead—other times they prayed to be spared. There were times when their hopes plunged to pits of despair—other times their faith soared to infinite heights.

And they had prevailed. The journey had ended.

Rebecca continued her stroll, enjoying the solitude. When she came to a cascading waterfall that fed the flowing river, she sat down on the riverbank and removed her shoes and stockings, then dangled her feet in the river. It was surprisingly warm after those cold mountain rivers and streams.

On impulse, she removed her gown and underpants, and waded into the water. Wishing she had a bar of soap to bathe herself, she closed her eyes and lazed in the water and let it wash over her.

She suddenly sensed she was no longer alone, and opened her eyes in dismay.

Clay stood on the riverbank staring at her. "You've strolled pretty far from camp, Becky. You never know what you might encounter."

"I know there's nothing to fear here, Clay. This valley is too peaceful."

"How's the water?"

"Wonderful."

He sat down and pulled off his boots and stockings, then striped down to his drawers. "You're right," he said, wading in. "It's almost as warm as a bath. It must be fed by a hot spring."

Rebecca followed him when he swam over to the waterfall, and disappeared into the rainbow-streaked mist. She took a deep breath and walked into the plunging spray.

To her surprise, she found herself in a cave hollowed into the granite rock. "I've never seen anything like this before."

"Interesting, isn't it?"

"But noisy," she said, trying to be heard above the roar of the falls.

He came over to her. "You're shivering, Becky."

Too late she realized her wet camisole was clinging to her, the taut tips of her breasts showing through the thin fabric. Her heart began to hammer against her chest. She backed away, but was halted by the granite wall.

"I guess I should get back into the water."

He moved even closer.

"Clay, this is wrong," she said breathlessly when he pulled the wet chemise over her head. The granite wall was cold and damp against her back, but did nothing to lessen the heat burning through her

"Why is it wrong, Becky, when we both want this, need this? If you tell me that's not true, I'll stop."

Already weakned by her own desire she said, "I can't, because it wouldn't be true. I do want you to make love to me, though I know I shouldn't."

His mouth claimed hers and her desire blazed higher. She flung her arms around his neck, matching his passion with her own.

Without breaking the kiss, he lifted her higher and she locked her legs around his hips.

The thrill of her arousal coursed through her, incinerating any reservations. Flesh on flesh, she clung to him, burningly aware of every spot where their bodies touched.

His warm palms cupped her rear and lifted her higher until his mouth found her breasts and teased the sensitive nipples to aching peaks; then he cut off her moans of ecstasy with a kiss filled with urgency, desperation, demand. His masterful tongue set her aflame, and she dug her fingers into the corded sinew of his shoulders for support as she began to tremble. Then he drove into her—and she lost all awareness of time or place. She matched her rhythm to his thrusts as his tempo increased; the escalating mindlessness soared; and their bodies shuddered in the divine release of climax.

He lowered her to her feet, but she couldn't stand, so he swept her up in his arms. Abandoning his drawers and her chemise, he carried her back through the waterfall and onto the riverbank.

While Clay pulled on his Levi's, Rebecca quickly put on her gown and slipped into her drawers. Then they sat in the warm sunshine to dry their damp bodies and hair.

"You know as well as I, Clay, that it was a mistake," she said regretfully.

"I'm not sorry it happened. Why should I feel guilt or regret over being intimate with my wife? It's part of a husband's—and a wife's—obligations, and we both enjoyed it.

"Besides, the damage was done when we made love in the cabin. An annulment is out of reach now Becky."

Obligation? She was damn tired of being seen that way. She started to put on her shoes and stockings. "But a divorce isn't out of reach, Clay—and that's what I intend to do in Sacramento.

"We both have plans to go our separate ways, and an involvement would just make it harder when we part." She stalked away.

"*If* we part, Mrs. Fraser." Rising to his feet, Clay followed her.

The discovery of gold nearby in '49 had turned the once-tiny town of Sacramento into a bustling city whose growth could not be slowed by even three floods and a devastating fire. It became the state capital five years later.

As they drove through the city, seeing the people dodging the flow of carriages and wagons, brick buildings three and four stories high, sidewalks, paved thoroughfares, lampposts, hotels, restaurants, and merchant stores, made Rebecca yearn to jump off the wagon and run from store to store, just to peer into the windows.

Scotty led the train to the stockyards, where everyone would be saying their good-byes. The Garson and Davis families were headed farther southeast, to locate the parcel of land on which they would build their future. Howard Garson had offered to buy Clementine and the two chickens, but Rebecca wouldn't take his money. She was satisfied just to know that someone she trusted would take good care of the animals.

After a tearful farewell to Etta and Tom, and their promise to write to her as soon as they got situated, Rebecca said goodbye to Clementine, Katharina, and Lady MacBeth.

"How does she know which chicken is which? They look alike to me," Garth said as he and Clay watched Rebecca's sorrowful parting with the chickens.

"I once asked her the same thing, and she said that since parents can tell their twins apart, why wouldn't she be able to tell the hens apart?"

"How long you figure she's going to stand there, watching them wagons pull away? We've got a lot to do."

"You want to go and tell her that, Little Brother?" Clay said.

"She's your wife, Brother Clay."

Mike Scott came over and shook hands. "You boys were a big help on this trip. Don't know what I'd have done without you. Once you find your sister, if you decide to go back East, I'll be pulling out of here in a week. I figure we can get across the mountains before the snow starts to fall. You boys are welcome to join us."

"Can't make any promises right now, Scotty," Garth said. "We've got to settle this business with our sister, and I've been thinking of staying in California for a while."

"What are your plans, Clay? You and your wife staying in Sacramento, or are you planning a real honeymoon somewhere else?"

"I don't know yet; there are several matters to settle here. I think we'll be sticking around for a while, but I'll let you know."

"You plan on selling your wagon, Clay?" Scotty asked.

"I imagine so. There's no use for it here in the city."

"I was looking it over, and it's still in damn good condition. I'll take the team and wagon off your hands for five hundred dollars. If you decide to head back East with us, I'll sell it back to you for what I bought it for."

"I heard that," Becky said, joining them. "I paid seven hundred dollars for that wagon and team."

"Mrs. Fraser, the team and wagon have deteriorated since you bought them."

"Some would consider the team is better trained now, sir," Rebecca countered in defense of her beloved mules.

"Five hundred's my top price. I'll throw in another

hundred dollars for whatever utensils and supplies you want to get rid of."

"Far as I know, we'll want to sell everything," Clay said. "Right, Becky?"

"I haven't thought about it yet, but I suppose you're right. I really won't have much use for most of that here in the city. And you're never going to get me in a covered wagon again."

"Well, Clay, that sounds pretty final. Looks like we can do business."

Becky made a final check of the wagon to make sure there was nothing she wanted to keep, then she signed the bill of sale. Sighing, she put the check into her purse, then walked over to the corral to face one last painful parting.

"Uh-oh, brace yourself, boys," Clay murmured.

"Not again!" Garth exclaimed. "I haven't fully recovered from the farewell to the cow and chickens."

"This will probably be worse—there's six mules."

All six trotted over to the fence when they saw Rebecca, which was an amazing sight for a breed that took indifference to a higher plane than even a cat.

"Now, Desdemona, you be kind to Othello. You know he's got a hankering for you," she said, hugging and kissing them. "And Mark Antony, I don't want to hear that you've been nipping at Cleopatra just because she's a little slower than you. Mr. Scott has promised me he'll take good care of you and see that no one takes a whip to any of you. And Caesar, I told him that sometimes your leg is sore, and he said he'd team you up with Brutus or Cleopatra since they're slower. I'd take you all with me, if I had a place of my own where you could graze in a field of clover, instead of pulling heavy wagons up and down mountains."

"Did she always talk to them like this?" Scott asked. Clay nodded. "But they're just dumb mules."

"Doesn't look like that to me," Garth said. "They seem to understand what she's saying to them."

"Becky insists that animals have feelings and like to be told they're loved, just like humans do," Clay said. "Funny thing about it is, they never acted up for her like most mules do. Docile as lambs whenever she spoke to them."

"Mrs. Fraser, I have to admit there were times I thought you were more trouble than you're worth," Scotty said when Rebecca rejoined them. "But all in all, I'm sure going to miss you. You made this trip interesting. I wish you and Clay a long and happy life together."

"Thank you, Mr. Scott. And despite the times I found you to be officious and overbearing, I thank you for bringing us through safely. I can't imagine why you want to do it all over again."

"I'm a single man, ma'am, with no roots. This life keeps me from being lonely."

"Perhaps if you'd plant some roots, sir, you wouldn't have to be a single man. Thus, no loneliness." Her eyes flashed with the spunk Clay so adored. "Take care of those mules, sir, or I shall haunt you the rest of your life."

"Yep, Mrs. Fraser, no doubt about it. I'm sure going to miss you." He tipped his hat. "Well, it was a pleasure to have met you folks, and good luck in the future." He winked at Clay. "I think you're going to need it, son."

"And good luck to you, Scotty," Clay said as they shook hands.

"My offer's still open if you change your minds in the next week," he said, slapping Garth on the shoulder.

"Good man," Garth said after the wagon master left.

While Clay got her trunk out of the wagon, Garth went off to hail them a cab.

Rebecca took a deep breath and said a quick prayer to get her through the next few minutes. "I guess this is good-bye, Clay."

He looked at her inscrutably. "I'll see you safely to your brother's."

"That won't be necessary. I'm sure you and Garth are eager to find your sister. Besides, I thought I'd stay in a hotel tonight, to freshen up before going to find him."

"Then come with us to see Lissy," he said. "I'd like you to meet her."

Rebecca hesitated. Why not? After tomorrow, they might never see each other again. Why not put off the parting as long as she could?

Garth returned with a cab, and after the men loaded the trunk and saddlebags onto the rear of the carriage, they went to the nearest hotel.

Fittingly named "The Prospector," the hotel appeared to be new and was much fancier than the one in Independence. More important, it offered two attractions that Rebecca hadn't known for over four months: a solid roof over her head, and an actual bed to sleep in.

Clay registered them as husband and wife, and once

upstairs, Rebecca discovered they had a connecting room with Garth, as in Independence. Clay wordlessly settled any doubts she had by putting his saddlebags in Garth's room.

Rebecca looked forward to the first hot bath she'd had since they left Fort Laramie. After pouring bath salts into the steaming water, she slowly lowered herself into the tub until the water covered her shoulders. Then she leaned back and relaxed as the hot water surrounded her tired body in a warm and fragrant cocoon.

Closing her eyes, she thought of that night in Fort Laramie, when Clay had made love to her and they'd almost consummated their marriage. Inevitably that memory led to the memory of the ecstatic night in that cabin, when they did consummate it.

Though it seemed so long ago, every detail of that night was vivid in her memory. Could she ever put it out of her mind? Did she really ever want to?

When the water began to cool, Rebecca scrubbed her scalp vigorously to make sure she rid it of every speck of sand, then she left the tub and returned to her room. She had just finished dressing when Clay tapped on the door and came in.

"All set?"

"Yes, all but my hat." She removed her hat from the trunk, adjusted it to a saucy angle, and pinned it on. Then she spun around to find him staring with a bewildered look at her.

She glanced quickly in the mirror, but nothing appeared unusual. "What's wrong, Clay?"

"You were wearing that hat the first time I saw you," he said.

"I imagine so, it's the only hat I own. Is there something wrong with it?"

"No, I was just remembering. Seems a long time ago." His smile was unconvincing.

"Everything seems a long time ago now, Clay."

"Yeah. Sure does."

25

The Frasers stood in front of a white clapboard house adjacent to the stagecoach office. In answer to their knock, a young red-haired man opened the door. He nodded and offered a friendly smile, and Rebecca liked him on sight.

"Howdy, folks."

"Are you Stephen Berg?" Clay asked.

"Sure am. What can I do for you?"

"I'm Clay Fraser. This is my wife, Rebecca, and my brother Garth."

"You're Lissy's brothers!" he said, shaking their hands. "I'm Lissy's husband. She figured you'd show up. Come on in."

Once inside, he pointed to an armchair. "Please sit, ma'am. That chair's the most comfortable. Lissy's tending the baby, but I'll go get her."

As soon as he left the room, Rebecca teased, "So which one of you boys is going to shoot him?"

They both were still chuckling when a whirlwind blew into the room.

"Clay! Garth!" The young girl was stunningly beautiful. Her long hair was as black as that of her brothers, and her tiny frame was engulfed by her tall brothers when she flung herself at them. Her brilliant blue eyes flooded with tears as they hugged and kissed, and Rebecca would have sworn she saw tears in Garth's eyes, too.

When they all finally settled down, and Clay had introduced her to his sister, he said, "Well, where is it? You don't think we came all this way just to see you."

Lissy giggled. "Your nephew Theodore just went to sleep."

"So you had a boy," Garth said.

"Yes, and do you believe Stephen wanted to name him Ulysses after General Grant!"

Stephen looked sheepish. "That appealed to me more than Beauregard, which Lissy wanted. So I suggested we name him after her father."

They all laughed, and Garth walked over and slapped him on the shoulder. "You did good, brother-in-law."

Rebecca saw Lissy's face light with joy at the remark.

After Theodore awoke and had been introduced to his uncles and aunt, Lissy let Rebecca help with the baby's bath. Rebecca marveled as she gently cleansed the tiny arms and legs, and the little round cheeks of his rear end. Tiny toes, fingers, arms and legs; each part a perfect miniature. She couldn't help smiling as the two uncles cooed over their nephew, and she was surprised to see how adept Clay was when he picked Theo up when he began to cry. Clay grinned with pleasure when the baby's little fingers curled around his large one.

*   *   *

Later, when they decided to leave, Clay went into the bedroom seeking Lissy and Stephen. He stopped at the doorway when he saw them standing at the baby's crib. Stephen's arm was around her shoulders as they gazed down at their sleeping child.

He brought her hand to his mouth and kissed the palm. "I love you, Lissy."

She leaned her head against his chest and smiled down at the infant. "And I love you, Stephen."

"And thank you for our beautiful son. You're our life, Lissy. We both need you, love. You fought so hard to give him life, just as you gave life to me when you became my wife."

Clay felt guilty eavesdropping on this private moment, but he was too moved by it to leave. The resentment he'd harbored toward Stephen was obliterated by his sense of shame. What made him and Garth think they had the right to try to meddle in that love?

A matter of honor? Whose honor? These two people in love had done the honorable thing. They admitted their love, and were willing to risk the consequences of their actions—not out of some self-imposed sense of duty or honor, but for love.

Clay started to turn away, and discovered Becky was beside him. How much had she heard of the conversation? For a long moment they stared at each other, and then he took her hand and they slipped away quietly.

Garth had romance on his mind, and as soon as they returned to the hotel, he took off. Clay tapped on the connecting door.

"You hungry?" he asked when Rebecca opened it.

"Famished."

"Then let's go downstairs to dinner. Unless you'd rather go somewhere else to eat?"

"No, here will be fine."

Clay's palm lightly rode her back as they followed the waiter past a satin-draped alcove, where a string quartet was playing the soothing strains of a Mozart sonata. After seating her, the waiter gave them menus and Clay ordered wine.

Rebecca looked around with pleasure. A flickering candle cast a shimmering glow on the delicate crystal glasses. She lightly traced her hand across the luster of the white tablecloth; it felt cool and smooth beneath her fingertips. A whiff of jasmine drifted up from a bowl of yellow and gold flowers, and she dipped her head to it and took a deep breath of the fragrance.

"This is all so wonderful." She leaned across the table to whisper softly, "Clay, can we afford this?"

"If this is our last dinner together, I would like it to be a special one."

His words were a jarring reminder of how little time they'd have together. The candle suddenly lost its glow; the music became less sweet.

The return of the waiter gave Rebecca a chance to restore her composure, as he poured the wine and Clay gave him their order.

Then Clay picked up his glass. "This occasion calls for a toast to the most incredible woman I've ever known. I shall never forget you, Becky. May you find the happiness you deserve."

Rebecca's hand trembled as she reached for her glass. "And to you, Clayton Fraser. You're the finest man I've ever known." She didn't know if she could get through the dinner without breaking out in tears. "But good-byes are so painful, Clay. Let's not say them here, with candlelight and soft music. It would be too poignant to bear."

She met his beautiful brown-eyed gaze. How would she ever forget him? To change the mood, she added, "Even if you are a Southern secessionist."

He understood, as she knew he would, and broke into laughter. Lord, he was handsome when he laughed! They clinked their glasses together.

As they ate their meal, both concentrated on other subjects to avoid an awkward silence.

They didn't speak on the way back to the room. Rebecca unlocked her door, thanked him again for dinner, and entered her room.

There, she changed into her nightgown and climbed into bed. She tried to read herself to sleep, but thirty minutes later she hadn't read beyond the first page.

She'd made a drastic mistake when they arrived in Sacramento. She should have said a final good-bye to Clay at the stockyard. Prolonging the inevitable was just making it harder. Her control on her emotions was slipping, not strengthening. How could she get over loving this man, as long as she remained with him? She had to keep him entirely out of her life. No more meals together. Avoid any further contact, even the sight of him, the sound of his voice.

The way he'd talked at dinner, it was evident that he had no qualms about parting. He clearly couldn't wait to get back to Virginia.

Face it now, Rebecca. Once and for all.

First thing in the morning she would locate her brother, and then hire a lawyer to dissolve the marriage.

Just as she rolled over to blow out the lamp, a light tap sounded on the connecting door.

"Becky, are you awake?"

Rebecca bit her lip. She'd be much wiser to pretend she was sleeping, but what if it was something important?

"What is it, Clay?"

"May I come in? I have something that belongs to you."

Rebecca got up, pulled on her dressing gown, and unlocked the door. "What is it?"

He stepped into the room and closed the door. He was barefoot and bare-chested, and his hair glistened with moisture from the bath he had just taken. A faint scent of bay soap carried to her nostrils when he handed her Charley's ring, which she'd lost when Eagle Claw had taken her. "I thought you might want this. I found it the day—"

"I know."

"I forgot I had it. It must have been mixed up with some of my clothes and ended up on the bottom of my saddlebags."

"Thank you, Clay." Grateful for the thoughtful gesture, she rose up on the tips of her toes to kiss his cheek just as he turned his head. Her lips brushed his.

Startled, they stared at each other. Then the warmth of his palm curled around the nape of her neck, as he drew her gently into his arms. Her breath quickened, and the flutter of her heart became a hammering in her ears.

Clay lowered his head, covering her mouth with the warm, moist pressure of his own.

His lips were firm and searching. The kiss, demanding. When he held her tighter, she curled into the curve of his muscled strength, her body tingling from the contact.

Breathlessness forced their lips apart, but her passion soared from the tantalizing slide of his lips along her neck before he reclaimed her lips, where his tongue explored the heated chamber of her mouth.

Her emotions whirled. This would only make their parting more difficult to bear; but how could anything that felt so wonderful be wrong? Why not make the most of whatever time remained?

She surrendered to the swirling passion of the kiss.

With a ragged gasp, Clay broke the kiss. Burying his hands in her hair, he cupped her head and forced her gaze to his. His warm brown eyes looked deeply into hers.

"Are you sure this is what you want, Becky? It's not too late to stop,"

"If this is to be our last night together, let it be our final memory, too."

His smile was as tender as the kiss he pressed to her lips. Then he slipped her dressing gown off her shoulders. Her loving gaze never strayed from his beloved face as she memorized every feature, while he undid the buttons of her nightdress. Then he pulled it over her head and cast it aside.

She felt neither shame nor modesty as she stood naked under his sweeping perusal. Rather, she gloried in the knowledge that her female sensuality could match the cravings of his male passion. He had taught her that lesson.

He released his pants and stepped out of them, naked beneath them. She studied him boldly, memorizing the beauty of his long, muscular body.

Then she reached out and lovingly followed the width of his shoulders and breadth of his chest with her fingertips. Lowering her head, she placed a light kiss in the midst of the dark hair, the quickening of her breath matching his.

"Becky. Becky," he moaned. He whispered her name against her lips, and then lifted her into his arms.

Easing her gently down on the bed, he covered her with his own body, the warmth of her flesh as tantalizing as the hardness of his body. His tongue caressed her taut nipples and the silken skin of her stomach. She matched his passion with her own uninhibited exploration.

Their lovemaking was tender as they explored, aroused, and satisfied each other. Giving, taking, sharing in an unspoken expression of love that neither would admit aloud.

She fell asleep with his name on her lips. He slipped into slumber holding her in his arms.

*   *   *

Clay awoke to find Becky curled up beside him. After last night he knew he was in much deeper than he'd originally planned—but he guessed Becky was in the same situation, which could work in his favor. There were several obstacles to overcome, though, and he had to keep a clear head and work it out so he could convince her.

He eased himself out of bed, and then, grabbing his Levi's, he opened the connecting door and closed it carefully behind him. He was surprised to see Garth sitting at the table with pen and paper.

Garth looked up and gave Clay's nakedness a once over. "Well, Brother Clay, you've either lost your drawers in a poker game, or you were in bed with your wife."

"Shh, keep your voice down," Clay said. "You'll wake Becky." He found a pair of drawers in his saddlebags, then dressed.

"Took you long enough," Garth said. "For a while, I figured you'd never make it. So what are you going to do about it? Kind of blows the plan for an annulment, doesn't it?"

"That plan went up in smoke the night Becky and I stayed in that cabin."

"Took you that long, huh?"

Clay glared at him. "Garth, get off the subject, or I'm going to start busting up this furniture with you."

"Easy, Clay, I'm only kidding. What's chewing at your craw?"

Clay dropped down on the bed and stretched out with his hands under his head. "Sorry. I've got myself pinned into a corner and can't get out."

"You mean with Becky?"

"Yeah. I've got to figure out what to do about it."

"You really want to get out of this marriage?"

"That's what she wants."

"I can't believe that. Becky strikes me as a woman who wouldn't go to bed with a man if she didn't love him. How do you feel about her?"

Clay stood up and began to pace the floor. "Confused. I'd like to give this marriage a chance, but it seems like she can't wait to get it over with. And even if I tried to convince her to try it out, I know she'd never go back to Virginia with me. She hates Southerners, remember?"

Garth grinned. "I think the journey here got that out of her blood."

"But, it's a double-edged sword, Garth. She'd be miserable living in the South; there'd be people there who wouldn't accept her just because she's a Yankee."

"Both of you are damn fools if you let other people live your lives for you. Forget Virginia and build a life here. This is as good a time as any, Clay, to tell you I've made up my mind that I'm not going back yet."

"You aren't really going to go chasing after that pot of gold, are you?"

Garth held up the sheet of paper he'd been working on. "I've been thinking about that gold mine my whole life, Clay. Even drew up this map from memory. And I'll never have a better time than this. I figured you'd join me, but since you and Becky might stay married, I'll do it on my own."

"When do you plan on going back home?"

"I figure that in a few years they'll have a railroad running across this country from shore to shore. By then, maybe I'll be ready to go back and settle down."

"Part of Fraser Keep belongs to you, Garth."

He shook his head. "Fraser Keep belongs to Will— he's worked his ass off to keep that place going. I love our home, but I've got to find something that's mine alone. Something that I created with my sweat and blood."

"I can't imagine what the place will be like without you." Clay slumped down and buried his head in his hands. "This is a double blow—losing a wife and a brother at the same time."

"You aren't losing a brother. And as for your wife, Becky is the kind of woman a man dreams about his whole life. Why would you ever consider giving her up?"

"You've got that wrong, Garth. She wants to give *me* up."

Garth chuckled. "You gonna let a Yankee win this battle?" He folded up his map and put it in his pocket, then shoved back his chair and stood up. "I'll wait for you in the dining room."

Garth paused on the way out and slapped Clay on the shoulder. "Swallow your pride, Brother Clay. Don't let her get away from you. Why don't you come right out and tell her that you love her?"

Clay was taken aback. "Who said I love her? She's my wife; she's my responsibility, I have an obligation to—"

Garth cut him off. "Brother Clay, face the facts: you know damn well you love her."

Clay grinned widely. "You can tell I've really got a problem, if I have to take my younger brother's advice."

"Who happens to know a damn sight more about women than you do. You forgetting about Ellie?"

"Ellie who?" Clay said, grinning, and gave his brother a light kick in the butt as Garth left the room.

Why was he trying to fool himself? There *was* a good reason why he wanted them to stay together. He had done the unimaginable: He'd fallen in love with his wife.

26

Rebecca had opened her eyes in time to see Clay leaving. Sneaking away, more like it. It was just as well; what do you say after a night of making love to your husband when you know he intends to leave you the next day? When she had promised to give him his freedom, she hadn't planned on falling in love with him.

And making love made it even harder to say goodbye to him. Now she couldn't even look at him without remembering the thrill of his kiss, his touch, the feel of his arms around her. Worse, she'd miss his grin, the warmth of his chuckle, and the sound of his voice.

If only she could sneak away without having to face him again . . . but that was impossible. They had to meet with a lawyer to terminate their marriage.

What if she suggested they try to make a go of their marriage? He would probably laugh at her. She had dug this hole for herself, now she had to live with it.

As if he could read her mind, Clay rapped on the door and called out, "Becky, are you awake?"

She appreciated his courtesy in knocking before entering her room. But that was Clay; a gentleman to the end.

She rose from the bed and pulled on her robe. Now

he was free to return to Virginia. That's what he'd wanted from the beginning. And then she could begin to put her life in order—but Lord, it would hurt.

"Yes, come in, Clay."

Clay opened the door. "Good morning."

He didn't look the least bit uncomfortable about last night. Maybe she had just dreamed the whole incident. She might try to convince herself of that if he hadn't just stepped on her nightgown where it lay on the floor.

"How about breakfast?" he asked. "Garth's waiting for us downstairs. He's leaving today, and wants to say goodbye to you before he goes."

She felt a sadness that he'd no longer be around with his cheerfulness. At least he'd be remaining in California; maybe their paths would cross again.

"You go ahead. I'm not dressed yet," she said, picking up the nightgown.

"I can wait."

She began to collect her toilet articles. "That's not necessary. Order me whatever you're having. I'll be down in a few minutes."

Rebecca gave herself a hurried sponge bath and returned to her room, where she dressed quickly, groomed her hair, and pinned on her hat.

Clay and Garth were at a corner table in the dining room. Both men rose to their feet when she approached. That Southern chivalry hadn't been exaggerated; she couldn't think of a time when Charley got to his feet to help seat her.

But making comparisons between the two men wasn't fair to either one. They were raised in different worlds—and so were she and Clay. *Face it, Rebecca, you could never fit into his world.*

The waiter immediately brought her a large glass of orange juice that Clay had ordered for her.

"Thank you," she said. "I love oranges."

"I've noticed," Clay said.

"If I were rich, I'd plant myself an orange grove so I could just pick one off a tree whenever I wanted to."

Garth chuckled. "Some women would have dreams of fancy gowns, others expensive jewels. There's no accounting for the female mind."

"Is that right, Garth Fraser? And what do you men dream about?"

Garth's grin was endearing. "A woman who prefers oranges to diamonds and pearls." He winked at Clay. "You've struck gold here, Brother Clay. I'd hang on to her if I were you."

Garth was about as subtle as a sledgehammer, and sat there looking pleased with himself.

Try as he might, Clay couldn't keep his eyes off Rebecca. He would not accept that this would be their last day together. As soon as they were alone, he would try to convince her that they should make the marriage work.

Hadn't her life been tough enough without adding the stigma of being divorced? Society accepted a divorced man with some qualms, but practically hung a scarlet letter around the woman's neck.

After breakfast, they went through the painful parting with Garth. Clay wished his brother well, and told him to be sure to keep in touch so the family would know where he was.

It was impossible for Becky to avoid tears when he kissed her good-bye and she watched another dear friend ride away.

Then Clay insisted upon accompanying her to her brother's house.

A young woman opened the door when she rang the bell. "May I help you?" she asked with a pleasant smile.

"Is this the residence of Matthew Brody?"

"Yes, it is. I'm Mrs. Brody."

Matt was married? Though why shouldn't he be? After all, she was on her second husband.

The woman was very lovely, with long-lashed brown eyes that were regarding her with friendly curiosity at the moment.

"How do you do," Rebecca said. "I'm Matt's sister. And this is my husband, Clayton Fraser."

"You're Becky!" She stepped aside. "Please come in."

Once inside, the woman hugged and kissed her. "I'm Virginia. Matt speaks of you often, and he'll be so glad to see you. Sit down while I get him. He's right outside, in the backyard."

Rebecca sank down in an upholstered chair, eager to see her brother after almost seven years.

"Becky!" Matt came rushing into the room. She jumped up and they hugged and kissed, then he stepped back and looked at her. "I can't believe it's really you, after all these years. You look wonderful."

"Oh, Matt, it's so good to see you." Her eyes misted with unshed tears. She hadn't realized how much she had missed him until she saw that boyish grin of his again.

He reached for his wife's hand. "And this is Ginny, my wife. She tells me you're married."

"Clay Fraser," Clay said offering his hand.

"A pleasure to meet you, Clay. So tell us, when did you get here? *How* did you get here? And why didn't you write and let us know you were coming?"

Same old Matt, she thought affectionately. He hadn't changed a bit. "Hey, slow up. One question at a time," she said.

"Why don't we go into the kitchen?" Ginny suggested. "There's coffee on the stove, and we can have a cup while the two of you get caught up."

"And there's a lot of catching up to do," Rebecca said.

"Becky, you should have let me know you were coming. What if I'd moved out of Sacramento?" Matt asked.

"I did. Didn't you get my letter? I wrote it about six months ago."

"No, I've never received it."

Rebecca described to them the hazards of the trip, her kidnapping by Eagle Claw, and her ultimate arrival in California. "Now, tell me all about yourselves. How did you meet? How long have you been married? I want to hear all about it."

They found out that Ginny was the daughter of one of the prospectors Matt had met while he was panning for gold; they'd fallen in love and gotten married.

How simple and uncomplicated, Rebecca thought. Why couldn't she and Clay have done the same?

"Are you still prospecting, Matt?" Clay asked.

"No, I gave that up when Ginny and I married. I'm an agent now for Leland Stanford. He's president of the Central Pacific Railroad out here."

"What do you mean by agent?" Rebecca asked.

"Mr. Stanford owns a lot of land and property in this area. I sell it for him. With this population influx, due to the war, it has been a very profitable venture for me." He grinned at Ginny. "Certainly more profitable than prospecting was."

"I'm going to have to decide what I'll do for a job," Rebecca said.

If Matt found the statement strange, he didn't indicate that. "What are you qualified to do, Becky?" Matt asked.

"I think I could do anything I set my mind to," she said. "I'm good with figures, and I love to cook and bake—I worked in a bakery for years. Maybe I can find a job working in one, or in a restaurant."

Matt leaned forward. "Have you considered opening your own bakery?"

"I would love to, but I . . . we don't have the money to get started."

"Don't be too sure about that. There's a property for sale just a few blocks from here that used to be a bakery. It's in excellent condition and there's living quarters above it."

"Oh, Becky, that would be ideal for you two," Ginny enthused.

"We only have six hundred dollars. I'm sure it would cost much more than that to buy a building and the supplies I'd need."

"Why not consider leasing it for six months and see if it will work out? It's in a good location, and I would think you could attract a lot of customers. The town's full of single men who would love fresh baked goods."

"Do you think it would be possible to lease it?"

"I'm sure of it. I know the agent who's handling it, and he's very easy to do business with. His name is Matthew Brody."

It was too good to be true. "Can I see it now?" Rebecca asked.

"I don't have the key here. How about tomorrow morning? Then, if you like it, you can sign a lease."

Clay couldn't wait to get out of there. Matthew Brody and his wife couldn't have been nicer, but now her brother had convinced Becky to open a bakery! That would make it even harder to dissuade her from a divorce.

As soon as they returned to her room, he broached the subject. "I noticed you didn't mention your intention to divorce me to your brother."

"I thought it better Matt didn't know."

"You know I have not agreed to a divorce. And I think we have a lot more to discuss on that subject."

"We *discussed* it in Independence. We *discussed* it numerous times on the trip to California. What more is there to *discuss*?"

"We've shared the same bed, and we *are* husband and wife. And I take my oaths seriously, Rebecca."

"Doesn't that armor you clank around in begin to feel heavy after awhile?"

Rebecca slumped down on a chair at the table, crooked her elbows, and cradled her head in her hand. She looked so desolate, he wanted to hold her and comfort her, but he was fighting to hold onto their marriage.

Clay sat down across from her. His anger had run its course, too. "So you're back in the bakery business."

Call it exhaustion, despair, or just having him sitting across the table from her again. Rebecca started to giggle. "That's right. I came all the way to California to end up moving in above a bakery again."

"Well, once they taste your peach pie, you'll have more customers than you can handle."

His remark surprised her. "I didn't realize you liked it. You rarely said anything about my cooking."

His gaze swept her face. "There were a lot of things I never said and should have."

She couldn't bear to meet that intense gaze of his. Her fingers itched to just reach out and touch his hand. An awkward silence developed between them. She finally asked, "I imagine you'll be going back to Virginia."

"I'm not sure. That long trip back is enough to tempt me to stay right here. Howard Garson tried to convince me to buy some property near him in a place called Napa Valley, southeast of here. He got it under the Homestead Act. If they occupy and farm the land for five years, it will belong to them."

"You mean you would consider doing that?"

"No, the Homestead Act prohibits anyone who bore arms against the United States from benefiting from the program. That eliminates any of us Confederates."

"That seems unfair. After all, the war is over and we're all Americans now."

"Yes, we are, aren't we?" he said, amused. "But I'm sure I could raise the money to buy some land out here, if I decided to stay."

Rebecca's heart began pumping so quickly, she thought she would swoon. Was it possible Clay was considering not returning to Virginia? Remaining in California?

"Aren't you needed on the plantation?"

"No, my brother Will has plenty of help now. That's why Garth decided not to return."

"He's following a dream, Clay. Why didn't you go with him?"

"Because it's his dream, Becky. I have my own."

"Another Fraser Keep?"

"No. You'll laugh if I tell you what I'd really like to do."

"I won't laugh, Clay."

"I'd like to start a vineyard."

"A vineyard! What do you know about growing grapes?"

"I've been reading about it on the trail. My grandfather had about fifteen acres of grapevines and made as good a wine as you could buy. He'd hand out bottles of it to our family and friends at Christmas."

"Can you support yourself raising grapes?"

"Same as any other farmer who's raising fruit or vegetables. If it worked out, eventually I'd like to build a winery. I always loved following Grandfather around, helping him." He looked embarrassed, like a little boy caught with his hand in a cookie jar. "It probably sounds silly and impractical to you."

"I don't think it's a silly dream at all, Clay. If that's what you want, you should try it."

"What I *want* is to talk about our marriage. I don't want a divorce, Becky. I refuse to abandon you."

Rebecca exploded. "Oh, please! I was on my own before I ever met you. Is this where I get the lecture about your honor again? I am so tired of hearing that I'm your responsibility, Clay Fraser. If I'm going to be a wife, I want a husband who wants me for myself. Who doesn't look at me as an unwanted obligation thrust upon him!"

She took a deep breath to hold on to her control. "I owe you too much, to expect you to spend the rest of your life upholding an oath you were tricked into taking."

Clay stood and stomped to the connecting door. "Forget it, Becky, I will *not* give you a divorce. And if you don't want a conjugal visit from your husband tonight, I suggest you lock this door."

27

Rebecca could barely keep from skipping when she left the doctor's office the next morning. She had to find Clay! Hurrying back to the hotel, she tapped on the connecting door, and opened it.

A startled maid was making up the bed.

"Oh, I'm sorry. I'm looking for Mr. Fraser."

"He just checked out, ma'am," she said.

Her heart sank to her stomach. "How long ago?"

"Not more than fifteen minutes."

Rebecca began to feel panicky, and she hurried back outside. Her worst fear was realized when she saw that Scott and his men were on the verge of moving out. Clay was driving her old wagon, with her beloved mules harnessed to them.

So he was leaving—and without even saying goodbye. In her heart she had hoped he wouldn't go back to Virginia, but this wasn't the time to stand on vain hopes or false pride. She loved him too much to let him go without telling him. Then, she hoped, he would ask her to go with him. He'd said he didn't want a divorce, that he was willing to give their marriage a chance. And whether he meant it or not, she was going to take him at his word.

She was about to call out to him, when he pulled out of the line and reined up in front of the hotel. Her spirits buoyed when he waved to Scott, and the wagon master waved back. If that wasn't a good-bye wave, then she was the Queen of England.

For over four months, concealing their true feelings for each other had come easily to both of them, and she tried to appear nonchalant when he caught sight of her.

"That's a fine-looking rig and handsome team of mules you have there. Where are you heading with them?"

"Southeast of here. A place called the Napa Valley. I've got some good friends there."

"Could you use some company?"

She saw his start of pleasure, which he quickly concealed. "I'm not looking for company, lady. I'm looking for a wife—in the full sense of the word."

Joy surged through her in a floodtide, and she felt as if she were floating on air. She'd never known such a feeling of exhilaration. It was grand. It was glorious. She wanted to throw her arms around him, and shout, Yes! Yes!

"You see, I'll need a lot of help if I settle down there and build a house."

"Didn't you once tell me your great-great-great-granddaddy built his plantation by himself?"

He arched a brow. "Guess I must have failed to mention that great-great-great-grandma was right there with him."

"I guess you did," she said, her lips curving into a suppressed grin.

"You have to understand that choosing the woman you want to be your wife takes a great deal of consideration. It takes a clear head."

"And I'm sure you'll keep a clear head when you do."

"You bet. There's a lot more to choosing a wife than choosing a horse or a pair of boots."

"There is indeed." She folded her arms across her chest.

"There'd be a lot of hard work, she can't be afraid of that."

Nodding, Rebecca agreed. "Hard work never hurt anyone."

"And she'd have to be a good cook. It's important she knows how to make a decent pot of coffee."

"Ranks right up there with a good horse and pair of boots."

"And I'd expect her to be able to make dried beef taste like French cuisine, or prepare a buffalo steak tender enough to cut with a fork."

"I don't think they have buffalo in California, Clay."

He grinned, and her toes curled. "That's good, because I never want to see one of those stinking animals again."

"Sounds to me like you'll be one fortunate fellow when you find her," Rebecca said, suppressing her own grin. "What other qualities must this miraculous woman possess?"

"I'd kind of like to hear her hum when she cooks, and talk to animals because she knows they've got feelings, too."

"I suspect so. And what would she have to look like?"

"Hmm, what would she have to look like?" He gazed up at the sky in deep contemplation. "I had always imagined she'd be tall and willowy, with dark hair and blue eyes. But I guess if she had all the other qualities I mentioned—especially brewing a decent pot of coffee—I'd be satisfied if the top of her head only comes up to my chin, that her hair's the color of honey, and her lips taste just as sweet. She can even have green eyes as light as jade when she's feeling happy or as dark as emerald when she's romantically inclined. Oh, and, that's another very important point. I'd want her in my bed when I need her . . . or when she needs me."

Rebecca was bursting with excitement. If he didn't get down and kiss her soon, she was likely to climb up on that box and throw herself into his arms.

"You haven't mentioned children. Isn't that part of being a wife in the full sense of the word?" Rebecca asked.

"Of course, she'd have to want children as much as I do. I'm not getting any younger, so I'd want to start a family once I get settled."

"How about before you get settled? You see, I pretty much fit all those other qualities you mentioned, but I already come with a baby."

"A baby!"

The game had just ended.

Clay jumped down from the box and grabbed her by the shoulders. "You're . . . we're . . . going to have a baby!" He pulled her into his arms joyously and kissed her.

"Why didn't you tell me sooner, sweetheart? Were you just going to let me ride away?"

"I'd never have kept it from you, Clay. I've only suspected it for the past week, and the doctor confirmed it this morning. But even if I weren't expecting a baby, I'd already made up my mind to find you. I couldn't let you leave without admitting that I love you and wanted us to be together, no matter where we lived."

"You'd do that for me? God, sweetheart, I love you," he murmured through the kisses he rained on her face and eyes. "I'm so crazy in love with you that sometimes I feel like I'm going to burst apart if I can't see you, touch you." He reclaimed her lips in a deep kiss that left them both hungry for more.

"Becky, Etta and Tom's love taught me how fragile life can be. That time is too precious to deny what's in our hearts. Let's not waste another moment of our time together. We've been through so much together, and now that we're having a baby, we have to start building on that.

"I love you, Becky, and I want us to spend whatever time we have on this earth together. Because I can't imagine going through the rest of my life without you."

"Then why didn't you say so sooner, Clay Fraser?" she demanded. "Do you have any idea how long I yearned to hear you say that?"

"Why would you doubt it? How could you not know it?"

"There are some things a woman must be told. Oh, Clay, I love you, too. I think I've loved you from the time I picked you out of all those hundreds of other men in Independence. And I've agonized over the way I tricked you into marrying me."

"But if you hadn't, you wouldn't be here now, in my arms. The Lord works in mysterious ways."

"But can you ever trust me again?"

"I'll let you know when I put the question to our grandchildren."

"Our grandchildren—what a beautiful sound." She sighed in contentment. "Oh, Clay, I'm so happy to be having this baby. What could be a greater gift from God than bearing a child conceived in our love?"

He tipped up her chin with a finger. "You understand, sweetheart, that child will be part Reb."

"All that matters to me is that the child will be part you. And if you want our children raised in Virginia, my love, we'll go back there. I'll be content wherever you'll be the happiest."

"No, we'll stay here and start new lives, just like the rest of our friends. No more living for—or in—the past. We've got our future ahead of us right here in California." He kissed her again.

Her heart overflowing with joy, mischief gleamed in her eyes as she looked at him. "Sounds like it's certainly worth . . . discussing."

He chuckled and grinned back at her. "And my guess is that the *discussing* will take most of the day."

"Possibly even into the night."

Pulling her back into his arms, he kissed her again, then cupped her cheeks between his hands in a tender caress. "Oh, Lord, I love you, Becky. And I've made so many mistakes."

"We both have, my love."

"Do you still have your hotel room?" She nodded.

"Well, then, it's high time we get on to the discussing, wouldn't you say?"

Sighing, she slipped her arms around his neck. "I thought you'd never get around to it. It's no wonder you Rebs lost the war."

Throwing back his head in laughter, he swooped her up in his arms and carried her into the hotel.

Later, as she lay in his arms, Becky asked, "Clay, were you really going to ride off with that wagon train and leave me behind?"

"No, but I wasn't sure what would happen. For the first time in your life, you had the opportunity to become financially independent, to run your own business. Part of me wanted to give you that chance, then return when your six-month lease was up in the hope of convincing you to give it up and go back with me. But I really wanted you to choose me—so I bought back our wagon and mules in the hope that I could bribe you back with them."

"You don't fool me anymore, Clay. You bought them because you knew it broke my heart to see them go. But what makes you think that a bakery is what I've hoped for? It would be a way to support myself, but I don't want to spend the rest of my life baking for other people. My dream is to find a man who loves me, and to have his children."

She sighed deeply. "Clay, I'll always express my own opinions and make my own decisions. I'll never rely on other people to do my thinking for me. That's what in-